A QUEEN'S MERCENARY

by Sam Burnell

•

First published in eBook and paperback 2018

•

© Sam Burnell 2018

•

The right of Sam Burnell to be identified as the author of this work has been asserted by her in accordance with the Copyright, Designs and Patents Act 1988.

All rights reserved. No part of this publication may be reproduced, stored in or introduced into a retrieval system, or transmitted, in any form, or by any means (electronic, mechanical, photocopying, recording or otherwise) without the prior written permission of the writer. Any person who does any unauthorised act in relation to this publication may be liable to criminal prosecution and civil claims for damages.

Thank you for respecting the hard work of this author.

Please note, this book is written in British English, so some spellings will vary from US English.

DEDICATED TO

Clive Andy Lomas
and
Nickelback

CHARACTER LIST

Fitzwarren Household
William Fitzwarren – father of Richard, Robert and Jack
Eleanor Fitzwarren – William Fitzwarren's wife
Robert Fitzwarren – William's son
Jack Fitzwarren – William's son
Richard Fitzwarren – William's son
Harry – Cousin to the Fitzwarren brothers
Ronan – William's steward
Edwin – Servant
Charles – Servant
Jon – Servant
Master Juris – William Fitzwarren's physician

The English Court
Stephen Gardiner – Bishop of Winchester
Wriothsley – Privy Councillor
Kate Ashley – Elizabeth's governess
Travers – Controller of Elizabeth's household
William Cecil – Secretary of State
Christopher Morley – Cecil's man

London Law Firm
Geoffrey Clement – Lawyer
Marcus Drover – Employee of Clement

Richard's mercenary band
Dan – Also a family servant
Mat
Froggy Tate

Marc
Pierre
Andrew Kineer
Thomas
Master Scranton

Other characters
Lizbet – A London prostitute
Hugo Drego – Captain of the Dutch Flower
Christian Carter – Richard's friend
Catherine De Bernay – Daughter of Peter De Bernay

CONTENTS

Chapter One – The Crossing
Chapter Two – An Error of Judgment is Addressed
Chapter Three – A Lawyer's Trial
Chapter Four – A Knight's Entrance
Chapter Five – The Future of War
Chapter Six – Shaping Destiny
Chapter Eight – The Forgotten Lady
Chapter Nine – A Fools Regret
Chapter Ten – Forged in Fire
Chapter Eleven – A Warning Ignored
Chapter Twelve – The Unavoidable Trap
Chapter Thirteen – A Hunter's Folly
Chapter Fourteen – The Alaunt
Chapter Fifteen – A Narrow Escape
Chapter Sixteen – The Bond is Cut
Chapter Seventeen – An Inevitable Ending
Chapter Eighteen – A New Master
Chapter Nineteen – The Day Of the Innocents
Chapter Twenty – A Reckoning Welcomed
Chapter Twenty-One – The Payment
Chapter Twenty-Two – A Search For A Knave
Chapter Twenty-Three – The Fallen Knight
Epilogue – Introduction to A Queen's Knight

Chapter One
The Crossing

Of every kinnë tre,
Of every kinnë tre,
The hawthorn blowëth swetest,
Of every kinnë tre.
My lemman she shal be,
My lemman she shal be,
The fairest of every kinnë,

☦

In April, the church bells in London rang out with news of the birth of Mary's child. Londoners, ever tuned to the mood of their monarch, took to the streets in celebration. A preacher proclaimed loudly that he had seen the babe and it had the fairest countenance of any child ever born to a woman. The news did not stop at London; soon it spread to the continent, letters of congratulation making their way to the shores of England. It seemed that the political map had changed once again. For the child Mary had been delivered of was a son, a new prince for England.

Whoever had released the news could not have known the devastation and damage this would cause; Mary's humiliation was complete. There wasn't a child. Her attempts to bolster her rocky position by proclaiming that the babe was still unborn and would arrive later in the year were believed by very few. By July, the Queen, with a flattened belly, was back at Court preparing for Phillip's imminent departure. She had lost a child and a husband in a few scant months.

†

"They're going to kill it! Jack, they're going to kill the horse! Jack, where are you?"

Both men heard Lizbet before she'd even got up the stairs to the cabin. They all met in a jam on the steps. Lizbet flattened herself against the wood panelling, letting them press past her, Richard in the lead with Jack hard on his heels.

Corracha, Richard's horse, was housed in a makeshift stable on the Fluyt. The crossing to Holland was to take only three days and, for a fee, the Captain had agreed to take the animal. A makeshift stable had been rigged between two lots of packing cases. With the passage being so short, only a minimal amount of feed was needed. So far, the Arab had been happy with the stall and with the journey but not anymore, it seemed.

They heard the constant pounding before they arrived. Corracha was kicking out wildly, sometimes with both rear hooves and sometimes with one. The wooden partition was being opened and the ship's cook, a burly Dutchman with a hatchet in one hand, was being goaded on by his shipmates standing at a safe distance behind him.

A meaty hand flexed round the wooden shaft of the weapon. He was watching the horse closely and gauging when he could safely take a swing at the animal with the blade.

"Stop!" Richard commanded. "You touch that animal and I'll put that blade between your eyes!"

The Dutchman hefted the axe in his hand. "Then you put a stop to it! Leave it much longer and the damned thing will have holed the hull."

Corracha continued with his incessant kicking. Iron-clad hooves were indeed splintering the wood.

"That hull is a hand's width thick. A horse isn't going to kick it through." Richard moved himself between Corracha and the man with the axe.

Jack was even quicker and slipped between them both. Richard heard him talking calmly to the stallion behind him.

"Donny," the Dutchman called over his shoulder at the group of men, "get Captain Drego now. He'll settle this. I'm not waking up in the night to find myself up to my bloody armpits in water."

One of them ducked reluctantly away and went in search of Drego.

The horse's eyes were wide, his coat slick with sweat as he continued to kick blindly at the wall behind it. Jack, his head against the horse's cheek, smoothed his hand down the serpentine neck, his voice level, calm and easy, speaking quietly to the animal.

Twice Corracha pushed him away, the first time hard into the wooden partition and the second time backwards out of the stall, sending him reeling into Richard. When he went back the third time, he wound his hand round the animal's head collar, firmly pulling Corracha's head down to meet his own. All the time he kept talking in a level voice. The hooves finally missed a beat.

The arguing outside the makeshift stable stopped as the deafening crashing halted. The horse kicked out again, just once more but with less conviction. Jack's hand hard on his head collar, he allowed Jack to turn him in a tight circle in the stall. He neighed and stamped but the kicking, the incessant kicking, had stopped.

The Dutchman dropped the hatchet to his side and a cheer went up from the men standing behind him. Lizbet, watching from the top of the steps, felt the tension subside. Drego had arrived and was talking with Richard, but Lizbet was watching Jack. His whole attention was given to the animal. Wearing only a linen shirt, it was soaked with the horse's sweat where he had pressed against it. Still his voice spoke quietly to the horse. She couldn't make out the words, but Corracha was listening and let Jack lead him in another circle around the stable as she watched.

The situation had been defused and Lizbet silently made her way down the steps once the rest of the crew slunk away after Drego spoke scathingly to them. Richard closed the partition that acted as the stable door, and Jack remained with Corracha, an arm around the horse's neck and his body leaning against him.

When he spoke to Richard it still sounded as if he was addressing the horse. "He's got a bad cut on his hind quarters – it'll need stitching. I should have seen the row of nails sticking through the wood at the back. I'm cursing myself for not noticing them." Jack continued to run his hands firmly down the horse's neck. "I'm not leaving him, get me some

11

rope and a broom handle and send Lizbet. I'll tell her what else I need."

Jack told her what he wanted, finishing his instructions with, "…the thickest needle you can get me, and make sure it's sharp."

When Lizbet returned, Corracha, snorting and stamping, was agitated again. Richard motioned Lizbet to be quiet and she sank down onto the bottom step to watch.

Jack, holding the horse's head collar, was trying to slip a loop of rope over his nose. The horse, his ears back and eyes wide, seemed to sense what Jack was trying to do and repeatedly pulled his head back just as the loop started to tighten. Lizbet realised she was watching a battle of wills. Jack calm, his movements economical and voice quiet yet commanding, was giving the Arab a clear message. Corracha was, by degrees, accepting it, and finally Jack got the loop of hemp rope over his soft nose.

Three rapid turns fastened it tightly in place. The shaft from the wooden handle was twisted in the rope. Jack, turning it, forced the rope to tighten into a hold that the horse could not pull away from. Corracha took a faltering step backward. Jack held fast to the rope; man and horse eyed each other for what seemed an age. Neither Richard nor Lizbet saw a change in the horse, but Jack felt it and twisted the rope quickly, pinching the Arab's upper lip in the rope loop.

"What's he doing to it?" Lizbet's eyes were wide; surely the horse was going to kick out against the vicious knot held round his nose.

"Shh, just watch," Richard warned, quietening her.

The horse's head, by degrees, lowered. The ears that had been laid flat back against his head in an attitude of aggression twitched forwards. As she watched, the tension left the taut body and the sleek neck, corded with muscle, relaxed. Lizbet was sure she even saw it sway a little on unsteady legs.

"Richard, hold this." Jack, his fist still tightly gripping the wood, held it out for his brother to take. "Lizbet, bring everything over here." Jack spoke quietly, but loud enough for them both to hear.

Richard took the wooden shaft, careful not to let the rope loop slacken. Standing close to Corracha, he spoke in level tones and ran his hands down the horse's neck as Jack had done.

"Right lass, you can give me a hand." Jack pushed open the stall door to make space for her to enter.

"I'm not coming in there with that mad beast!" Lizbet held out the needle she had borrowed and the canvass thread but made no move to step into the stall. "Get him to help you." She nodded in Richard's direction, and then added, "It's his horse."

"I've got my hands full," came the silken reply and a boot was swiftly planted on her backside, propelling her into the stall.

Lizbet flattened herself against the partition wall, as far from the horse's heaving sides as she could get. So close was she to the animal, she could smell the acid tang of sweat and feel the heat coming from the lathered flanks. Lizbet swallowed hard, her heart hammering in her chest.

"Come here, you can't help me from there." Jack reached out and pulled her by the arm to the back end of the horse. Lizbet stared nervously at Corracha's rear legs but they were stilled now, one even pointed, as if he was standing on his tiptoes.

"He's asleep. He'll be fine as long as Richard keeps a tight hold on him," Jack reassured her.

The cut was clean and straight and with Lizbet's help, holding the torn edges together, Jack slowly stitched it back together. Under his breath he complained endlessly about the needle Lizbet had brought him. Meant for sail repairs, it was long enough to stitch the animal's hide back together, but the needle was blunt and thick and forcing it through Corracha's skin was making holes in his own hands. Finally, Jack cut off the end of the thread with his teeth and nodded with satisfaction, his hands covered in a sticky mixture of his own blood and that of the horse's.

"Hold him tight," Jack said to Richard, and then to Lizbet, "Give me your shoe."

Lizbet gawked at him as if he were mad.

"For God's sake woman, give it here. I need something to bang these nails flat."

Lizbet complied. Unhooking a wooden clog from her foot, she passed it to Jack and was forced to hop from the stable. Richard tried, and failed, to hide a smile.

Jack banged the nails in with the heel of the clog. Each sharp, staccato sound twitched the horse's ears, but the noise didn't startle him. Jack swapped places with Richard, taking the wooden shaft with the twisted rope from him.

"I'll stop with him," said Jack, beginning to slacken the rope and talking in a low, calm voice all the time to the horse.

Richard pushed the partition back in place, fastening Jack in with Corracha.

"Give me my bloody shoe back," Lizbet hissed.

A moment later the wooden clog sailed over the partition to be neatly caught by Richard. He hefted the wooden shoe in his hand before offering it back to Lizbet. "Well, at least we know that if you fall overboard you'll float!"

Scowling, Lizbet snatched the clog back from his outstretched hand and rammed it back on her foot.

✝

They left Jack with Corracha and returned to Drego's cabin. Then Richard arranged for a quantity of aqua vitae to be delivered to Jack in Corracha's stall. He knew Jack's intention would be to get drunk for the remainder of the journey; Jack had no love for boats, a fact that always amused Richard.

Lizbet stood on the deck, the air chilled and her clothes invaded with a feeling of damp that never seemed to leave them. Unlike Jack, Lizbet did not dislike the Fluyt. When she was on deck standing next to Richard and gazing out across the sea, she knew that she had never looked so far before. There wasn't a house, a tree or a wall obscuring her view and she had a view right to the very edge of the ocean.

She'd heard from men who'd been to sea, of course, but had always just imagined it to be very much like a wide river, with the land visible on the other side. That the waves rolled on and on, she had not been prepared for. She didn't mean to, but her hand reached out and squeezed Richard's arm as she stood and found herself, for once, lost for words.

Richard didn't pull from her hold. Instead, sensing her wonder at the sea before her, he asked, "Did you ever imagine it would look like that?"

Lizbet just shook her head and, loosening her hand from his arm, placed her hand on the wooden gunwale as the ship heaved beneath her, lifted by the swell of the waves.

"It's so…" Lizbet paused, "… I can see so far. I wonder if I can see right into Heaven."

Her reply was not one he expected. "If there was a window into Heaven then it would be here," he said.

"I didn't know it was possible to see so far. I can see to the very edge of the world, and, if there is an end to the world, then what is it that I can see after that? What it must be to get so close to God."

Richard was about to reply, but stopped himself. He had been about to tell her he'd known a good few sailors and none of them had been touched by the grace of God. It seemed unfair to steal her sense of awe simply because it was not a feeling he shared.

"Why does the horse let him do that?" Lizbet asked, changing the subject.

"In truth, I don't know," Richard replied. "It sends them to sleep."

"It's a useful trick," Lizbet remarked. "Shame it doesn't work on men."

Richard laughed. "Well, it might. You'll have to try it and let me know. If you could do that, there would be no need for dwale."

The memory of Colan and the poisoned wine she had given him was one that still disturbed her sleep; not particularly because of his slobbering and drooling demise, his face flat against the table, but more for the death Richard had delivered when he had ripped Colan's cousin's throat out without even hesitating. The image of the man, standing for a brief second before his body collapsed, an expression of stricken terror on his face, air whistling from the incision and blood splattering across the wall pumping from his neck like some dying animal, was an image she was trying to bury.

†

The Dutch Flower completed her voyage without further incident. Jack remained with Corracha, in a drunken stupor mostly, which was his preferred state when travelling at sea. Before he left England, Richard had sent a final message to Dan's sister. In it, he told Dan that there was a crossing on the Fluyt paid for in advance, if he wished to join his former Master in Holland.

The weather at the start of 1556 was good for trade and the Dutch Flower made a swift crossing back to England. Richard waited, and when word came that the ship had come back into her berth three days earlier than expected, he was at the quay wondering if she carried the men he sought.

A smile crossed his face when he saw them; it heralded a feeling of relief he had not expected. He saw Dan first, the big man was never hard to find in a crowd; next to him, dark haired and looking mutinous was Mat, and Froggy Tate was bringing up the rear.

Richard walked straight towards Dan and when the big man saw him, he stopped in his tracks.

Mat, on seeing the Master, leant his head a little closer to Dan's. "So the De'il himself is in Holland. You could have bloody told us."

Richard held Dan's eyes and, with a slight smile still on his face, he said evenly, "Welcome. I trust the passage was a good one?"

Dan grinned back, pleased to see the Master looking so well. "A good one, and all that salt air has given us a thirst. Hasn't it, lads?"

Richard led them to the inn where they had taken lodgings. When Jack saw them coming through the door one after the other, he was out of his seat and across the room, calling their names, grinning like an idiot – utter disbelief plain on his face.

"Good God! Dan, Mat, Froggy!"

A grin split Mat's face, revealing his broken front teeth. "Aye, we've not changed our names!"

"I'll be guessing then that the Master didn't tell you we were following you from England on the Dutch Flower then?" Dan said laughing.

"Bloody right he didn't! God, it is good to see you!"

They drank all afternoon and all evening, stopping only when the new day was upon them and Mat, sprawled across the table, began to snore loudly. They left him where he was and Jack, Dan and Froggy made their way unsteadily up the stairs to fall into drunken slumbers.

†

"This is the best I can do, so don't go complaining at me." Lizbet backed into the room, opening the door with her rear, her hands carrying a laden tray. "It's some sort of bread, God knows what they make it from. You could hammer nails in with it."

Richard, seated at the table, watched Lizbet as she negotiated a chair and a pair of boots that were discarded on the floor, before placing the tray in front him. "Jack, is he awake?"

Lizbet's brows raised. "I'd have thought you'd know better than to ask that. The lot of them went to bed when the larks got up and kept us awake half the night with their drunken laughter." Lizbet had slept on the floor at the back of the inn, in a communal room.

"I know. You weren't the only one to suffer it," Richard said, then smiling, added, "Lizbet, could you get me a bucket of water?"

Lizbet read what he meant to do from the mischievous expression on his face. "Really? I'll make sure it's bloody cold." And with that, still grumbling under her breath, she left to find a pail.

Richard kicked open the door, the smell of sweated beer fumes wrinkling his nostrils. His sudden entry though had not breached the sleep of any of those within. Froggy, sat on the floor, his head resting on the end of the bed, one boot on and one off, appeared to have succumbed in the act of trying to remove the second boot. Dan was sprawled face down, head pillowed on his arms, and Jack had made it to the bed where he lay flat on his back, open mouthed and snoring.
Richard considered them all for a moment, before taking a firm hold of the bottom of the bucket and throwing half of it over Dan and the other half square in Froggy's face. Jack he spared. Lizbet, hovering behind him in the doorway, released a squeal of pure delight.

†

Dan stared mutinously at the Master over a cup of restorative ale. "Aye, well it did get late quick," he offered by way of an apology.
Mat was still asleep on the floor where he had landed after sliding from his perch on the table during the night. Froggy was in the yard trying to dry himself. Only Jack, still asleep, remained blissfully unaware.
"Now the happy reunion is over with, do you want to tell me what happened after I left?" Richard enquired equably.

"After you left?" Dan was dismayed. "You hardly left. We all thought you were dead."

"As you can happily see, that did not come to pass. I sent word to you via Jamie, did I not? To stay with Jack?" Richard's grey eyes held Dan's until the other was forced to look away shamefully.

"You did, but you don't know what he was like. I tried to help him, it wasn't easy." Dan knew his words sounded poor.

"No one would ever accuse Jack of being easy. Nevertheless, he ended up in London on his own. Why did you leave him?" Richard's tone was still conversational but experience warned Dan of the temper that lay behind the words.

"He chose to go his own way. I couldn't stop him, could I?" Dan replied carefully.

"He ended up in Marshalsea, Dan, in just a few weeks and you could have stopped that. I left him with you. He was in your charge." Richard's voice bore a hard edge now.

"Why does that not surprise me?" Dan said, a little too quickly, shaking his head. "Do you think I could have stopped him gambling his way into gaol? Do you?"

Richard slammed his fist down hard on the table, making Dan jump. "My family put him in Marshalsea, not his own actions. Had you been there, it might not have happened. I didn't leave him alone. I left him, so I thought, in your care, and what did you do?"

Dan, staring firmly at the table, chose not to answer.

"Tell me, why?" Richard demanded again.

Dan glanced up and met Richard's cold steel eyes. "Because you were dead. And he's not you. I couldn't make him into something he's not, could I?"

Both men stared at each other. The silence was suddenly broken by a women's voice.

"Shift your elbows otherwise I've nowhere to put the plates."

Richard, sitting back, removed his arms from the table but ignored her. Dan did the same as a plate of cheese and ham was banged down noisily between them and, a moment later, a wooden board topped with bread was dropped next to it. Dan scowled at the woman who had delivered them. The sound from the clanking plates grated inside his head painfully. Lizbet held his eyes as she loudly thumped down a pitcher of beer between them. Turning on her heel she left them, Dan muttering swear words at her retreating back.

"If I may continue…" Richard drew Dan's angry gaze back from where it rested on the girl's back.

Dan returned his attention to the Master, though not particularly wanting Richard to continue. He had tried to help Jack, but he'd been shown the door, more than once. Jack had not wanted anyone's help. Finally he said, "I tried, I truly did, but there was no persuading him."

"There is never any persuading Jack when he has a temper on him, and you know that," Richard said coldly. "You should have followed him."

The words hung between them.

Dan knew he should have followed him, but he'd had his own grief and he'd not wanted to deal with

Jack. Jack had reminded him too much of Richard, and Jack had been making a mockery out of everything he had been left.

Dan realised he was going to have to say something. "I know. I should have…" and when he spoke, he knew his words sounded like a poor excuse.

The silence lengthened between them.

Dan added, "I'll not make the mistake a second time." Then when the Master remained silent, he said with finality, "I'll not make…"

Richard regarded him with cold eyes. "I got Jack out of Marshalsea, but I didn't save him from it. He's not the same, Dan. He'll never be the same."

"Looks fine to me," Dan retorted, glad the conversation had moved away from his own failings.

"Well, now you are back, you make sure he stays that way." Richard, changing the subject, asked, "And the others? Where did they go?"

"Pierre and Marc went back to France. As far as I know, they will still be there. They were going to Pierre's father's home in Lille. The others, I don't know. After we'd left Ayscough's man dead on the road, we needed to get away from Burton quickly and no one stopped to take their leave."

"Well, we have a new start." Richard, rising, clapped Dan on the shoulder.

The impact made his head rock, as it was designed to do, and Dan groaned inwardly as his brain inside his skull throbbed.

Chapter 2
An Error Of Judgment is Addressed

Foulës in the frith,
The fishës in the flod,
And I mon waxë wod;
Much sorwe I walkë with
For beste of bon and blod.

†

Pierre and Marc had been with Richard and Jack in England in the summer of 1552 when Mary took the throne from Northumberland's hands. Richard hoped Dan had been right and that they had returned to France and to Marc's father's house. The house was near Château de Malbrouck, about five miles on the wrong side of the French border. Jack and Richard left the men at Eft-Hellendorf and set off over together. Richard very much wanted to increase the number of men under his command again, although what his plans were he did not share with Jack.

They went at dusk. France was at war with England and it made sense not to get caught on the wrong side of the French lines. Both spoke French, however neither would pass as a native.

Between the border and the Château de Malbrouck was open farmland. The terrain was impossibly flat and what trees grew there were sparsely placed, offering little cover. The road was raised from the fields with a deep ditch on either side. They made their journey heavily cloaked, Jack with a hood over his blond hair.

Jack was still enjoying the freedom. The voyage from London had been a trial. Jack hated boats, and he'd spent most of the time at sea drunk, sharing Corracha's stall. Since they had arrived in Europe though, he'd felt a freedom that had not been his for a long time. The weather was good, he was outside. Time in the saddle with his steel back in his hand, he felt his skill returning. The shakes in his hand had lessened to a point where he now thought he'd sometimes imagined them, and the soft flesh on his belly from enforced captivity in London was gone. Jack liked to feel the ache in his body when he'd used it and recognised his skills rising to their old level. Never a complacent man, he'd been taught well, and he knew his continued existence rested upon him following a few simple rules strictly.

They arrived finally at their destination. A few quiet enquiries led them to Marc's father's house. Marc's father's face was grim and his mother, her apron clamped to her face, was crying silently.

"Tomorrow, they'll hang them in the square," Marc's father revealed.

The man before him enquiring after his son was cloaked, but what he had been able to see told him of a wealth his son would never have. Well-stitched, soft leather boots were showing from the edge of the cloak he had wrapped around himself; there was a sword belt beneath it for sure, and his eyes were drawn to the elegant and expensive jewelled rings that crested the man's fine hands.

His son, Marc, and his friend Pierre, had been arrested three days ago for the murder of a man in the village. He'd been found behind the church wall with his head staved in, and seemingly two witnesses had seen Marc and Pierre delivering the fatal blows and then fleeing the scene. It was a fabrication. Everyone knew it. But as recent newcomers to the small town, the pair had been elected as scapegoats for the crime. A crime which everyone also knew had been committed by the son of the Comte de Malbrouck, but for which someone else would have to pay.

"Could you perhaps intervene, put a good word in on their behalf?" Marc's father pleaded.

Richard placed a hand on the man's arm. "I wish that I could, but I am English, and France, where we stand, is at war with England. It's unlikely a word from an enemy is going to offer your son any help. Come on, Jack, let's go into the town and see what we can do."

They left the shack, and behind it their horses, and made their way through the dusk-darkened streets to the town square.

"Are you sure this is safe?" Jack hissed in his ear.

"Not at all," Richard replied, and then added, "Didn't you tell me once that you declared yourself a Scot when in France?"

"Aye, I did. The French have no idea what a bloody Scotsman sounds like, so it's usually fairly easy to confuse them."

"Well then, let us be two travelling Scots from Edinburgh. Have you ever been to Scotland?"

"You damn well know I haven't."

"You're lucky then; it's a damp wet land swarming with midges and mites, and clans that have as yet to accept that there is a world beyond their border and whose principal pastime is fighting amongst themselves," Richard replied cheerfully.

"Perfect place for you then," Jack commented sourly.

Richard declined to reply.

†

In the square there was a tavern with benches outside and a good view of the open square where the empty wooden market stands stood in two long lines. By virtue of an economy of materials, they used the structure of the gallows platform to bolster the ends of the two rows of stalls. Behind the stalls was a pen, and from the noise coming from it, it was full of cattle, as the market would take place tomorrow. Entertainment would be provided early on and then the market would take over. The empty wooden boards would be filled with fabrics, pottery, hides, earthenware, ribbons, fowl and vegetables. The cattle to be sold, though, were already installed.

The brothers sat quietly outside the inn and Richard ordered ale and pies.

It was Jack who finally broke the silence. "What are you thinking?"

He'd spoken in English, quietly so as not to be overheard, but the reply from Richard came in his neutrally accented French. "Still your words. I'm trying to think."

"This is going to go wrong," Jack observed morosely.

"Stop complaining, you wanted to be here," Richard replied, stilling Jack's words, if only for a moment.

"Wanted to be? If I remember, it was you who invited me?" Jack retorted.

"Only to save you having to beg to be asked." Richard grinned. "I'm trying to think."

Jack, still grumbling, took a long draught of ale and looked in the direction of Richard's gaze. His brother's assessing eyes were scrutinising the gallows platform.

It was not a new structure. Fresh planking showed where the platform has been repaired, especially at the end where the pillory post stood. Nagging wives, poor apprentices and lazy servants would find themselves chastened and tied to it for a day, shamed by the villagers and unable to avoid any unpleasant missiles aimed in their direction.

The gallows to hang a man were both simple and cruel. The neck nooses were currently looped away over the framework. The platform provided only two steps for the condemned to step up to receive the noose and then they would be either pushed or forced to jump from the top rung. The drop was not long. Jack doubted it would be long enough to break a man's neck. Their feet would dangle only a short distance above the platform so there was no way helping hands could grab their legs and bring on a swifter end by breaking their necks.

A shudder ran down Jack's spine. He'd liked Marc and Pierre, and somewhere, not far from where he sat now, he knew they would be contemplating their final moments the following day.

Jack pulled his gaze back from the gallows and attempted to gain his brother's attention. "Come on, we can't sit here all night."

Richard gave him a withering glance. "There are two of us. We need to create a lot of confusion if we are to stop this tomorrow."

"Well I'm fairly confused already as to how we, just the two of us, can take on the whole town," Jack complained.

"We are going to recruit a dozen or so able helpers, each with the strength of ten men and all of them eager to escape themselves." Richard laughed quietly at the expression on his brother's face. Clapping him on the arm he added, "I'll show you later, when it gets a little darker."

They would need rope, Richard had said, lots of rope. Some of it they filched from the back of the blacksmiths and some they liberated by silently loosening the rope bindings holding the stalls together, rendering the rickety structures even more susceptible to collapse. More they took from the gallows platform, including a good length which had been rigged as a hand rail around the edges, to keep the prisoners from the spectators. Jack shook his head as he laid out the lengths as directed; how his brother's mind worked was beyond him, and what he needed the rope for, he had no idea.

When Richard finally told him what they were to use the rope for, his initial reaction was to tell his brother he thought he was mad. But then, as Richard explained in patient detail, Jack began to see how it could work and silently, under the cover of night, he set out to lay the ropes where his brother wanted them.

The final tasks Richard needed performing found them under the gallows platform. An oil lamp stolen from a baker's window cast lurid yellow light around the interior and upon Jack, sweat beading on his brow, muscles in his neck corded as he stood, arms above his head lending a steadying hold to his brother who was stood on his shoulders.

"Will you hurry up?" Jack hissed.

As if in answer, the feet on his shoulders shifted their weight and Jack cursed as he fought to keep his balance, and that of the man above him who seemed to have total faith in Jack's ability to keep them both upright.

"I can't see," Richard complained. His weight shifted again causing Jack to sway. "Pass me the lamp."

Loosening a hand from his brother's calf, Jack reached tentatively for the oil lamp where it sat on a planking shelf. It was just too far away from him to reach without leaning, and lean at the moment he could not. Shuffling his feet in the dirt, he closed the gap.

"Hurry up!" Richard said, using the wall for support. He leant down and an impatient hand opened and closed above Jack's head.

"Have some bloody patience or you'll be on the floor with your skull cracked open," Jack growled. He had a hold on the lamp now and, keeping it carefully level to stop the flame from being drowned, he passed it up. The lamp was taken quickly and disappeared up over, taking with it the light. Jack, returning his hand to the steadying hold on Richard's leg, could see little below him but above him when he tilted his head back he saw the knife in his brother's hand and the roped joints he was methodically applying the blade to.

All of Richard's weight shifted to his left leg as he leant to cut the next rope fixing.

"For God's sake, tell me where you want me to move to. Don't make me guess," Jack complained, moving quickly to centralise the weight again.

"I would have thought it was obvious," came the quick reply from above him.

"I'm in the damned dark, in more ways than one. I cannot read your mind." The man above him sawing at the ropes seemed to be totally unconcerned that his footing was not on solid ground. "Will you stand still?"

"Look, if I could swap places with you, I would. But really, it's not that practical, is it?" Richard's knife severed the rope and his body lurched as the support it had offered gave way.

"For God's sake!" Jack staggered two paces forward trying to regain his balance.

"Go left, not forward. Two paces, and another, stop there – I can reach now."

"What do you mean 'it's not practical'?" Jack, feet slightly further apart now, had better control over his balance.

"Exactly what it sounds like," Richard replied. "I'm far lighter. It would hardly make any kind of sense, now would it, to put the lighter, smaller man on the bottom?"

"Are you accusing me of being fat?" Jack blurted, and when his question was met with stony silence, he continued, "Well, are you?"

"Not fat exactly. More well-built, like a cart horse, whereas I'm more a hunting hound," Richard replied.

Jack couldn't see his face but knew his words would be accompanied by a mischievous grin.

"Come on left, left horsey, renvers three more paces. Well done." Richard added in the dressage command and Jack cursed.

"Just remember whose shoulders you are stood on," Jack shuffled the last step and stood still. He felt Richard's movement above him as his knife set to work again.

"How could I forget? Right, that should do it. Let go and I'll jump down," Richard commanded.

Jack loosened his hold on his legs and Richard jumped down, his hand using the top of Jack's head for support on the way. He still had the lit baker's lamp in his other hand and greeted Jack with a raised eyebrow. "Come on, we haven't got all night."

Jack, lost for words, was forced to follow in his brother's wake as Richard dropped to his knees and crawled out from under the edge of the platform.

✝

The morning found them back in the square. A cart, high-sided and containing the miserable forms of the condemned, was already waiting at the end of the gallows platform. Through the slatted sides they were providing caged entertainment for the gathering town's folk who hurled insults and worse at them. Watching from the back of the crowd, Jack couldn't see the men he knew; they had their backs to the crowd to protect themselves from the hurled filth, and it was further complicated by there being four men in the cart awaiting the rope and not just the men they sought to save.

"Shall I go now?" Jack asked under his breath.

"No, wait. Let's see who they bring out first," Richard cautioned, and Jack waited.

Eventually, on horseback, the town officials arrived along with a priest and took up positions on the platform. It was with some satisfaction that Jack noted that none of them had seemed to notice the missing rope that had ringed the platform, separating them from the crowd.

The condemned men in the cart had their hands tied behind them, and around their necks a second rope was looped to lead them by. The cart was opened and one of the guards, who had been cheerfully encouraging the gathered crowd to assail those within with insults and worse, picked his first victim. Winding a sinewy hand around one of the trailing ropes attached to the condemned man's neck, he pulled. A vicious tug brought the man to land cruelly on his face, much to the amusement of the spectators.

Spurred on by the popular support, as the man got back to his knees he was pulled over again. Jack didn't know the man, but he felt his stomach twist and his face harden as he watched him being dragged as he tried to crawl up the steps to the platform. There was a vicious cut above his left eye and his mouth was split, blood running into his eyes and mixing with the tears.

The second man avoided the humiliation suffered by the first and jumped quickly from the cart, landing squarely on his feet. Jack didn't know him either. His feet were bare and bleeding and he shuffled slowly up the steps to join his companion.

Their crimes were read out to the assembled crowd. Death for stealing a goose.

Well, thought Jack, *a man is worth much less than an animal. Christ, what a crime to go to your death for, stealing a bloody goose of all things.*

Observing the pair closely, it was plain to see why they had wanted the fowl. Both their faces wore the pinched appearance of hunger, hollow-cheeked and slack-skinned. Beneath their shirts, ribs pushed through sunken flesh. The crime they had committed was the simple one of wishing to survive. Survival was something a choking rope was about to deny both of them very soon.

The priest took over then. Broad chested with a barrel of a stomach protruding from his Christian robes, he stepped to the edge of the platform to address the assembled crowd. Jack wondered if he would notice the missing rope, but the cleric was too interested in delivering a diatribe to the assembled on the Ten Commandments and in particular 'thou shalt not steal'. He finished by lecturing the convicted, delivering the solemn judgment of a vengeful God upon them for breach of his rules.

Jack's face darkened. He had no love for this robed, judgmental breed. Suddenly he received a hard jab in his ribs from an elbow, reviving his attention. Richard did not want Jack's disapproving stare that he laid on the priest to attract the attention of the people pressed close to him. Jack cleared his face and watched blankly, as the men were forced to take their final two steps on earth. The nooses were slipped over their waiting necks and pulled tight. The town executioner moved behind them and pushed each of them in the small of the back. Both fought to retain their balance on the narrow perch, but both lost the battle.

The crowd cheered.

Jack had been right. There was hardly any drop and they swung frantically on the rope. Legs jolting, bodies convulsing, piss running down their legs, soaking their hose. You can't scream when you are being hung, the rope chokes off the sound in your throat, but a rattling, coughing gasp reached Jack's ears, one he recognised. Their eyes were popping from their heads, spittle running down their chins, mouths open, expressions those of panic. The man with the bleeding face swung on his rope and his eyes, for a moment, seemed to connect with Jack's. His mouth was wide open in a silent scream, tongue protruding from his mouth a seemingly impossible distance. Jack didn't break the stare – it was the rope, twisting, that took the man's gaze from his.

Jack watched them dance, the Devil's death indeed, as he'd called it when he was a child. The sinners' torment in Hell, starting before they'd even had their souls ripped from their bodies. The kicking lessened and after a few minutes lessened to a twitching. The shouting crowd quietened and their interest switched to the scaffold's next two victims.

As Jack watched, there was a hurried conversation between those gathered on the platform. The officials had their heads together and after a brief moment there seemed to be some agreement reached. A liveried servant drew a knife from his belt and dropped easily down the steps from the platform to where Jack's old companions waited. The men he had looked for, he now recognised as they stood in the cart ready to meet their end.

As Jack's body stiffened, a restraining hand with steel fingers bit into his arm to hold him still.

"It's good, Jack, I think they are going to get Marc and Pierre to move the bodies for them so they don't have to," Richard said quietly in his ear, and it was true.

The liveried servant slashed the binding ropes and both men, their arms free, walked up the platform. The hangman had unwound the securing rope for the first noose and the body dropped, to the crowd's delight, in a crumpled heap on the planking. The noose was loosened and slipped over the purple, swollen neck and between them, Marc and Pierre hefted the body by its legs and underarms across the platform and down the steps, rolling it into the cart before returning for the corpse of the man with the blooded face.

Richard still had hold of Jack's arm, and now pushed him. "Go, go."

The crowd were pressing forward, eager for the next display, and Jack, unseen, skirted quickly around the back of them, making his way to the back of the market stalls and the rear of the hangman's platform. Dropping to his knees, he ducked under the fencing and disappeared between the warm, brown flanks of the cattle.

Last night, at Richard's direction, he had fashioned nooses of his own and they now lay amongst the bovine feet. Shoving and coaxing first one and then another to move, he retrieved each one and slipped it over a wet, black nose and past a pair of gentle eyes. The pen was crammed and there was little space for the cattle to move, that was until the entire back fence suddenly fell flat. Jack, seeing it, raced to the back to avoid being trampled and then stabbed first one and then another thick hide rear with his poniard. The cows bellowed in fury and charged towards the opened fence. Jack kept up his encouragement, unsure which of the brown rears with their thin, tufted tails, belonged to the cattle harnessed unwillingly to the platform behind him.

The animals as a mass suddenly surged forward towards the large opening and Jack immediately heard the fierce cracking of the wooden joints behind him as the staging began to give way.

Jack pressed forward so he was amongst the escaping cattle and avoided the platform as it finally tipped and then fell, propelling dignitaries, priests and the condemned into the dirt. With a nimbleness borne of desperation, Pierre jumped first; landing squarely on his feet, he began to run as the splintered wooden platform being pulled by the herd overtook him and dragged him beneath it. Marc, not so lucky, slithered over the edge of the bouncing woodwork and fell, landing awkwardly on his knees, the platform only inches behind his heels. Jack's strong hand pulled him forwards and forced him into a stumbling run, preventing his body from being smashed beneath the wood. The joint-wrenching hold saved him. Jack grinned at him as he dragged Marc through the jostling cram of bovine bodies.

Jack shoved and pushed them, and their thick hide bodies buffeted him back in return. If he tripped, he knew they would be firstly trampled by the hooves and then further flattened by the gallows that they dragged behind them. A fierce grip under Marc's arm, he pulled him along, forcing his way through the melee and towards the edge of the running herd.

Ahead was a wide exit from the market square. On the right was a brazier, lit with orange coal where a chestnut seller had set up his stall. The coals tumbled from the iron basket onto the mud and onto something else which could be hardly seen.

Glowing and hot, the coals lit the black powder trail laid on the ground, spitting and hissing and showering sparks on the mud. A hessian bag thrown amongst the tumble of coals quickly burnt through and the powder ignited with a dull thunder clap.

Twenty-three panicking animals dug their cloven hooves into the soft earth of the road and brought themselves to a skidding, jolting halt. Jack, pulling Marc behind him, did not stop and emerged at the front of the cattle a moment before the lead beasts changed their course. The cows stampeded left in panic and headed back towards the market place, still dragging the platform behind them.

Bellowing, the cattle ran, and on foot the townspeople scattered from them. Behind the cacophony, Richard, Jack and two grateful men made a neat escape through the quiet streets.

They ran from the village towards Marc's father's house where their horses, already saddled and ready, waited for them. In the confusion of their escape, Jack had not chanced a backward glance and had missed the liveried men who had witnessed their escape and skirted round the edge of the cattle to give chase.

Jack, leading his mare from the back of the house, was preoccupied and unaware of the pursuers and met them head on. He was alone. Marc was taking leave of his father and Richard and Pierre were with them.

There were four of them.

The two directly in front of Jack grinned maliciously and the two on either side moved round to give his attackers space, and worse still, moved to a point where they knew his vision could no longer see them. Two in front, two behind.

Jesus!

Jack gripped the hilt in his right hand tighter. He couldn't win, but every move he was going to make was going to damn well count. Of the two before him, the one on the right was the natural target. But was he going to get an attack in before it was two against one? He doubted it. On his left, just on the edge of his vision was another. Jack shifted the poniard in his hand. It would be a hard throw, and if he turned to put some power behind it, the two in front of him would be on him.

Jack pulled up his left arm, readying to make the throw – and that's when he felt it, the forceful jolt in his back as his brother's shoulders connected with his own.

The odds changed.

Jack grinned.

The two behind him were no longer his concern and the two before him, their confident smiles falling from their faces, knew it.

Fighting back to back was an art. You needed to communicate your position to the man behind you without wrong-footing them, or banging into them hard and affecting their swordsmanship.

Jack heard the clash of steel behind him; his brother had engaged and Jack sent his blade towards that of the more confident of his two attackers. The other, he gauged, would wait to see what the outcome was, or he might chance an attack if Jack gave him an opening, which he had no intention of offering.

Neither were skilled and in a moment the man before Jack realised that greater numbers did not mean greater skill as he found his blade deflected back at him a second time. Jack couldn't take the two killing steps forward he needed, as he had to remain closely linked with his brother. Otherwise, both their backs would be exposed. So when his blade connected with his assailant, it was only the bare point that cut through a sleeve to carve a scarring cut across the other's upper arm.

It drew blood, a gasp from the man and a moment's pause. Jack reversed the poniard in his hand and sent it on a powerful flight into his opponent's thigh. The blade buried itself in muscle and flesh down to the bone. There was a scream and his sword dropped. His partner was already backing from the fight, recognising that he was next.

Wisely, Jack didn't turn. A boot to the injured man's leg caught the hilt of the poniard, sending him falling to land on his back screaming. The other ran backwards until he judged himself a safe distance and then turned and took flight.

Then Jack did turn. Richard also had one man down who he was now rolling on the road, blood bubbling from his mouth, hands clasping his chest where his brother's blade had pierced his lungs. The second had dropped his sword and was stepping slowly backwards, his hands up in a gesture of supplication.

Jack clapped his arm around Richard's shoulders for the briefest of moments before turning to deal with his fallen foe.

He pulled the poniard from the man's leg, and the man emitted another agonised howl as the blade was wrenched from his flesh.

☥

The horses worked hard for them, carrying a double load and at a gallop most of the way. A coppice of trees provided some small shelter and they finally broke their flight there, resting the sweating mounts.

There were tears in Marc's eyes. He dropped to his knees in front of the Master.

"That was a kindness I don't deserve, Master." His voice was the accented French Jack remembered.

Pierre joined him, kneeling, head bowed. "Neither of us can thank you enough."

There was a silence. It was uncomfortable to Jack, but if it was to Richard, he didn't show it.

Finally Richard spoke. "Let us hope that you are both afflicted with very long memories."

Swallowing hard, Pierre met the Master's eyes. "Very long, Master, you can depend upon it."

Richard nodded. "Get up. We will give the horses a little longer, but we dare not stay longer than that. It'll not take them long to realise they have been duped and send out men to hunt for us, and there is a chance they saw us riding this way."

Jack, a bone scraper in his hand, was wiping the lathered sweat from his mare's neck.

"That was a good start to a day, don't you agree?" commented Richard, leant with his back against the mare's saddle.

Jack was astounded. "I like women, I like ale, I love good food and the feel of a great horse. I don't overly like being nearly trampled to death, only you could find some pleasure in that."

Richard, laughing, bent his head close to Jack's. "Yes, you did. Admit it to yourself. We are not out of this yet, but I will lay a wager you'll be telling a good story over ale to Froggy and Dan when we return."

Jack, pulling up the girth strap he'd slackened when he'd dismounted, shook his head. "As you say, we are not out of this yet. I suggest we leave, and soon."

"As you say, come on then."

Within a moment, Richard and Jack were mounted again, each with a pillion and they set their horses' heads back in the direction of the border.

Chapter 3
A Lawyer's Trial

Ich have y-don al myn youth,
Oftë, ofte, and ofte;
Longe y-loved and yerne y-beden –
Ful dere it is y-bought!

✝

It had been a confrontation that Clement knew was coming. He very much wished he had never heard of the name Fitzwarren.

Robert had summoned him to his London house a week ago. Clement had penned a rapid reply declining the invitation and pleading an infirmity for his lack of attendance. He knew his refusal would bring Robert to his offices, but it put off the meeting for another few days and Clement was, above all else, a coward.

He was now stuck between the lot of them. Richard Fitzwarren was a calculating cur, too clever for his own good, but it was his bastard brother Clement was justifiably terrified of. He'd been quite sure that the one who had escaped Marshalsea had been set to kill him if the other brother had not laid a controlling hand to stop him. Clement had drafted the legal documents for the bastard's father to sign to acknowledge him as heir. Since then, he had not heard from them.

Richard Fitzwarren had provided him with an address he could use to send messages should he need to, and he had agreed that should he hear of anything that might be of interest to Richard, that he would communicate it promptly. If he failed to, then Richard had made it quite clear he would remove the restraining hand from his brother, and then Clement rightly feared he would be torn limb from limb by the dog. Robert Fitzwarren he feared, but he was utterly terrified of the blond bastard he'd helped to put into Marshalsea.

Robert was here now at his offices. He heard Marcus yelp as he was pushed out of the way and Clement braced himself for the confrontation. This was not his fault, it was that fool Kettering's fault. Clement was going to stand by that.

The door slammed open, rebounding against the wall and sending a cloud of dust into the room.

"You had better make this good," Robert Fitzwarren warned from where he stood in the doorway.

There was little Robert could do other than threaten, and threaten he did. Clement's heart was in his throat and his knees shook. But Clement was not one of Robert's servants, and the lawyer knew that no matter however much Robert wanted to beat him, he knew he couldn't.

Clement swallowed hard and nodded.

"Him and that bastard are wanted for murder, not once now but bloody twice!" Robert stormed, pushing a stack of papers off the end of Clement's desk and sitting on the edge.

"Murder?" Clement squeaked. Why did this not surprise him? Clement pushed his chair away from the desk in an attempt to put some distance between himself and his angry client.

Robert rounded on Clement. "Aye, not one but two it seems. They argued over a whore and killed two men. One of them had his throat cut so badly his body was drained of blood and there was little but a few strings of flesh holding his head on, by all accounts."

Clement paled even further.

Robert sneered, "And the other one got a knife through his ribs. A knife in the back would be more to my brother's liking, but never mind."

"And have they caught up with them?" Clement was for a moment hopeful that his nightmare might come to an end if the blond bastard ended up swinging from a rope for his crimes.

"No. They're cowards, tricksters. They'll not be around now. They will have fled from the city," Robert spat. Little did Clement know that Robert was trying hard to bury the uncomfortable memory of his meeting with Richard and the bastard he called a brother. Clement would have been heartened had he known as well of the painful cut, still tender and healing under Robert's hose, where Richard's blade had torn through the skin on his thigh. "That bastard will wish he was back in Marshalsea when they catch him."

Robert went on to tell Clement of the enquiries his men had made which had eventually led them to the location of the inn where Richard and the bastard had been lodging. Robert had taken himself to the inn, and an open purse and his obvious rank had produced the information that linked Richard to the deaths of Colan and his cousin. When pressed with silver, Fendral had confessed to having been forced at knifepoint to help Richard move the bodies from the room upstairs. Fendral had gone further and told Robert of a whore who had also helped in moving the bodies, her name was Lizbet.

Clement took in all the details silently.

When Robert was finished, Clement did have some news that he thought might cheer his client. "I have had some communication from the lawyer in the De Bernay case, and there's good news." He hoped this would divert Robert's attention away from Marshalsea and the missing man.

"Go on." Robert was not going to be easily diverted.

"The woman's family have sent through a deposition." Clement fished through the papers on his desk. "Ah, here it is. He states that Peter De Bernay, as her closest living relative, will be happy for the girl to join his household and he states that her own family are rightly placed to manage her property affairs until the girl is wedded."

Robert sounded horrified. "What's in it for me? What do I get out of this?"

"Well, they say they will welcome her back to the family and..."

Robert's fist hit the table hard, stopping Clement's words and sending more files to slither to the floor. "Know this, you fool, I want control of Assingham. I took over as her guardian when her family spurned her. I'm not handing her back so they can dispose of her and her inheritance as they bloody well see fit!"

Clement's hand, holding the papers from De Bernay's lawyer, shook.

"I have the girl, and I should have control of her lands. Why can't you see that?" Robert continued.

Clement was forced to speak. "It's not that simple, sir. Her family have accepted her and they are her legal guardians. We would have to assert that they are not suitable for this role and ask for you to be legally appointed her guardian."

"Of course they are not suitable. It's been nearly three years since her father was killed, and since then they have taken her lands and refused to acknowledge her as her father's daughter. If she goes back she'll not be safe, they only want her so they can control her wealth," Robert spat.

"That very well might be the case," Clement replied. Then more to himself, he added, "We would need to apply to Chancery for a writ of guardianship. That would provide you with the legal right to control her manor and lands until the girl is wedded."

"Well, what are you waiting for? Get it done," demanded Robert, sliding off the end of the desk.

†

William had sent for his physician, Master Juris. He had not wanted to, but in the end there was no one else, and he wasn't prepared to spend his last remaining days alone in this room. There had to be something that could be done.

Juris arrived, and Edwin and Jon carried the aged lord as steadily as they could to the bed so Juris could examine his patient.

Propped up on pillows and panting from the exertion, William banished his servants from the room, leaving him alone with Juris.

"Well man, don't bloody stand there, take a look," William barked.

William was wearing a linen shift only, and his legs, bare and pale as bleached bones against the rich counterpane, lay outstretched and unresponsive. Strong muscle and taut sinew had withered, skin hung on the emaciated legs and the joints at the ankles and knees protruded viciously. The narrow thin legs looked not at all like they belonged to the man propped up on the goose-feather pillows.

William was suffering a wasting sickness that was slowly stripping his legs of strength. It had started almost two years ago with an acute pain in his legs and a swelling at the base of his spine. His physicians had bled him, attempting to balance the humors, confining him to his bed, forcing vile smelling concoctions on him and wrapping his legs in a red curative cloth that had stunk of piss. William was convinced that they had robbed him of the last of his strength, for within a month he could no longer walk, and from then he had been confined to his room on the top floor of the house, transported between his bed and his chair by servants.

Juris laid his cool hands on William's legs; the slack skin lay in loose folds where once it had housed muscle. William tolerated his prodding and poking fingers through gritted teeth. He was not prepared to concede defeat, not just yet. Richard might have removed a sizeable portion of his wealth from his rooms, but William had plenty more. If he made Juris understand just how much he was willing to pay, he was sure there must be something that he could do. He knew Juris worked with the monks at St Bartholomew's in Smithfield, and perhaps they could offer him some earthly salvation from his condition.

"Well? What do you think?" William felt he'd waited long enough.

"My Lord, do you still have full feeling in your legs?" Juris enquired, and then pinched the skin of William's feet. "Here, can you feel that?" William nodded. "And what about here? And the lump on your back, is that still troubling you?"

"Not so painful. It's more a damned discomfort than anything else." With Juris' help he rolled onto his side so that the physician could view the swelling at the base of his spine.

Juris ran his hands over the darkened lump. There would be more, much more inside, hidden between William's organs, pushing them apart as it grew within the man, slowly taking over his body. Juris knew there was little he could do for William. That, however, was not what his patient would wish to hear.

"I think the swelling is lessening, and the heat has left the skin which is a very good sign." Juris pulled down the linen shift and helped William to roll himself back to sit up once more on the bed.

"Is there anything you can recommend?" William asked, then, getting to the crux of the matter, added, "I am a man of means. I am aware that you work with the monks at St Bartholomew's – perhaps they have some medications, some skills that might bring me some relief?"

Juris nodded. "I can certainly take your case to them, discuss it with Father Landown. He runs the hospital. If I have your permission, my lord." Juris did not like the slur on his professional knowledge that William had just made. However, he could smell money and that would more than make up for any slight made against him as doctor.

"You have my permission. Do it with all haste. I am sick of being tied to these rooms," William replied shortly.

Juris left him soon after, a new salve on the cabinet to be rubbed into his legs twice a day and powder to be added to wine three times a day.

William summoned Edwin and watched as he added the reddish powder to a glass of wine. It settled like dust on the surface. Taking a spoon, Edwin stirred it, and the spoon sent some of the powder into the air. Edwin grimaced as his nose registered the odour and the smell reached William's nose as well, reminding him of the stench of rancid leather from the tanner's yard in Grace Street. Christ only knew what Juris had put into it.

Edwin held out the glass, and William's trembling hand knocked it, splashing a red stain across his linen shift.

"You imbecile! Once more and I'll turn you out into the street with nothing but the clothes on your back, do you hear me?" William roared.

Edwin, eyes fixed on the floor, nodded and mumbled, "Yes, my lord."

"Speak up man!" William had heard perfectly well.

"Yes, my lord," Edwin said a little louder.

"Get out of my sight." William waved towards the door.

Edwin needed no further invitation and, backing to the door, had it open in an instant and was through it before William could send another tirade in his direction.

All the drapes were drawn back around the bed and William could clearly see his wife watching him haughtily, her eyes staring into his from the painting that hung on the wall near the fire. Blue eyes, as bright as sapphires, held his own.

"You think I deserve this, don't you, woman?" William said to his long-dead wife.

†

Pulling the door closed and hearing the finality of the latch click shut, Edwin met Jon's eyes and shook his head. "It doesn't get any better."

"It's words, Edwin, that's all. It's not like the young Master – he'll leave you with a bleeding ear for just looking at him," Jon answered from where he sat on the edge of the makeshift bed in the corridor.

"You're right. It could be a lot worse," Edwin accepted.

"You're lucky to be just working in here for him. Look what happened to young Walt after that bloody horse was stolen from the stables? It was hardly the lad's fault, was it? The Master beat him so bad he couldn't walk for two days!"

Edwin's expression twisted at the memory of it. Walt's face had been left nothing but a blackened bruise; both his eyes were swollen and closed, and when they had opened again one was a milky white, the sight hopelessly lost forever. The other lad, Hal, had hidden, and it had been Ronan who had delivered that beating when he found him squeezing out from under a cupboard in the kitchens. Ronan's temper had flared, but it was nothing compared to Robert Fitzwarren's and Hal got away with boxed ears and a bleeding nose. He'd been lucky.

"Christ, the Fitzwarrens are a bad-tempered lot, down to the very last man," Edwin grumbled, settling down next to Jon. It was a fairly safe place, as William couldn't move. He was bound to his chair and all he could do was shout or pull on the bell-chain fastened to the table at his side, and Robert was not at the London house at the moment.

"What I want to know was what happened a few weeks ago. You've heard what old Charles said, haven't you?" Jon mused.

"Everyone's heard about that. He said it was Richard, back from the grave, but we've never seen him since and no one apart from Charles saw them on that night either. It could have been anyone.

Charles can't see past the end of his nose on a good day," Edwin scoffed.

"Charles said it was Richard Fitzwarren who recognised him, and Charles said he recognised his voice. If you ask me, there is something going on. Master had a sore temper on him when he thrashed Walt, and I'm telling you, it was more than just a lost horse that put him in that mood," Jon continued.

"Maybe, but I'm starting to think it'll not be such a good thing when the Lord dies. We'll not be sat like this then, will we? Robert'll be in there and there'll be no bloody hiding from him like we are now," Edwin grumbled.

"There's no bloody pleasing you, is there? One minute you want the old bastard dead and buried, the next you want to preserve him in his dotage!" Jon rebuked, spreading his hands wide.

"We shall have to wait and see what happens when Robert takes the title. He's not like his father. William liked to be in London, close to Court, but Robert's not bothered; he'd rather be out hunting, he's hardly ever here. I'd wager that we'll have a quiet enough life in London, and he'll be away at the Kent manor. It's a much grander place than here." Edwin settled his back against the wall.

"Let's just hope he leaves us here to manage this place rather than dragging our backsides there. My Marie will not be happy if I have to tell her I'll be moving out of London, and I doubt she'll want to come with me," Jon said, shaking his head.

Edwin laughed and clapped him on the back. "And is that such a bad thing?"

Jon screwed his face up in thought for a moment. "You might have a point. A life without a woman might be a damned sight less complicated."

☦

William was not a man who had ever felt that his spiritual values were under attack by the changing religious mood in the country. The break from Rome established by Henry VIII and the disbursement of the monastic wealth had been a programme William had not only helped enforce, but he had directly profited from it as well. Well placed, and in favour at Henry's Court, parcels of monastic land had been his to purchase at prices that could not be turned down. Henry's coffers swelled, and his key nobles exerted influence over land and property formally under the control of the Catholic Church – it was a mutually beneficial arrangement.

When Henry died and Edward firmly marked England as a Protestant realm, William was happy to believe as his sovereign dictated. With the re-establishment of Catholicism under Mary, William happily switched back and accepted the Mass once more. His property rights were not assailed even if his religious freedoms were – but William was not troubled by this. He would worship where his sovereign directed and questioning the changes was not in his nature. Creation owed its existence to the Creator, and William took his lead on how to worship the Lord from the sovereign. If William believed in anything passionately, it was sovereignty and the divine right of kings. He respected the power he could see, not the one he could not.

Juris had close links with the Church at Bartholomew's. He worked there offering his skills for free to the poor in the infirmary, and two days later Father Landown from the infirmary called to visit William.

Father Landown was shown into William's room, where he sat as usual fastened to his chair. Edwin brought a second chair for Father Landown and set it at a respectful distance from where the lord sat.

"I believe Juris asked you to visit me? I am grateful, father, I had hoped that you may be able to abate my suffering," William said hopefully.

Father Landown nodded. "Master Juris is a godly man. He helps weekly at the infirmary where we treat the poor, and has done so for years. He asks for no payment and uses his own salves and balms in the treatment as well."

William nodded, although he had little interest in how Juris spent his time when he was not attending William, and even less interest in his help of the poor and destitute. He did wish, however, to avail himself of the expertise at Father Landown's disposal, and he had more than Juris working for him. There had to be something they could do. "He has suggested that you might be able to help me. He has done much, but perhaps you can offer me more."

Father Landown smiled. "There is much we can offer, my lord. It would be a simple matter to arrange."

William smiled as well. This was what he wanted to hear. "I thought so. Juris has only so much expertise. With your infirmary and the brothers in your service, you surely are so much more knowledgeable."

"We can start now. We can include your name in our daily mass. The brothers would lift your name higher so the Lord God would hear your name and grant your passage to Heaven. A perpetual mass in your name. God notes such devotion and you can rest assured that your eternal soul would…"

"… I understand, Father, what you can offer my eternal soul. I have not invited you here to discuss my funeral! Your infirmary, your medical advice, are you not experts in this field?"

A confused expression settle on Father Landown's face. "My Lord, we are. Our Order has been offering salvation to the sick and injured since its foundation. Master Juris has discussed your case and he has done as much as he can. It is your eternal soul we can assist."

"I don't want my eternal soul assisting," William said through gritted teeth. "I want earthly assistance to get my legs moving and get me out of this damned chair, you hear?"

Father Landown paled. "My lord, we can offer hope and salvation. Earthly suffering is but fleeting in comparison to a…"

"Get out!" William barked.

Father Landown, even though he was seated, jumped and the chair legs scraped on the floor.

"Edwin, get in here." William was yanking insistently on the chain to summon his servant. Edwin arrived almost instantly. "Get him out of my sight. Now!"

William closed his eyes and rested his head back against the chair and listened to the noise of Edwin closing the door and their footsteps as he walked with Father Landown along the corridor towards the stairs. Such a simple thing. To be able to walk. Damn them all to Hell.

When he opened his eyes again, he found he was not alone. Eleanor's gaze lay upon him, and he was sure he could detect scorn in her eyes.

The following day saw Edwin and Jon labouring as they moved William and his belongings from the top floor to the ground floor. The house had a large hall affording spacious dining, and another smaller room which had been his wife's, and it was here he moved. His bed was dismantled, carried down the stairs on the backs of his servants and rebuilt. His coffers, books and shelves were all brought down and the wall cleared of hunting trophies so that Eleanor could watch over her husband once again.

Sitting back in his chair, William smiled up at his wife. "You were right, I was giving in." The scornful expression seemed to have left Eleanor's face now and her eyes smiled at him once more.

The room was noisier, the sounds from the street making it inside. He heard the servants in the hall outside, and if the door at the end of the corridor were left open he could even hear the noise from the kitchens as well. The noise was better than the oppressive silence of loneliness.

Chapter 4
A Knight's Entrance

Sing cuckóu, nou! Sing cuckóu!
Sing cuckóu! Sing cuckóu nou!
Somer is y-comen in,
Loudë sing, cuckóu!
Growëth sed and blowëth med
And springth the wodë nou
Sing cuckóu!

†

Lizbet had a tray with a breakfast of bread, cheese and ale and efficiently placed a wooden trencher before Richard where he sat outside the inn. The low sun rising to a clear sky was the herald of a pleasantly bright morning and preferable to the inside of the inn, which was filled with smoke from the cooking fires. Lizbet put half of what she had on the tray before him and prepared to leave.

"Who's the rest for?" Richard asked as he tore open the fresh warm brown bread.

"Jack. I thought I'd take it up to him," Lizbet replied, before ducking back through the inn door and making her way to the stairs for the rooms above.

Richard had been about to say something, then changed his mind. Instead he listened closely and smiled when he heard Lizbet's raised voice swearing. Her feet tramped noisily back down the stairs and he called her over as she passed the open doorway.

Lizbet, her eyes blazing and her cheeks hot with anger, stood before him, the tray clutched in white-knuckled hands.

With the eating knife he was holding, Richard pointed to the trestle opposite him. "Sit down."

Lizbet didn't move. Her mouth opened, about to speak, but she thought better of it and closed it again.

Richard raised his eyebrows, nodded towards the seat, and Lizbet grumpily obeyed, noisily banging the tray down on the table.

Richard continued to eat, and Lizbet sat and watched him, her eyes still bright with unspent anger.

After a few minutes he took a draught of ale and his eyes held Lizbet's over the rim of the cup; she met his challenge with her own capable stare.

"He's not your charge anymore," Richard said calmly, then added, "And he's not the man you knew who was fastened to a bed not that long ago. You'll not control him, Lizbet; not even I can do that."

Lizbet didn't reply, but continued to glare at him across the table. Finally unable to contain herself, she spoke. "You knew! And you let me go up?"

The expression on Richard's face was answer enough, and Lizbet swore.

"Come on, Lizbet, you know how it is. He likes women, and, I'm afraid they like him," Richard said. "I'm guessing you found him too busy for food? Well then, you know what you can do with his breakfast, don't you?"

"Shove it down his bloody neck, tray and all?" Lizbet couldn't help herself.

Richard laughed. "No, you eat it. He can go hungry. Then, if you still want to batter him and his new wench with the tray after you've finished, I'll come and watch."

Lizbet couldn't help herself and a grin spread across her face; moments later she was halfway through Jack's breakfast.

By the time Jack arrived outside the inn and found his brother, Lizbet had eaten her fill and left. Jack cast his eyes over the remnants of food on the table.

"It seems you are too late. Sleep in, did you?" Richard queried.

Jack, ignoring him, found two decent sized pieces of bread and stuffed them into his mouth and then tipped the earthenware ale jug to inspect its contents. "Did you leave me nothing?" he complained as he righted the jug.

"It seems not. You could go and find Lizbet and ask her to get you some?" Richard ventured.

Jack's face twisted into a grimace. "Maybe not. She'll be busy enough." Jack rounded up a few more morsels of bread from the trencher and sniffing first at half a cup of ale Lizbet had left, he drank it.

"Is that so?" Richard replied.

Jack declined to reply and said instead, "So, where to next?"

"We are leaving here in a day or so, and I need good horses. Can I trust you with the task of procuring us all some?" Richard fished inside his jacket and threw a purse at Jack that the other intercepted neatly.

Jack, loosening the strings, peered inside, hefting it in his hand so he could fully see the funds he had been provided with.

"You don't have to spend it all," Richard said, reading the calculating expression on Jack's face.

"Would I?" Jack sounded hurt.

"You would. We both know you were born with holes in your hands from which coins trickle."

Jack, about to speak, was stopped when his brother said quickly, "You are the best judge of a good horse. I trust you to spend our money wisely."

"Our money?" Jack repeated slowly.

Richard smiled. "Of course. I'm just not letting you look after it. Think of me as your banker. So when you are spending that money you can keep half of what is left."

"That'll sharpen my bargaining up," Jack said grinning.

"I thought it might. We need a horse for yourself, then there is Dan, Mat, Marc, Froggy, Pierre, and I need a dray for the cart and one for Lizbet and a spare." Richard ticked each of them off on his fingers.

Jack smiled; the thought of getting back on a good horse again was one that appealed, and the opportunity of going out to buy horses appealed even more. When it came to gauging a good horse from a bad one, few were better than him. So far, apart from Richard who had brought Corracha with him, he had been making do with a mare hired from the inn. Docile and obedient with a steady pace, but she was not at all what he was used to.

When Jack awoke the following day he found that Richard, along with Froggy Tate, had gone. He'd left brief instructions with Mat for Jack to wait for his return once he had purchased the horses. Jack was less than pleased that his brother had kept his impending and obviously planned departure from him.

†

Gunpowder might have originated in China but Europe in the renaissance charged its chief alchemists with the task of perfecting this lethal recipe. The simple ingredients of saltpetre, charcoal and sulphur when combined produced this explosive powder. The Liber Ignium, Book of Fires, was Graecus' own collection of incendiary recipes. Over time more ingredients were added, quantities and weights refined. Military might could indeed be couched in terms of gunpowder; when Henry VIII had invaded France in 1544, he got his supplies so catastrophically wrong that he ran out, having to suffer the huge expense of buying extortionately priced powder from Antwerp, much to the profit and delight of the merchants involved.
    Froggy had spent time in Antwerp and had more than a few stories to tell about his narrow escapes when manufacturing black powder. He had been the

ideal companion for the trip to the city that Richard was about to make.

It had been via enquiry in London, before Richard left, that the name of Master Scranton as an expert in the field had arisen, as had his departure two years previously. Seeing the threatening clouds of Catholicism rolling towards him, Master Scranton had taken his family and run. He knew very well Antwerp was not only a centre for alchemist learning, but also the largest producer of black powder in Europe and black powder was his own specialty and trade. He'd arrived hopeful to secure another significant post, but as a foreigner he'd found his way blocked. His expertise had been shunned and Scranton had eventually settled for a job managing black powder production in a warehouse for a Master who cared little for him and even less for his expertise.

Froggy and Richard were in Antwerp now at Master Scranton's rooms above a printers in the Lombardenvest quarter of the city. Beneath them they heard, and to a lesser extent felt, the incessant clack and thud of the mechanical presses, the floor reverberating with the noise. Scranton had spread on the desk between them a copy of the revered Liber Ignium, the thumbed and blackened pages telling of use.

"And why should I share with you anything?" Master Scranton sat back heavily and regarded the pair across the table from him over steepled fingers.

"Vanity," Richard said smiling. "Such a thing as knowledge for knowledge's sake is of little use.

You cannot yourself profit from it. I, on the other hand, can."

"You'd steal my secrets for your own ends? I hardly think you are recommending yourself to me, sir."

"Steal is a perhaps an overstatement. I rather think you'll share them freely." Richard continued to smile and Froggy, sitting next to him, continued to stare between the pair uneasily.

Master Scranton dropped his hands to the desk with a thud. "Do you think I am simple, sir?"

"Not simple, but perhaps expedient. I can profit from them, and you can't. So the simple solution is a sharing of your knowledge in exchange for some of my profit, is it not?" Richard explained simply. "And vanity."

"Vanity," Master Scranton echoed.

"In England, Master Scranton, before your unfortunate forced retreat to Europe, you were a man of some note, I believe, in charge of the powder rooms at the Tower and His Majesties Keeper of Munitions. In Antwerp, as an Englishman, you are always suspect, always the outsider. Such a position here would be impossible."

Master Scranton's face crumbled, his voice when he spoke was bitter. His visitor's assessment of the situation had been far too accurate. "They suspect me always, the Guilds are tightly knit. Without recommendation or a forwarder I have no way in. Skills and knowledge count for naught here. It is money and names that pave the way."

"Well I assure you I have a new Master for you in mind that will not baulk at your heritage, and will indeed weigh you by your knowledge and skills alone," Richard replied, the silence between them lengthened as Master Scranton considered his words.

Master Scranton raised his eyes to Richard's. "Tell me, who your Master is that could offer me such a post again?"

"I will let you think on it." Richard pushed himself from the chair and stood quickly.

Froggy surprised, scrambled up quickly to match his Master.

"I cannot consider it, sir, unless I know for whom you work," Master Scranton complained.

Richard smiled. "One a step at a time. I'll call again tomorrow evening if I may?"

They had left and were in the street before Froggy spoke. "I thought you wanted to recruit him? He was the best you know?"

"I do," Richard said. "I've fed him hope, now he just needs a little time for it to take root and we shall see if from it some commitment might grow."

"God, I don't understand you, I bloody don't," grumbled Froggy.

Richard clapped Froggy on the back. "Master Scranton is not in an uncomfortable position. His wife and family are housed in Antwerp, he has a job, an income, even if he does not like his Master, and even if he feels he should have a better position in life." Froggy's face was still blank. "It is, as I said, vanity. I can offer him back his professional pride. So let him think on that for a while."

Froggy grumbled under his breath; this was all just wasting more time, he was sure.

But the next day the reception they received was markedly different. Master Scranton's eyes were more focused, he moved with an energy that had been previously absent and it was obvious he had been waiting expectantly for them to arrive. Froggy smiled. Master Scranton was acting like a man ready to be bought; the Master was indeed a crafty bastard.

Master Scranton showed them into the same sparsely furnished room they had visited the previous day and bid them be seated. The Liber Ignium still lay on the table, open this time at a different page. Master Scranton may indeed have been a Protestant, but the Liber Ignium was his bible. Next to it lay a calf skin wallet; the leather thong ties were loose, and an eating knife was wedged in between the pages. Evidently Master Scranton had something he would like to share.

"So gentlemen, I considered your words, and I am hopeful that you will tell me more," Master Scranton asked smiling. He offered Froggy wine which he accepted, though the Master declined, making Froggy instantly regret his decision so he decided to ignore the wine in the cup and leave it untouched on the table.

Richard reached into his doublet and pulled out a letter. The seal was broken and the paper somewhat creased, and he handed it to Master Scranton without a word.

Master Scranton unfolded the single sheet and angled it towards the candle flame to read the words. It was the brief note from Tresham recommending Richard Fitzwarren to the Order of St John, and in particular to their outpost in Venice. It spoke of little else, but the name of the Order was enough; Master Scranton's eyes widened and his jaw dropped. Froggy wished he knew what was on the page that had such an effect on the man, and when Scranton spoke, Froggy's eyes opened wide as well with shock.

"You are working for the Order of St John?"

"Hoping to, yes," replied Richard upon receiving back the sheet from Master Scranton's hands.

"Sir, I fled England to save myself and my family from the unholy wrath of Rome. The Order is not so different."

"The Order is not Rome, indeed rarely do those two esteemed organisations see eye to eye. The threat the Order seeks to prevent is from Saladin, not from within Europe. What we can offer them I think would make them overlook your adherence to the Protestant cause," Richard replied. "They are not linked to the inquisition; you would have my word that you would be safe on that level."

Froggy raised his eyebrows, but said nothing. He wondered exactly how the Master would seek to protect one man's life if the Order of St John decided it should be forfeit. It would be a quick end, Froggy did not doubt.

"I am interested. Please tell me why you need my skills," Master Scranton asked carefully.

"I am hoping you can tell me that. You are the best, so I hear, sir," Richard said and Master Scranton grinned. "So tell me why do people say that?"

Master Scranton liked to talk, and it became painfully evident to Froggy that he had a lot of talking bottled up inside of him waiting to come out, and it had been a very long time since he had been afforded an opportunity to converse on his favourite subject, himself.

For an hour with little input from either of his listeners, Master Scranton took them through a history of his own personal career. Of his triumphs, of decisions he had made that had been of monumental occasion, of figures he had met, and of feats he had performed. Eventually he pulled the leather bound volume towards him and flipped it open where the knife had been placed.

"Back in '52 we had a big explosion at the powder store in the Tower. The walls were thick enough to withstand it, and luckily there was less than half as much as we normally kept in the store. Seven men met their deaths, two died instantly and the other three later from the burns. Anyway, I was charged with trying to find a way to store the black powder more safely. The sensible place to keep it would be off site, but then when you need it it's not much use having it half a mile away on the wrong side of the walls in enemy territory. No, it has to be inside, and the powder stores need to be safe. I started here, can you see?"

Master Scranton stabbed a finger at his notes.

"There were a known number of additives from the Ligur but I had some ideas of my own, and I worked through them. The secret for a safer production was to grind it as a paste. They do that here, but not as wet as I found it needed to be. Reduce the ingredients to a slurry and they can be safely worked and ground without risk of ignition. The secret is consistency; and we could work and then re-work the same material to produce a finer grain. Once we'd done that we laid it out flat, a finger's thickness deep, and let it dry off for two days. You know when it's ready as it forms a sticky paste; it's like bread dough that's stuck to your hands. From this you can draw it up and roll it into pellets, tray them out again and let them dry for a day. After that they will not stick together and they can be packed in casks."

"And this stopped the explosions," Richard asked.

"It seemed to, but the other advantage we found was that the pellets in themselves when used to charge a cannon were far more powerful than simply using ground powder on its own. Far more."

"How much?" Richard asked.

"Here, look for yourself," Master Scranton said and spun the volume round so Richard could view the list of results from Master Scranton's experiments penned neatly on the page before him.

"Here we are using conventional powder, and here is the distance the gun fired. Now here is the same gun fired with pellets and look at the distance now," Master Scranton said, pointing at his results. "What is even better is that we found we could achieve the conventional distance with just one third of the black powder charge when it was converted into pellets. Just think, powder produced like this will go three times as far, three times!"

Froggy grinned, but Richard just nodded even though his grey eyes were unusually bright.

✝

There was one more man Richard wanted to meet in Antwerp but this time he left Froggy and went alone.

Andrew Kineer had been a part of Thomas Seymour's household when Richard had been there. Half a score older than Richard, he had been Seymour's Master of the Horse until Seymour's downfall. From there he had gone to work for Northumberland. After Northumberland's fall, Andrew and Thomas Gent, who had also been part of the same household, left England and had worked in Antwerp ever since, as part of the force that manned Antwerp's fortress, Het Steen. The richest city in Europe, Antwerp's sugar merchants, moneylenders and financiers took their security very seriously.

Richard had kept in touch and it was in a crowded inn in the Lombardenvest quarter that he met with him again.

The man he sought was there already, seated at a table with his back to him. Richard recognised the broad profile and the long brown hair that was tied tightly and spilled down his back. He'd not changed. Richard hid a smile.

He owed the man much; when he had been at Seymour's house set adrift from his father's house, it had been under the tutelage and friendship of Seymour's Master of Horse, Andrew Kineer, that he had honed his skills at arms.

Not saying a word, Richard rounded the table and dropped into a seat opposite Andrew. Their eyes met, and it was Andrew whose face split first into a happy smile.

"I am heartened to see you." Andrew leaned across the table and took a firm hold of Richard's arm in a welcoming grasp.

Richard nodded. "It is good to see you. It has been so long, and yet you look the same."

Andrew laughed. "Hardly! I've grey hairs aplenty these days and I've not the energy I used to have to chase after young idiots like you anymore."

Richard couldn't keep a smile from his face. Andrew's warm laughter was infectious. "I am not as young as I was, but I am probably often still an idiot."

"What brings you to Antwerp?" Andrew said, swivelling in his seat. He gestured with his arm for ale.

"Commerce. Isn't that what brings everyone to Antwerp?" Richard replied.

Andrew groaned. "It is a city of bankers, merchants and money lenders. All of them greedy and self-seeking."

"Not a place for a principled man then?" Richard asked.

"They try my patience. I often think Antwerp is quite a Godless place," Andrew replied gloomily.

"Believe me, working for the sugar merchants here would make a cynic out of saint."

"Trade often becomes a religion for many," Richard observed.

"That's a truth indeed. Profit, capital and supply – those are my Master's holy trinity." Andrew laughed bitterly.

It was later that night that the conversation turned to the past and Andrew's face became serious. "I am sorry about what happened. If I could have stopped it I would have."

Richard nodded, accepting his words. "No one could have stopped it."

Andrew's expression became serious. "Seymour was a hard man to divert from a course when he'd set his mind on it."

"I was there when he walked to the block." Richard's voice bore a hard edge.

Andrew's eyebrows raised a degree. "Well, you'd more reason than most to want to see him meet his end."

"I had hoped it would help. Somehow I thought if I was there I would have a sense of justice." Richard spoke thoughtfully.

"And did it help?" Andrew leant forward observing his companion closely.

Richard shook his head. "It didn't."

"Justice often fails to heal the wounds caused by the wrong it sought to redress, I am afraid. All we can do is leave the past where it is and concern ourselves instead with our current deeds. As I told you when you were younger, a wrong cannot be undone, so strive not to stray to it in the first place.

William Marshall's own words. Do you remember?" Andrew said, his voice still serious. "That's all any man can do. Marshall was an exception, and he was cast in a chivalric mould that God will not use again. Some standards are there not to be equalled but just to be aspired to, and I believe that is what Marshall's were." Andrew spoke as if delivering a sermon.

Richard was not the boy he once was, and he made that plain with his next words. "Chivalry, Andrew, is often a worthless cause."

"Worthless maybe, but worthy yes," Andrew rebuked, waving a finger at Richard.

"I remember. His tenets are hard to live by, but I try," Richard replied, a little wearily. "I shall have to share them with my brother, especially the one about not straying in the first place."

"Robert? You are reconciled?" Andrew sounded shocked.

"Not Robert. It would be a cold day in Hell before we saw eye to eye again. No, one you've not met. He is called Jack."

Andrew looked clearly confused.

"He's my half-brother," Richard supplied by way of explanation before changing the subject quickly. "I have new Masters, and I am looking for men, good men."

Andrew smiled. "It would not take much to tempt me away from Antwerp. Guarding greedy merchants' wealth and listening to them gripe over the cost of their security is something I could live without."

It was a long night, a night of reminiscences and long-lost memories. Andrew's company was like a well-worn comfortable jacket. As the evening wore on, Richard realised this was the nearest he had ever come to being welcomed home. Andrew wanted to know every detail of his exploits since they had last seen each other. He didn't judge, didn't dampen Richard's endeavours with tales of his own, Andrew just listened and laughed, and when Richard paused he'd throw in a question to keep the narrative going.

"Good God, lad, I would have given anything to have been with you last year rather than being here. If only I had known. Maybe it would have ended better for you as well. Who can tell," Andrew concluded.

"I've missed your guiding hand, and I've even missed your bloody sermons on chivalry as well, but most of all I've missed your company," Richard said with sincerity.

Andrew, reaching over, clasped the other's wrist. "You don't need me to guide you. You've got what's inside here to do that." Andrew banged his fist on his chest.

"My judgement on occasion is not always that sound," Richard laughed.

Much later, when Richard finally asked, Andrew agreed to join him without hesitation. His only caveat was that he brought with him another man, Thomas Gent. He had also been part of Northumberland's unfortunate household who had been forced to find other employment.

Chapter 5
The Future of War

Say me, wight in the brom,
Teche me how I shal don
That min housëbondë
Me lovien woldë.'
'Hold thine tongë stillë
And have al thine willë.'

†

It took Jack longer than he had thought it would to buy the horses he wanted. Two good mounts were bought locally, but then he had a long ride to see more and pick out the final ones that he needed. Jack arrived back with his purchases a day after Richard returned with his new companions from Antwerp.

Mat found Jack in the inn stables where he was ensuring his new acquisitions were being cared for.

"And I will be having that one," Mat announced, pointing at the dappled horse Jack was leading into a stable. "You tell the other lads that this one's mine, I saw it first."

"You damn well won't be getting her." Jack gave the horse a kindly pat on the neck. "This one's mine. You can pick any of the others. They are all in the next five stalls, but if I were to choose I'd be taking the chestnut rouncey; take a look and let me know what you think."

A rouncey was a good horse, not quite in the same league as the courser that Jack had bought himself, but still an excellent mount. They provided the rider with a horse that could be used for hunting as well as for day-to-day riding. They lacked the speed of the courser, but Mat knew Jack all too well, and if there was an opportunity to show off on horseback Jack would rarely miss it.

"You're right, I'll take the chestnut," Mat agreed, emerging from the stable, then noticing the horse next to his new mount, he frowned. A small fourteen hand mare, almost white, pressed its head over the stable partition and tried to gain his attention. Mat rubbed his flat palm against the mare's nose. "What's this one for then? Looks a bit small even for Froggy."

Jack didn't answer him, and Mat, glancing between the mare and Jack, just shrugged.

Wandering back across the yard, Mat located Froggy and Dan in the inn and sat down to join them. "I tell you, I might not be happy to be away from England but what I've just seen in the stable makes up for it. Master's not short of coin, that's for sure."

"Jack's back with the horses?" Froggy was already rising from the bench.

"He is, and the chestnut is mine, so don't go getting any ideas," Mat shouted at his retreating back, and then he added, chuckling, "He's got you a white mare that's in the next stable."

"What's the joke?" Dan asked.

"Jack's bought a little mare. Lord knows what for. It's no more than twelve hands, maybe thirteen at the most. Can't see it pulling the cart either."

"I've no idea. But you know what Jack's like when it comes to horses. He wants to own them all," Dan replied.

"I know what he's like, but what's he want a lady's horse for…" Mat's words trailed off and his eyes met Dan's. "Jesus! You don't think he's bringing his woman with him, do you?"

Dan shook his head. "I hope not."

Mat's eye's suddenly widened and his face split into a huge grin. Leaning across the table, he said quietly, "You don't suppose the fool got himself wed whilst he was in London?"

Dan snorted in his beer, spraying Mat across the table as he exploded into laughter. "There's a thought I'd not had until just now."

"Come on, Dan, you've spoken to the Master. Have you asked him what happened since they left Burton?"

"I have," Dan conceded.

"Well? Go on then," Mat pressed, leaning forward, very much wanting to know what had happened to the Fitzwarren brothers.

Dan shook his head slowly. "You don't need to know." Then seeing Mat's glowering expression, he said, "We have a new course, the Master has put coin in your pocket, what else do you need to know?"

"Hmmppphh, I suppose I didn't expect you to say much more. I asked Jack and got a slap round my head for my pains. He's still got a temper on him," Mat replied.

"Well, if they don't want to tell you, leave it. It is, after all, not your business, is it?" Dan said quietly.

"No, it's not." Mat was grinning. "But I'd still like to know what happened. I can see with my eyes that Master has been ill and Jack's got a secret or two he would rather not have. I want to know who the lass is that they've got traipsing around after them. Do you want to put a coin or two on a bet, Dan?"

Dan was not one for idle gambling, but on this occasion he could not resist. Before the bells struck for the next hour, Mat had taken bets from everyone in their group on whether or not Lizbet was Jack's wife.

Dan watched the girl as she left Jack's room and made her way down the stairs and he wondered. Neither of the brothers referred to her, but she was overly familiar with Jack, and Dan found the way she spoke to Richard nothing short of alarming. He'd assumed she worked at the inn, but he was not so sure. So who the hell was she? Jack's woman was his guess, which surprised him. Jack was well noted for changing his woman every time the wind swapped direction, so to have one in tow was most unlike him. Dan resolved not to ask questions, not yet anyway. However stupid he often thought Jack was, he could not see him as wedded to the girl and he'd placed coin on that which was currently in Mat's keeping.

✝

Jack took an instant dislike to Master Scranton, and it seemed the feeling was fairly mutual. Master Scranton, small, bespectacled, with thick greying hair and an acid tongue in his head, had been a man used to being obeyed when he was in England, and he took no time in asserting his authority amongst the group. He made it painfully clear that, with the exception of the Master, he was above the lot of them. When he'd found out from the others that Jack was a bastard, it had reinforced his firm belief that he was a man not at all worthy of his attentions.

This fact rankled with Jack even more, as Richard had wisely advised him to keep his counsel about the exact details of his parentage. The men with them had known Jack as Richard's bastard brother for years, and they cared little; he was widely accepted now as their second in command. If he announced that he was now indeed the Fitzwarren heir it was likely to attract little more than speculation, disbelief and a lot of ribald comments, all of which, Richard advised, they could do without. Jack was inclined to agree. Being heir to nothing, he had to admit, didn't exactly lend him much credibility.

He had, however, started to use the Fitzwarren name, and it was with some satisfaction now that he occasionally heard himself referred to as Jack Fitzwarren rather than his previous title that had always been 'the Master's bastard brother'. He had even heard this on Dan's lips, which had pleased him more than he thought it would.

Andrew and Thomas, however, Jack found to be good company. Andrew appeared to have no problem with his parentage, and accepted immediately his seniority in the company without question. It did not surprise Jack that Andrew and Thomas had left what was probably well paid employment to join a small band of men led by his brother that was heading slowly south through Europe. Richard could be very persuasive when he put his mind to it and with the benefit of their father's money, they were, at the moment, an affluent group.

What exactly his brother's plans were he did not know, and Richard had told him repeatedly that he would let him know soon. Jack was happy enough, outside, with food in his belly and a good horse again beneath him. It was, he felt, going to be a good summer.

†

Lizbet, studying her hands, swore loudly. Tasked with cleaning the black oil from the flintlocks, a layer of it was now coating both her palms and with it there was an attendant noxious odour.

Hearing the door click open, she swivelled round to see the Master watching her as he closed the door behind him.

"They're all done. It's just me that needs a clean now." Lizbet held her hands up for him to see.

Richard, ignoring her, picked up one of the flintlocks and ran his hands along the deeply engraved barrels, his fingers tracing the fluid scrolling lines that decorated the barrel.

"Pretty as a crown of dancing garlands, aren't they?" Lizbet, reaching out a hand, ran her fingers over the decoration.

Richard battered her hand away. "They are filthy. Keep them to yourself."

"And they got that way cleaning them for you," Lizbet said hotly.

Richard turned the flintlock over in his hand. "The future it seems is made of such things as these."

Lizbet shrugged. "If you say so. I don't care to ask how much they cost. I would wager they would empty even a gentleman's purse."

Richard, smiling, said absently, "Indeed, however the purse I have in mind is a large one." He placed the flintlocks back on the table and twitched a cloth over them, before turning his attention back to Lizbet. "I've another task for you tonight."

Lizbet's shoulders dropped. "Another?"

"It's an easy one." Richard walked past her and flipped the drape from the window, revealing the stone sill. "Up you get, my pretty Erato."

"What are you on about?" Lizbet remained unmoving in the middle of the room.

"I need your ears, and your silence. I need you to know what is said within this room tonight and I need to know if any of them repeat it where they should not," Richard explained patiently.

"You want me to spy on them?" Lizbet's eyes widened in delight.

"I'd have you know as much as they do, but without them knowing; there is a difference." Richard's eyes twinkled in the firelight. "It is a venture that could become unstitched so very easily by a loosened tongue and I would like to know if they speak out of turn. I would wager they don't pay much heed to you."

Lizbet grunted. "You'd be right there. Skivvy and servant to the bloody lot of them."

Richard's eyebrows raised. "That is what I pay you for."

"I had thought I was seeing to you two, not mending the linen of a bloody army. I am fairly sick of having holed socks and filthy clothing thrown at me."

"And so you should be." Richard, still holding the drape to one side, motioned with his head. "Up you go and I in return will reduce your laundry burden."

"And another thing…"

Richard planted a finger across her lips. "No more. Now up you go and keep your counsel for an hour." Then leaning forward he asked, "You can be quiet for an hour, can't you?"

Lizbet opened her mouth to protest but this time he clamped a hand over her mouth. "I think we will start now. The same letters are used in listen and in silent, so be both for me."

Lizbet sat on the sill, her eyes blazing with fury and Richard, grinning mischievously, let the curtain fall back, concealing her.

†

The men filed into Richard's room and waited; the Master was not yet present. In the centre of the room stood a trestle table and upon it several items covered purposefully with a cloth. Jack was more than a little curious, and recognised that he was about to find out what they were doing in France. However he obeyed the unspoken tenant and restrained himself from inspecting whatever it was that lay beneath the cloth. The door opened and ten pairs of eyes fell expectantly upon Richard Fitzwarren.

Richard's gaze met those of his men regarding him, finally coming to rest on the most inquisitive pair. "Have a look," Richard invited, nodding towards the cloth.

Mat wasted no time, his sinewy hand pulling the cover away immediately. "Holy mother and all the saints," Mat gasped. "Look at these beauties."

Jack, Dan and Froggy crowded round the table. Andrew and Thomas, new to the group, stood back respectfully and Master Scranton, adjusting his spectacles, pushed Froggy out of the way to get a better view.

Lizbet from her concealed seat in the window knew what they were looking at. Her hands were still black with the pungent grease from the guns, but her work had been good and Richard was pleased with the elegant shining results of her labours.

Jack took the second pistol from the table and upon turning it over appreciatively in his hand said,

"I am guessing you didn't bring us all up here to show off your latest purchases."

"You ever fired one?" Mat asked Froggy.

Mat knew Froggy had spent some time in military service.

"Aye, the musket but not the pistols; those are gentleman's weapons. Although Lord knows why. They are less accurate than the musket, and fire over a shorter range." Froggy hefted the musket in his hand. "Facing down a line of these takes some nerve, I can tell you. We used these against the French at the Siege of Boulogne."

"Any good?" Jack asked, genuinely interested.

"If we'd had more maybe. There was about a double line of twenty, so they fire and then the row behind swap places while you reload. At least that's the theory. Trying to drop a musket ball clean down the barrel when your hands are shaking is a rare feat, I can tell you. Then you just fire smoke and noise and hope no one notices you dropped the lead ball in the grass." Froggy cocked the musket. The mechanism clunked neatly as he pulled the trigger. "This is a nice piece; much better than the ones we had. This pin here…" He twisted the gun so they could all see. "The one holding the frizzen, was forever coming loose, then the flint wouldn't strike straight and the damn things stopped firing. I don't think that would happen with this one. It's properly secured to the rest of the mechanism rather than just having a daft screw into the wood to hold it." Froggy turned his beady eyes on the Master. "These are fine pieces. I'd like a chance to fire them if I may."

"You may. I want you to know everything there is to know about them, and you will all get plenty of opportunity to train with these. In a month or so I'm hoping to show just how good these can be in the right hands. I want every one of you to know how these work and be more than proficient in their use," Richard said, then added, "Gentlemen, it seems we have moved into selling the wares of war."

"Nice as they may be, two pistols and two muskets are not going to raise a lot of money," Jack said, holding one of the pistols now.

Richard gave him a weary look.

Jack's eyes narrowed. "How many?"

"Enough," was the only reply he received, and upon meeting his brother's gaze, Jack realised that he was unlikely to say more in the presence of the others.

"Well, let's hope we don't end up on the receiving end of these." Jack changed the subject, quickly realising his error, and put the pistol back down next to its companion.

"I agree, two of these are never to be fired, and these are the ones we will use for show. Jack, pick up the two pistols and look at the end of the grip," Richard instructed.

Jack did and he saw it then. One had a neat cross indented into the metalwork, and picking up one of the muskets he found the same mark there as well. "Go on then, what makes these two different?"

"The barrels are not sealed at the mechanism end. Fire this and the charge will not expel the ball from the barrel but it will probably blow the firing mechanism into the face of the man who is holding it." Richard smiled.

"Just on these two?" Jack asked.

"Just those two," Richard confirmed.

Mat was examining one of the pistols with the notched mark. "I can't see anything that would show the barrel is defective. Are you sure?"

"Quite. These two have been adapted to come apart, so we can show the inner workings of them more easily. I am fairly sure that standing in front of it is the safest place to be when it is fired," Richard said, smiling.

Shortly after, they filed out, leaving Richard alone with a man who had a lot of questions.

The latch secure from the inside, Richard and Jack were alone again in the room.

"Come on out," Richard commanded of the room in general.

Jack looked at him in confusion until Lizbet suddenly emerged, grumbling from behind the curtain.

"I can't feel my arse I've been sat up there that long! An hour you said, it's been more like two," she complained, rubbing her hands over her numbed rear.

"Any reason why Lizbet has taken to residing in your window?" Jack asked, folding his arms, his eyes switching between the pair.

"Lizbet will be my listener for idle tongues, that's all," Richard said.

"What about Lizbet's idle tongue. She's not known for keeping her mouth shut," Jack pointed out.

"Silence I agree is not one of her virtues, however stupidity also isn't amongst her traits either, is it, my Erato?"

"Stop bloody calling me that. I don't know whether to be insulted or flattered." Lizbet's brows furrowed. "I'll keep my trap shut. Now, if you've no need of me I've a stomach that's rumbling louder than the thunder clouds in Hell."

Richard flipped a coin neatly into the air between them and, faster than a striking adder, Lizbet seized it, smiling. "That will certainly quieten my stomach."

"And when you've eaten, bring me something as well," Richard instructed.

Elbowing her way between them, Lizbet flicked the latch up on the door and left them watching her departure.

"So how many have you got then? And where the hell did you get them from?" Jack had been bursting to ask this all night.

"They are in London with a friend, but I have with me six muskets, four pistols and a selection of the spares that accompany them," Richard supplied.

"Who are we selling them for? How many do they have? Why didn't you tell me any of this before?"

Richard related the story Christian Carter had told him of the failed arms sale and how they had ended up in a warehouse in London.

"I only made the decision to bring them the night before London, and I didn't want to unpack the cases on the Dutch Flower. You never know who would have had a look inside them," Richard said.

"Anyway, as it happens I got my idea from you as to where to sell them."

"From me?" Jack said, surprised but also delighted.

"Indeed. Remember when we were riding down the Strand and we went past Thomas Tresham's house? Well, then you told me of your high respect for the Knights of St John, and that gave me an idea," Richard said.

Jack's eyes widened. "No, we are not peddling these to that bloody lot." Then his mind caught up. "How many of these have you got?"

Richard smiled broadly. "Enough to start a war."

"I do hope we are not on the field when it starts," Jack said sarcastically.

Andrew was leaning against the wall outside the room when Jack finally left his brother. That Andrew had been waiting there was evident, but he wasn't sure whether it was Jack he had wished to speak to.

"I've a thirst on me," Andrew said, meeting Jack's enquiring gaze.

Jack smiled. He guessed Andrew had probably been waiting to speak to his brother, and why wouldn't he be after tonight's revelations?

"If you are buying then I will join you," Jack said, setting his feet towards the steps to the inn below.

A moment later, the door opened behind them and Lizbet emerged. She met Jack's eyes and those of his companion. She didn't like Andrew. She had felt his eyes upon her more than once since he had arrived, and the way he spoke to Jack irritated her.

Chin in the air, she moved between them. Her eyes met Jack's for a moment, and in a parody of Andrew's address, she said, "Excuse me, Master."

Andrew waited until she had passed before he spoke. "That lass needs some respect beating into her."

"Aye, maybe," Jack replied automatically and then said, "Come on then, let's see if Mat is in the taproom. He's got a purse full of my coins that I've a mind to get back tonight."

If Andrew had wanted Jack's company to himself that night, it seemed he wasn't going to get it.

Andrew joined Jack and absented himself as soon as he could to go in search of the other brother.

Standing outside for a moment, Andrew hesitated before tapping on the door. He heard a voice from within and pressed the door handle to open it.

The expression on the seated man's face told him immediately that he had not expected to be visited by any man other than his servants.

Andrew smiled broadly. "Excuse me, I've a mind to talk with you if I may?"

Richard pushed a chair out for Andrew to take. "Join me. Lizbet has brought me more than enough for one."

Andrew seated himself and, taking a piece of the bread from the platter, tore off a chunk, crumbs scattering over the wooden table.

"I'm assuming it's not food that brought you to my table," prompted Richard.

"No, no, it's not," Andrew conceded, placing the bread down in front of him and meeting Richard's dark eyes. "Although in a way it is."

"Go on."

"Sugar. I've spent the last three years guarding it, protecting, keeping it free from prying eyes, stopping it from being pilfered and even tampered with." Andrew paused.

"And your point is?" Richard asked.

"If you've a cargo here that needs that kind of attention, then I feel I am well placed to secure it for you," Andrew said, and then added hastily, "I do not mean to speak out of turn or to denigrate the skills of your men, I just wanted you to know that I have some experience you can avail yourself of if you need it. You are paying me now and so place me where I can be of most use to you."

Richard nodded, but instead of replying he reached for his cup.

Andrew, forced to continue, said, "It is not my place to ask, but I can only assume there is a large amount of these muskets and if I can be of use in ensuring their security then use me."

"Thank you, Andrew. Their security is not a current concern for me, however our journey south is, and your skills to ensure an uneventful and smooth journey are most wholly appreciated." Richard twisted the cup in his hand, regarding Andrew over the rim.

"Thank you. I will of course do what I can. It would help if I knew where we are going," Andrew asked.

"Just south. For the moment that's all anyone needs to know," Richard supplied. "Where this route will end I don't yet know myself."

"I'm not prying," Andrew said hastily.

Richard smiled. "I know, Andrew. I'd never accuse you of such. I did tell you in Antwerp it would be a worthwhile venture. What do you think of them?"

"They are the future." Andrew leant back in the chair. "I wish it were not so, but time moves on and they are becoming more and more useful in the field."

"I agree, and cannon aside, these can take down men, horses, punch holes through armour – and all at hundred paces," Richard said.

"It will change the field. No commander would pit his mounted forces against a fully primed musket line if it was executed right," Andrew said.

"That's the point, I think. Froggy talks about the poorest soldiers being trained to use them and it should be the reverse. In the hands of skilled, trained and dedicated soldiers they would be a force to be reckoned with," Richard replied.

Andrew nodded, "I agree. So how many do you have that would make a commander want to rethink his offensive strategy?"

Richard's eyes darkened, then he smiled. "Enough to make the journey worthwhile."

Andrew's shoulders dropped. "I am a prying clod. I have no right to ask." He leant close to Richard across the table. "But what you showed us all tonight, what you showed me, raises a man's curiosity, forgive me."

Richard picked up the wine flagon, and filled Andrew's cup. "There is nothing to forgive. Indeed if your curiosity was not roused then I would be doubting this very endeavour."

Andrew picked up his filled cup and clanked it against Richard's. "To your success, lad. I am proud of you."

†

The following morning the company united and now with a purpose was assembled, mounted and ready for the start of a journey the destination of which only two of them knew. The cart was driven by Froggy, his own horse tethered to the rear, and was ready to leave, as were the other mounted men.

"I've never ridden a bloody horse in my life. I don't even know how to get on," Lizbet was complaining.

Jack, taking a vice-like grip on her arm that made her wince, leant close to her ear so only she could hear his words. "Get on, shut up, and don't make a fool of yourself in front of them."

Lizbet bit her tongue. Indeed all the men were staring at her, with the exception of Richard who had already set his horse to leave the inn. She felt Jack's hands on her, and none too gently he hoisted her up into the saddle. After some shuffling she got her skirts straightened and Jack pushed her feet into the stirrups then left her. Glancing round she saw they were still all staring at her. If she had known why they were all so interested in the fact that she was obviously now joining them for the journey, she would have lost her temper. Mat, grinning, was counting his winnings already.

Her hands found the loose leather strap on the horse's neck and taking it in her hands, she tightened her hold. The body beneath hers shifted and she wobbled and Lizbet's eyes widened in alarm. She heard laughter and her face reddened. The men rode from the yard, followed by the cart with the Dutch Flowers cargo strapped to the boards. Lizbet sat astride her horse and watched them all leave. The mare stood, solidly, as it had been trained to do, and waited.

"Come on then, you dozy animal." Lizbet slapped the reins on its neck, but it did little more than dip its head and it remained standing in the yard, teeth grinding noisily on the bit. The cart had now disappeared through the gates and she could only just hear the rubble of the wheels as it followed the mounted riders.

"Come on, come on, they are not leaving me here." Lizbet urged it forwards but it did little more than spin around on the spot. "You miserable beast, come on, go through the gate." Lizbet yanked hard on the reins and the startled mare pranced on the spot, ears back and eyes wide.

Lizbet screamed.

"Jesus, don't do that or you'll be sat on your backside in the road."

Lizbet thanked the Lord; it was Jack's voice behind her.

"I don't know what to do, do I? I've eaten a few horses but I've never sat on one." Lizbet's voice was filled with relief as Jack clipped a line to the mare's bridle and started to lead it out of the yard.

"Never?" There was disbelief in his voice.

"No, not much call for them when I was working in London, was there? And as if I'd ever earn enough to own one. Daisy had a man who took her out on his a few times, but I've never been on one in my life."

They caught up to the back of the cart. Jack leant forward and clipped the other end of the strap that was attached to the mare to the back of the cart. Froggy was driving the cart and his horse was tied to the back as well and plodded dutifully on.

"There you go, she'll just follow now. All you have to do is sit still, and don't pull on her reins, just hold them loose. Like this." Jack showed her his own hands. With that he pulled his own horse back a pace or two and set her to canter back to the front where Mat, Dan, Andrew and Richard were riding.

Lizbet felt fairly alone, but on the bright side everyone was facing forward and not one of them saw her jostling and bouncing along on the horse. After an hour she realised she wasn't going to fall, and the only injury she was likely to suffer was a sore backside; the hard leather of the saddle was already making itself known.

Richard and Jack had ridden ahead, leaving her alone with the rest of the men. When they had stopped for a meal and she had taken round bread, beer and cheese, every one of the bastards had taken a turn at slapping her sore behind and making fun of her. It had been Andrew who had started it, and the others had followed his lead, laughing at her reddened face and evident discomfort.

Lizbet, standing apart from them and leaning against a tree while she ate, had felt utterly miserable. Her humiliation was complete when there was no offer of help to remount, Froggy wouldn't let her in the wagon and she was forced to half walk and half run for the next four hours until they met back up with Jack and Richard and made a final stop for the day.

Lizbet sat down at last outside, her back to the inn wall. It was hard to say what hurt the most, her backside or her feet. Taking a firm hold of her foot, she pulled the wooden shoe from it. A painful cry escaped her lips as it came away, bringing with it a quantity of skin. The inside of the shoe was packed with sheep's wool for softness and warmth, but on the long walk the wool had compressed into uncomfortable lumps and had become a trap for stones and grit from the road.

As she examined her left foot, she found the skin on the top was rubbed away, and each of her toes wore a painful blister. The other foot had fared little better.

Lizbet's nose was running and she sniffed loudly, then rubbed the back of her hand across it to remove the drip.

"Are you getting us some food then?" It was Mat's voice calling out from the doorway of the inn. All the rest of the men had trooped in, tired and quiet, while Lizbet had chosen to stop outside and examine her sorrowful feet.

Grumbling under her breath, unshod, she stepped carefully towards the door. There was already cheese, bread, ham, platters and knives provided on the table. Lizbet eyed the gathered men coldly. They expected her to serve and she was in no mood for their ribald comments and unpleasant humour.

Accepting a serving of bread, cheese and ham in front of him, it was Mat who slapped her hard on the backside, and laughing said, "It'll be your rear that'll be covered in blisters tomorrow." Clearly, he didn't know that it was already sore and rubbed raw underneath her skirts.

Lizbet thought for a moment about boxing his ears with the ale jug, but too tired to fight, she settled instead for slamming it down hard on the table and sending his ale cup flying, spilling the contents over his platter.

"For God's sake, woman!" Mat exclaimed, and tipping the wooden trencher he poured the ale from it to save his food from a soaking.

"Ah, stop being so bloody fussy," Froggy called out. "It's all going down your gullet to get mixed together anyway."

Mat cursed at him, then said to Lizbet, "Get me some more bread and bloody get rid of these dripping sops."

"Get it yourself," Lizbet spat back.

The bench behind Mat scraped across the floor as he stood.

"Sit down." A silken voice, sounding oddly bored, called from the other end of the table. "You fairly asked for that, Mat, now sit down, and if you want to get served, keep a civil tongue in your head and your hands to yourself."

Lizbet's expression changed to one of triumph as Mat was forced to back down and reseat himself at the table. The Master had spoken.

Tasks finished, Lizbet took her food and settled to eat it outside. The light had gone from the sky but the warmth of the day was still in the air, and with her back against the wall she ate and let her eyes try to follow the flights of the darting bats as they silently and effortlessly cleared the night sky of insects. It was Jack who came and sat down next to her. Reaching over, he helped himself to a lump of bread from the hunk in her lap.

Through a mouthful he said, "What happened to your feet?"

Lizbet shook her head. "Nothing, they'll be fine in the morning."

Jack just shrugged. It was a lie and they both knew it. "You can't walk again tomorrow, Lizbet. You're not overly tall to start with. If you keep this up you'll wear your legs down, woman."

Lizbet, offended, straightened her shoulders and sat bolt upright. "I'll have you know I was the tallest of my mother's lasses by a head." Then she added, "And I'm not shorter than Froggy either, and he's a man."

"I'm glad you cleared that up, I was never too sure about Froggy." Jack sounded amused.

"You know what I mean," Lizbet scolded with good humour, jabbing an elbow into Jack's ribs.

Jack stood smoothly and held his hand out for Lizbet. "Come on in. Let's find you a place to sleep."

Lizbet didn't take his offered hand, but instead looking up at him, said, "And how come you are being so nice to me now?"

"I just don't want my food covering in beer slops," he replied, grinning. "Come on."

Lizbet took his hand. He pulled her neatly to her feet and she allowed him to lead her back inside.

†

If Lizbet thought the next day would be easier, she was wrong.

"Watch, will you!" Jack scolded.

Lizbet pulled a face and returned her eyes to the horse.

"Hold the bridle like this." Jack shook it again in front of her eyes, and then swore. "Woman! Will you watch?"

"I am bloody watching," Lizbet spat back.

"Hold it like this in your left hand and then you can put your arm round the horse like this and use your right hand to put the bit…"

"If you think I am putting my fingers in that bloody animal's mouth…"

Jack lost his temper and flung the bridle over the stall door. "Well then, you will be walking, won't you?"

"Look at its teeth. It'll have my fingers off!"

I'll give her one last chance, just one more and that's it. Jack retrieved the bridle and forced his voice to be level. "It won't bite you. Now come here, stand in front of me and we'll do it together."

Lizbet flattened her back against the stall walls and edged round the beast to stand near Jack.

"Here, stand in front of me and get hold of this bridle," Jack commanded.

Lizbet gingerly ducked under his arm and stood in front of him. Her hand reaching up, she clasped the bridle under his firm hold.

"Good. Now give me your other hand." Jack reached down and took her hand, and together they reached for the bit.

Lizbet's eyes widened. Her fingers were closer to its yellow teeth than Jack's. She tried to pull back but his hold on her hand was a firm one.

"Now you just gently push your fingers in here…"

Lizbet screamed and her elbow rammed back into Jack's ribs, while the horse panicked and shied in the stable away from them.

"God damn you woman!" Jack took hold of Lizbet's arm and propelled her from the stable. "I have few rules." He still had a bruising hold on her arm. "You never act like that near a horse, especially one of mine."

"Bloody well let go." Lizbet struggled against his hold. "What the hell have I done? It was going to bite me!"

Jack took a calming breath. "The horse…"

Lizbet cut him off. "The bloody horse nearly…"

Jack clamped a hand across her mouth, silencing her violently. "Give me strength, woman. The horse will carry you, will save your feet, will take you from danger, will be more loyal to you than any hound and will ask for nothing from you other than a little kindness."

Lizbet made to speak and Jack pressed his hand harder across her mouth, the bridle still over his arm, rattling.

"I see lessons are going well." The amused voice was Richard's. "Are you trying to put a bridle on Lizbet? To be fair, her mouth is probably big enough."

Lizbet's eyes widened in anger but the filthy hand across her mouth prevented her from throwing insulting words at the Master.

Jack laughed. "That's probably where I was going wrong. I should have put one on her to start with to shut her up." Jack released her suddenly pushing her away; he didn't want another bony elbow in the ribs.

Richard switched his gaze to Lizbet, his expression not overly kind. "Settle your temper and learn your lesson or as Jack says, you can walk."

✝

Lizbet, seated at the end of the table, strained her neck to see the two cards Mat had just placed face up. She could view his triumphant smile but not the hand that had gained him the victory. Rising from her seat to get a better view, she was just too late as Dan's paw of a hand swept all of the cards back into a pile, reuniting the deck for another game.

"What did he win with?" Lizbet called down the length of the table. Her question though went unanswered as their eyes were on the quickly dealt cards that Dan flicked out at each of them across the table. Lizbet dropped back in her seat moodily. As a woman in public, none of them would let her take part in the game, and she was left with nothing better to do than watch.

"He had a pair of tens."

She hadn't realised the Master was standing behind her.

Lizbet swivelled her head around to view him. "The way he was crowing, you'd think he'd got a primero with aces."

"Agreed, but then it doesn't take much to get Mat excited, does it?" Richard sounded in good humour.

He was regarding her with steady grey eyes, the anger in his face he had turned on her earlier that day now absent, she noted with relief.

The sound of his voice brought the men's attention from the cards to their Master.

"Will you join us?" Jack asked, expecting a refusal. He was surprised when his brother accepted the invitation and there was a hasty reshuffling of seats to make room for him.

It was Froggy Tate sitting to the left of Dan who took up the stack of cards and began to shuffle the worn deck. He tried to riffle the cards but the act failed and a dozen escaped, flying up into the air, much to the amusement of his companions.

"I have a better idea." Richard leant over and claimed the deck from Froggy's hands, adding to it the scattered cards he had dropped. "Lizbet, you can sit in between Dan and Froggy and deal."

"What!" Mat exclaimed, and then seeing the expression on the Master's face, instantly regretted his outburst.

Richard's eyes narrowed.

Lizbet, utter delight painted across her face, was already standing behind Froggy, her bony finger prodding him in the shoulder.

"Come on, Froggy, shift your arse along then so I can squeeze in."

Froggy moved to his left. Lizbet had her feet over the bench and was settling into the gap a moment later, her hand outstretched for the cards still in the Master's hand. With slow derision he dropped the cards onto her palm and Lizbet, with all the eyes round the table fixed upon her, shuffled the cards with more expertise than Froggy had shown.

Banging the deck on the table to square up the cards, she announced, "Well then, lads, who's in? Get your coins ready or you'll not be getting any cards."

A shining coin skittered from Richard's hand and stopped in the middle of the table. Lizbet, a smile on her face, met his eyes and delivered two cards from the deck to land neatly before him.

Froggy sent in his stake next and received his cards and one by one all the others joined in the round. By the time that five hands had been played, the men were too intent on the game to notice the woman in the circle with them. As Richard had known, Lizbet's quick fingers and eyes that missed nothing made her the ideal head of the game. When Mat tried to avoid adding his stake to the pot to stay in the game, loud words from Lizbet brought an angry red hue to his cheeks and mirth to the rest of the players.

Late into the night the game concluded when Richard leant over and took the deck from Lizbet and declared the table closed. The game had been a good one; Richard's calculated losses had added fresh coins to those that passed through the players' hands that night and both Mat and Marc left the table with fuller purses than they had started with, and the rest of the players had, more or less, the same amount of coins they had joined the table with.

"So that there can be no doubt or lack of trust among you, I shall give the cards to Lizbet." Richard handed the now squared up, neat deck back to her. "If you want to play then find the lass."

Lizbet's eyes were bright, the grin on her face showing a line of neat white teeth. Taking the cards, she made a great show of storing them carefully in one of her pockets. The Master had not said it, but the implication was clear. She'd be allowed at the table, albeit as the dealer, but that was good enough for Lizbet, and preferable to sitting in the dark at the back.

†

"Did I hear right from Mat? Master let that woman, a servant, play cards with you last night?" Scranton sounded shocked and angry at the same time.

Froggy, who had little time for the powder expert, narrowed his eyes. "What if he did?"

"I know we are away from England, but surely we have not lowered ourselves to a state where women can play at the same table as men?" Scranton moved in front of Froggy, blocking his exit.

"Mat has it wrong. She didn't play," Froggy said and made to push past Scranton.

The wiry man grasped Froggy's arm stopping him. "He said the Master himself gave her the cards."

Froggy stopped, and pulled his arm free from Scranton's hold. "Well that is the Master's business, isn't it?"

"I agree it is his business, but I'd like to know what kind of group it is that I have joined. The Church warns us that such games lead to the sin of unchastity and that letting women play is an affront to God! What next?" Scranton continued.

"She wasn't playing!" Froggy repeated loudly. "Christ, man! The lass was dealing the cards for us. I don't think that's a breach of any of the Ten Commandments that I can recall."

Scranton's face darkened. "She's a tavern wench, or worse, and listening to her I've a good idea which gutter she crawled out of in London as well. Are those the hands you want on your cards?"

"Are you mad, man?" Froggy had taken a step back from him. This wasn't an argument he want to have, nor did he really understand Scranton's heated indignation. He was saved a second later when another voice ended the argument.

"Or worse? What exactly do you mean by that?" It was Jack who had spoken from behind Scranton.

Scranton turned round abruptly. The top of his head was level with Jack's chin but he stared up fiercely into the other man's eyes. "I shall tell you exactly what I mean. We all know she warms your bed when you've a mind for a woman, and she's a voice on her like a Southwark whore from the bawdy houses. Is that elaboration enough?" Scranton's voice was full of fury.

Froggy sensibly took a step back.

Jack swallowed hard, his mouth pressed now into a thin line. "I have been restrained, but now you have gone too far."

Scranton had no chance to move as Jack quickly twisted both hands into the material of his doublet.

Before Jack could lift him from the floor, or worse, there came a commanding voice from the other side of the inn, pitched to carry. "Jack, please go with Froggy. He needs help with setting up the range this morning."

The expression on Scranton's face was a mixture of relief and triumph as Jack, after only a moment's hesitation, let go of the little man and pushed past him, disappearing outside with Froggy.

Scranton made a show of smoothing out the front of his doublet and strode across the inn to where Richard was stood.

"He's out of control, sir. I am a man who wishes to meet God with a soul clean and free of sin, and associating with some of the members of your group here is more than I can tolerate. Bastards, sir, are an affront to nature, and whores are a blasphemy against women."

Richard took a deep breath. "I respect your convictions. Let God however, and not you or I, be their judges. Is it not Castellio who preaches of tolerance? Did he not say that to kill a man is not to protect a doctrine, but it is simply to kill a man?"

"Sir, he was speaking of heresy. I don't quite think that applies to the current situation," Scranton retorted.

"You and I are better placed to know of their sins. God will recognise this and association will not stain our souls. Indeed should we not try to bring them to God? Did not John make the unclean clean? Would that not be an act God would condone?" Richard said calmly.

Scranton's mood calmed. "Job 14.4 – you cannot make what is unclean clean again."

"Surely repentance, even that of the most grievous sinner can bring them to the Lord's grace," Richard's voice was serious, and with a hand on Scranton's shoulder, he continued, "I see the sins of both of them and I would bring both to the Lord. Every soul, sir, is precious in the eyes of God, even those of bastards and whores."

Scranton nodded sagely in agreement, his feathers smoothed by Richard's words. "What you say, sir, I cannot disagree with. Really though, it is for the house of God and its emissaries to bring people such as this to the Lord. It is admirable that you have charged yourself with the task, but I cannot see that you will succeed."

"I know. It distresses me as well, but I wish to try. I wish to offer these two souls to God that he may provide them with salvation," Richard did indeed sound distressed.

"But neither of them will thank you. They don't even recognise the Lord," Scranton pointed out.

Richard smiled benevolently. "And in that is the challenge that the Lord has set me."

"I admire your Christian spirit, sir," Scranton replied.

"Come, let us pray together for these two ragged souls that God has charged us with."

Scranton, unable to refuse, and pulled at the elbow by Richard found himself on his knees next to the Master, following him in the words of a prayer, his lips moving in silent repetition of Richard's loudly spoken words.

On the other side of the door, Jack, with his ears pressed to the wood, was holding back tears of mirth.

"What's he doing?" hissed Froggy from behind him.

Jack, knowing he couldn't contain the laughter, caught Froggy under the arm and propelled him across the inn yard. "He's got Scranton on his knees praying to God for my eternal salvation!"

"No!" Froggy exclaimed. "The Master's an evil bastard when he wants to be. Scranton deserves everything he gets."

Jack was now wiping tears of laughter from his eyes.

Chapter 6
Shaping Destiny

Good sir, pray Ich thee,
For of saynte charité
Come and daunce with me

✟

Progress finally halted. That Richard had a destination in mind became obvious when they arrived at the village of Elstepenn. Master Hinterton, owner of the inn, the blacksmiths and a large parcel of land behind the church, seemed to know Richard well. Jack's eyes narrowed as he watched the greeting between the pair, and he again experienced the uncomfortable feeling he often had when he was reminded that his brother had a past that he was not a part of.

Richard, Jack and Master Scranton were lodged at the inn. Jack had initially turned down the relative luxury of a room at the inn when he found out that Scranton would be there, but hastily changed his mind when it became clear that the alternative was a camp in the fields behind the church.

Froggy, at Richard's direction, had put together a training programme for the coming weeks that would make them more than proficient with the flintlocks. In small groups they would learn their new craft. Andrew, a disciplinarian second to none, would ensure they gave their full attention to the lessons delivered by Froggy, and added his own programme of training designed to make them into a small and formidable force.

Jack very quickly did not regret his decision to retain his room at the inn; the days were hard and long and the luxury of a comfortable bed was one he appreciated. The hard training and the competition amongst the men was very much to his liking, and when his brother was absent, to find himself in command was exhilarating. The group of men he had under his control at Burton had lacked the cohesion and singularity of purpose that he was beginning to see emerge under Richard's and Andrew's guiding hand.

Slowly they were moulding the component parts into one single deadly mechanism. Over the coming weeks Jack began to find his competence tested, and skills he thought he possessed he was shown lacked polish. Froggy's training sessions on the flintlocks in the field took up only so much of the day, and the rest had been segmented and planned out with a precision that could only be described as military by Andrew.

The initial reaction to this proposed training programme had been one of disbelief. None of them relished early starts, long hours and late finishes. Jack had stood next to Andrew while he had told them all what each day would contain, how the training would be divided up and what skills they would be learning.

After that Richard had told them that he intended to produce a unit of men of a standard rarely seen and if any of them wanted to leave, then they were free to go. If they remained however, he promised them hard brutal work, exacting tasks, long hours and vicious punishments for non-compliance. The men had exchanged nervous glances then.

The penalties he outlined were harsh, and varied from having their pay stripped to suffering a whipping, all depending upon the severity of the rules flouted, all of which would be administered by the Master. The lure though that he placed was a tempting one, professional pride in becoming part of an elite force, coupled with an increase in pay that not one of them could have ever considered earning, had near enough sealed the deal for them. However all of them would have given up the extra pay and worked for sustenance only when he revealed who it was that they would be demonstrating their field skills to. When the Master uttered the words, "The Knights of St John," the group had just gawked at him, from where they sat in stunned silence.

Richard continued, "So our discipline will be as theirs is, and our skills will not let us down." His eyes roved over the group. "And neither will our appearance."

Grey eyes assessed each of them in turn, and more than a few looked away, or squirmed under his assessing gaze, knowing that in appearance they certainly did not present themselves as a force to be reckoned with. Jack, standing next to Richard, was spared his brother's harsh glance, but glancing down he grimaced himself as he regarded the worn boots and a frayed cuff on his shirt.

His brother on the other hand was wearing clothes that fitted like a second skin, the black doublet neat, dust free and with a crispness that was completely alien to Jack who was still wearing the jacket they had taken from Robert. It fitted him well and it was also a trophy from that victory in London. However it was now less than clean and one of the buttons had come away. He had it in his purse, but had not thought much about its reattachment. Jack resolved to find Lizbet when he had time and get her to repair it for him.

It was further made clear that Andrew was in charge of the overall daily training programme. Froggy would supervise and deliver the field training with the flintlocks, and the Master would give his own lessons in theory, tactics and strategy. Scranton would provide them with everything they needed to know about black powder and training on horseback was to be organised by Jack.

After the Master had outlined the plan for the coming weeks, Andrew had taken over and delivered some detailed orders outlining how and where the camp was to be set up and organising two groups, one to assist Froggy Tate in building a training range and another to construct a cordoned off tilt yard and a powder store to be built to Scranton's design.

The men broke off and formed into the groups as directed. Scranton attached himself to Richard, talking endlessly, and Jack noted his brother was still doing a good job of trying to appear interested. *That'll not last long*, he mused, grinning as he walked away to join Mat and Andrew and help with the organisation of the tilt yard.

He was pleased to be in Andrew's group. Andrew had a seemingly endless supply of stories. He had taken to the battlefield during King Henry's time, and had held respected positions with men whose names secretly impressed Jack. Everyone liked Andrew.

Older by half a dozen years than Richard, he brought a capable and reassuring presence to the group. Richard sought his counsel, considered his arguments, and his position amongst the group was generally accepted as Richard's second in command. If asked, he would not accept that he held such a rank, deferring always to Jack, and placing himself beneath him in the hierarchy. But in terms of skills, in wisdom and experience, the men viewed Andrew as Richard's more than capable captain.

If Jack noticed, he seemed not to mind. Andrew was personable; he spent time with Jack who warmed to the attention in a way that seemed to delight Andrew. It was Richard's approval he wanted but in its absence Andrew's attention was sufficient and Jack basked in this new found and unlooked for praise.

Richard was happy to encourage their growing friendship. Andrew had much to teach, and in Jack he found a willing student. Much that was imparted were lessons that Jack would never have tolerated from his brother, but from Andrew he eagerly accepted the truth of them and rapidly sought more.

The muskets Jack did not particularly like. Their mechanisms could give a man who had little killing skill the ability to become level on the field with a man like himself, who had dedicated a large amount of his life to his skill at arms. It rankled with him that a musket ball fired at him could seriously wound or even take his life, and there would be little that his training and skill with arms could do to stop it.

Froggy had told tales of the firing lines smoking themselves out, of having to fire into their own foggy haze with no idea where their targets were. Jack took solace from this, hoping that their shortcomings would halt their progress and that battles would return wholly to the edged weaponry that Jack knew and liked. This had been the subject of the argument he had been having with Andrew for most of the morning as they hefted the wood needed to build the tilt yard rails.

"Jack, it's not a matter of if, it's a matter of when," Andrew repeated again, his voice patient. "If they can give a commander an advantage on the field then you can be sure they will not be overlooked."

"Perhaps, but their accuracy is often flawed. For God's sake, a simple bow is twice as accurate over easily three times the distance," Jack retorted hotly.

"Only in the right hands," Andrew replied, and then seeing the frown on Jack's face, continued. "Have you ever seen an arrow storm?"

Jack shook his head.

"When a line of archers fill the sky with arrows, it turns the sky dark. And the noise! It's one of the most terrifying sounds I've heard. It is like a wail from Hell, from some unearthly creature; makes the hairs on the back of my neck stand up even now just thinking about it."

"And your point?" Jack dropped the long pole he had been carrying on top of the pile they had already collected.

"My point is that the archers are firing together. They are pitching to fire the distance. Not one of them is aiming at a particular target in the opposing lines. They fire high. The arrows come down on top of the opposite lines – all the enemy can do is hold their shields over their heads to protect themselves," Andrew explained patiently.

"Yes, and that requires skill," Jack continued to argue. "The best are the Welsh with the long bows. They need years of practice to send an arrow across such a distance with the power to kill when it gets there."

"That's the point, Jack." There was exasperation creeping into Andrew's voice. "The muskets can create a storm, like the archers. They don't need to pick their targets, and sending such a hail of lead towards the enemy is a formidable weapon. You can train a man to do that in a lot less time than it takes to become a Master archer."

"You heard Froggy! The lines buckle. Using unskilled men, untrained men who lack the skills of the field, means they are rarely effective. They might get one volley off as a united force but after that they crumble," Jack countered.

"I agree. The temptation for a field commander would not be to use his skilled troops and divert them to a musket corps. What he needs is men skilled in their use, and many of them to make a force to be reckoned with."

"Exactly, and there are no quantity of such men," Jack replied as if this proved his argument was right, "and there is nowhere a commander could find such a group of men either."

"Not now, Jack, no. When they are trained and such a battalion is produced and they are skilled and disciplined then such a force will change the way men fight in the field." Andrew now had an edge of irritation in his voice.

"That's the point though, there are no such trained men. And no General will take good fighting men with hardened skills and move them to hold a musket. He'd be mad. It would immediately weaken his force. There are only so many skilled men they can have at their disposal, and placing muskets in their hands will lessen the effectiveness of the rest of his force."

Andrew turned his eyes skyward for a moment, but he was saved from having to reply when Corracha arrived and Richard leant forward in the saddle. "My brother, Andrew, as I think you are finding, feels he is always right."

The blue eyes Jack regarded his brother with were unusually dark. "My argument is simple. You put your skilled men where they are best placed. You don't take them from vital positions and give them a flintlock which is effective over about a third of the distance an arrow is."

Richard smiled. "Andrew, if you can change Jack's mind then you have greater skills of persuasion than I have. I do hear your points, Jack, very well, and with Master Scranton's knowledge and with Andrew's experience I think we can address some of them and show that a force equipped with flintlocks would be one that would be an incredible addition to any front line."

"How many could you put in the field?" Andrew asked Richard.

Richard considered his reply for a moment. His answer when he delivered it was vague. "Enough to be effective."

†

Scranton, for once, was not taking his meal with Richard, but instead he'd ordered food to be delivered to his room. The weather for the last few days had been unseasonably wet, and every one of them was soaked to the skin and had taken refuge in the inn for their evening meal rather than eat at the camp.

The little man met Jack on the stairs leading to the rooms on the next floor, and his brown weasel's eyes bestowed a hard stare on him, his hand gesturing for Jack to move back up the steps out of his way.

Jack's eyebrows raised a degree. About to force Scranton into a quick reverse, he read the warning on his brother's face from where he was sat in the room below and relented.

Smiling falsely, he stepped back up the stairs slowly. "Ah, Master Scranton, it seems the weather is treating us all quite equally today."

Scranton's mouth tightened into a thin line; he'd not missed the sarcasm in Jack's voice. "Out of my way."

With an agility that age had robbed Scranton of, Jack jumped neatly over the handrail and landed on a table top on the other side, stepping down into the inn room without giving Scranton a second look. Purposefully he joined his brother at the table and sat with his back to the stairs and Scranton who was still making his slow way up them.

Jack said quietly, "If in the morning he has difficulty speaking…"

Richard held his hand up to stop him. "I know, you'll have knocked his teeth down his throat. One more day of his incessant prattle and I may do it myself."

"How do you put up with him?" Jack said exasperated.

"At the moment it is a necessity," Richard replied wearily.

"We've got Froggy already, do we really need him? Froggy knows about as much as there is to know about flintlocks. With his training all of us will become well skilled with their use," Jack said.

"It's not just skill at arms we need, Jack. It's what he has in here." Richard tapped his head.

"Why didn't you just say so? I'd be more than glad to get whatever he has beneath his hat out in the open. Just ask."

"He's an expert with powder. He has years of experience in manufacturing it and using it, and that's what we need," Richard explained patiently.

"Have you heard him?" Jack blurted. "You do know the fool was using monk's piss to make his powder with? Monk's piss is the bloody same as anyone else's."

Richard laughed. "I bet if you were selling it you wouldn't say that, would you?"

Jack didn't reply. As usual his brother had an answer for everything.

On the other side of the room Lizbet continued to riffle the cards from one hand to another while the men sorted out their first round of wagers in the game of Primero.

"She brooks no cheating, no slight of hand and keeps the rules this one does," Pierre said, nudging Andrew who had joined their game for the first time.

"It's a new experience. I've never had a woman deal me a hand of cards before." Andrew took into his keeping the cards that had landed neatly in front of him.

"You'll get used to it," Marc chimed in. "She's nothing to lose and nothing to win so at least we know we are getting a fair hand."

"Now that is something I'm familiar with." Andrew grinned lasciviously at Lizbet. "A fair hand from a woman."

Lizbet locked her eyes with Andrew's for a moment, her brows raised. "And I wish I had a shilling for every time I've heard that one. Come on, if you are staying in, get your money on the table."

It was Andrew who won the first game.

"Lads, now come on, that round was beginner's luck," Andrew said as he gathered his winnings from the table and pulled the coins towards him. He had won the hand quickly. Marc, Pierre and Mat had all viewed the newcomer to the table as a new source of ready funds and all looked equally disappointed by his first win.

"Hand your cards back, come on." Lizbet held her hands out for their cards and collecting the worn deck, reunited and shuffled it. "Come on, wagers on the table, boys, or there'll be no cards dealt."

Lizbet flicked them all a new card, watching them carefully. Marc, she knew now, nibbled his bottom lip when he was trying to decide whether or not to fold, so the chances were whatever hand he held was not a good one. Pierre though had closed his cards together and was holding them flat to the table. A sure sign that he had confidence in his hand. No need to take a second look to check it, and sure enough, the fingers on his left hand were already selecting a coin to add to the pot.

Froggy Tate couldn't help himself, and if he had a good hand he'd constantly check the cards, lifting the corners an inch or so to view the tops of them where they lay on the table. He was doing that now and he had already three coins in a row in front of him so whatever cards Froggy had face down were, she concluded, probably good ones.

Jack was absent tonight, but when he played cards it was with his whole body. He couldn't sit still. If the hand was good, he'd be sitting forward on the edge of the seat, looking closely at the other players, trying to read their faces. If it was a bad hand, he'd invariably abandon it on the table, face down and sit back, arms folded, a dour look on his face. On the rare occasion when he held a winning hand, he'd tap his fingers impatiently on the table. Lizbet would find herself then having to stifle a laugh.

Mat was always a little harder to read. A skilled player who invariably never left the table with less than he started out with, sat now with an impassive face, and his movements were so economical that he was almost as hard to read as the Master.

Finally she let her eyes wander over Andrew and found his cold assessing gaze turned on her. He seemed to have little interest in the cards that he had been dealt.

She was right.

Marc folded, Pierre won and took the pot and Andrew lost the next three hands as well, making him a welcome addition to their card game. Mat, as she had expected, took a steady stream of coins from the pot to bolster his own pile in front of him.

"Where's Jack?" Andrew asked. "Doesn't he normally play?"

It was Pierre who answered. "He's probably still licking his wounds from last night. Mat took more than his normal quota from him, didn't you, Mat?"

"Well, if he was fool enough to keep going then that's his own fault. A man should recognise when the cards are against him and bow out," Mat replied.

"Jack's never backed down from anything in his life, be it a fight or a card game," Lizbet chimed in.

"It is wise sometimes to know your limits," Andrew added quietly.

"Well, don't go telling that to Jack, will you?" Pierre laughed. "We need him. He's a good source of coin for us, isn't he, lads?"

"Surely he's not that bad?" Andrew collected the cards Lizbet had dealt him and sent a coin spinning across the table to join the pot.

"When he loses, he loses a lot, and when he wins he goes to bed a happy man with a full purse," Marc supplied.

"He's not a cautious man then?" Andrew asked.

"Not when it comes to cards," came the automatic reply from both Mat and Pierre together.

Chapter 7
A Plan is Cast

Whoso list to hunt, I know where is an hind,
But as for me, hélas, I may no more.
The vain travail hath wearied me so sore,
I am of them that farthest cometh behind.
Sir Thomas Wyatt's 'Whoso List to Hunt'

✝

Froggy stood in the Master's room where he had been summoned. Richard wanted to know if he had the skill to make the lead shot for the flintlocks or whether he would need to buy it in. They had some ammunition already, but not enough to cover the training Richard had proposed. Froggy was confident, that with a little practice he was equal to the task.

"I'd rather do this on my own first. It's been a while since I last did it and there's a knack to it as well." Froggy turned the musket ball mould over in his hand as he spoke.

"Agreed. Find out then if you can still make them, before you show the rest. Lizbet will help you." Richard took the mould back from Froggy and flipped the catch open examining the inside.

"The woman!" Froggy exclaimed.

"Well, she's not likely to stand and criticise your every action, is she? And I'm assuming you'll need a fire? Do you want to carry your own wood?"

Richard held Froggy's gaze until the other backed down.

†

The next morning Froggy, with Lizbet in tow, went to find a suitable spot to set up a fire to craft the musket balls. Froggy told her he wanted the fire enclosed in a ring of stones, scraping a rough shape on the ground with the toe of his boot to show where he wanted them. He then tramped off leaving Lizbet to heft stones and collect a pile of dry wood.

It had rained hard over the past few days and finding wood dry enough to take a flame took her longer than she anticipated and necessitated walking further into the forest than she wanted. By the time she had enough wood and kindling, her skirts were soaked to the knee from the bracken and wild garlic leaves which all still held unshed raindrops. Her wool-lined clogs were also uncomfortably sodden.

When Froggy, a hessian sack over his shoulder, returned, Lizbet was rolling the last of the stones into place to make the hearth.

"Well, you timed that well, didn't you?" Lizbet complained, rising and dusting her hands off on her apron.

"That would depend on your point of view," Froggy said, grinning. He dropped to his haunches and set to lighting the fire.

Having worked out the direction of the prevailing breeze, Lizbet sat on the forest floor next to him and watched, avoiding the smoke that snaked its way silently though the trees. From the sack

Froggy produced another smaller one containing charcoal. When the wood on the fire was burning well, he used a stick to part the burning logs, revealing the glowing centre. He threw in several handfuls of the charcoal that he covered over again with the burning wood.

"What's that for?" Lizbet asked, pointing at the sack Froggy had taken the black coal like lumps from.

Frogging rubbed his blackened hands on the sack to remove the worst of the dust. "Charcoal. It burns slower and hotter than logs and we need it to get very hot to melt the lead."

Lizbet settled back, enjoying the silence of the woodland, and the warmth from the blaze. Froggy pushed the burning logs away to reveal the glowing charcoal and Lizbet felt the wave of heat from it on her face.

"I'd say that'd do us." Froggy used his stick to make a dent into the charcoal and then from his sack he pulled a broad ladle with a spout on one side and a short handle. The handle was hollow and, trimming one of the sticks from Lizbet's woodpile, he fashioned it to fit inside, making the handle twice as long and heat proof.

Froggy had another bag with what looked like grey pebbles, and one of these he dropped into the ladle and placed it in the delve in the charcoal. As soon as the ladle heated through there was a wisp of smoke from within and then, as quick as butter melted on warm bread, the pebble turned into a liquid silver bubble. Froggy, satisfied with the temperature, added half a dozen more pellets to the ladle and they both watched as they melted.

"Now this is the tricky bit, lass," Froggy said, producing the final part of the process from his sack. "This is the mould. We need to pour the lead in there." Froggy held it out showing her the small conical spout the lead would need to enter. "Spill it on the flames and it'll spit like a bantam at a cock fight. Do you have a steady hand?"

Lizbet nodded.

"Right then, get round the other side of the fire and hold the mould like this, nice and still." Froggy demonstrated before handing it to Lizbet.

It was hinged, and had a long handle to keep her hands away from both the lead and the flames. Lizbet took up a position opposite and held the mould ready. Froggy tipped the ladle's spout towards the opening in the mould slowly. Lizbet was amazed at how mobile the liquid lead was; it seemed to move quicker than water. Froggy poured it carefully in and there was another small plume of smoke from the inside of the mould.

"Right, lass, let's see what we have." Froggy held out his hand for the mould and taking it, unclipped the slides and opened it.

Inside, the chamber was only half full; the lead had solidified in the spout and the mould had not been completely filled.

"I was too slow. Look, it's set before I got it in and it's blocked the mould. Let's do it again."

Taking a knife he flicked out the still hot lead from the mould back into the ladle and the pair watched it return to a molten form for the second time.

"Here we go. Keep your hands steady." Froggy poured the lead, but the spout overflowed, molten lead dripping onto the charcoal.

It banged and spat.

Lizbet dropped the mould in the fire and jumped backward.

Froggy swore. "For God's sake, you are supposed to hold it still!" Froggy complained as he fished the mould out of the fire with a stick once the lead had stopped spitting at them.

"You poured it too fast. It wasn't my fault," Lizbet replied defensively.

"Let's do it again. Hold it to the left of the fire then if it drips it won't be trying to burn holes in us," Froggy instructed, returning the ladle for the third time to the charcoal.

It took three more attempts before they had the measure of it, getting the liquid metal into the mould at the right speed and enough of it to form the musket balls.

"There we go." Froggy opened the mould and the silver ball fell to the earth next to the fire.

"It's so shiny, not like the stuff you melted." Lizbet reached for it, Froggy battering her fingers away with his hand.

"That'll burn you still. Let it cool a while before you pick it up. They start out shining like buttons but in a day or so they dull and go the colour of pewter," Froggy said, rolling the musket ball over with a stick.

"What about that bit sticking out of the top of it like an apple stalk? Surely that's not supposed to be there." Lizbet pointed to the lead that had solidified in the neck of the mould and was still attached to the ball.

"That's called the sprue. When it's cool enough," Froggy touched it tentatively, "which it isn't yet, we can snip that off. In the middle of the mould there's a clipper you use to take it off. I'll show you in a minute when it's not trying to burn the skin off my fingers."

When it cooled and the sprue was clipped off, Froggy rolled the musket ball between his fingers, smiling.

"Here we go." He passed it over to Lizbet for her to admire and she took it from him smiling.

"Just another five dozen to make and we'll be finished," Froggy said catching her eye grinning.

It took all afternoon. After the first few were made, Froggy melted enough to make five balls at once, pouring it into the mould, and Lizbet quickly released it to the earth then the next was poured quickly in. With their sprues removed, Froggy lined them up in rows of one dozen.

Lizbet asked why they needed so many. Froggy told her that a dozen balls gave each of them twelve shots, which was not so very many for target practice, apparently the Master wanted each of them to be experts with the muskets before they reached wherever it was they were going.

"We'll make a target out of straw at the front, with clay at the back a hand's thickness deep.

That's enough to capture the balls, and if you keep the clay damp you can get the balls back out and reuse them so long as they don't hit another already lodged in there," Froggy explained. "We'll lose a fair few as well if they miss the target, so making musket balls, lass, is something we'll be doing quite often."

†

A day later, happy with their skill at making the musket balls, Froggy Tate was, for once, in his element. None of the others, apart from Richard, had seen the process and the rest of the men sat quietly and watched Froggy's alchemy, with Lizbet's steady helping hands, as he turned the molten lead into the small spherical musket balls.

Froggy picked up one of the round finished balls and passed it to Jack. "What you cannot see, and I'll show you tomorrow, is what happens to this wee fella when it hits something. You'd think, wouldn't you, that it would punch a hole straight through and pop itself out the other side, but it's not like that," Froggy said, shaking his head.

"What's it do then?" Mat asked.

"Like I said, I'll show you."

There were two targets set up the following day, one of which buzzed with flies.

Hung by a foot, and blessedly upwind, the ripe carcass of a sheep, its eyes already picked out by the birds, swung from a tree. Froggy had positioned a second target fashioned of straw, and backed with clay, to the left of the unfortunate beast. The centre of the target was picked out with a disc of dark brown leather. Froggy had one flintlock musket, the musket balls, paper, and a flask of powder.

"This is going to take all bloody day if we've only one between us," Mat complained, already looking bored.

"Well, there's more, but today I'm not willing to let any of you loose with them before you've had some practice. I'll not be stitching your head back on for you when you've blown it off your shoulders, and I'll not be fishing musket balls out of Dan's arse when you've shot him by accident either," Froggy reprimanded.

"If Dan gets a musket ball in his backside, there'll be no accident about it," replied Mat mischievously.

Richard's voice cut through the laughter. "It will indeed be a long day if you don't shut up and listen."

The rebuke was enough to silence them and Froggy had their attention again.

Andrew's sensible voice spoke in agreement with the Master. "Come on, lads. We are here to learn. Let's show Froggy here some respect. He's far more skill here than we have."

An appreciative grin split Froggy's uneven features at Andrew's words.

Froggy spent a long time, too long for Jack who was impatient to actually fire one, explaining how they worked. Starting at one end, he named every part and made them name them back to him. He took apart the firing mechanism and showed them how it screwed back together and how tight it needed to be. Finally, they moved on to how to fire one, going over and over the process without actually adding the gunpowder, but just dry firing the gun.

"So," Froggy announced at last, "who's first?"

Jack stepped forward, and the rest were forced to defer. Dan glanced at Mat who raised his eyes to Heaven. Dan grinned back. Despite Jack's outspoken dislike of the flintlocks, he'd still want to be the first to try them.

"Right then, let's see if you were listening then, shall we?" Froggy announced and everyone watched as Jack prepared the musket.

The charge went in the barrel first, then the ball surrounded by paper was rammed home down the barrel next. Then the hammer was half-cocked and the charge added to the pan, and finally the hammer was fully cocked.

"Right then, aim at that sheep and let's see if you can hit it," instructed Froggy from where he stood next to Jack.

Jack took aim and squeezed the trigger. As he did, the barrel dipped and they all saw the plume of dust some ten feet in front of the dangling sheep where the ball hit the earth. There was a round of jeering laughter. Jack scowled.

"What did I tell you? Hold it true. When you pull the trigger, hold your breath and don't let your trigger hand pull the barrel down," Froggy said. "They are heavier than you give them credit for and the barrel will drag itself downwards."

Jack's second shot hit the sheep.

The woolly carcass swung wildly on the rope from the impact as the lead ball ripped through the flesh.

"You can't see where it went in," Froggy said, advancing to the stinking animal, "but you can certainly see where it came out." With a stick, he rotated the carcass and on the reverse was a reddened mess of ripped flesh and splintered bone poking past the fleece where the ball had left the body. "So it's not what it does to you on the way in but on the way out that makes the bloody mess."

All of them were fighting men, and they looked with new respect at the flintlock; it was a weapon that seemed able to blow a man apart from the inside.

Froggy was still talking. "A leather jack will give you no protection against one of these at all, and plate, well at thirty paces it will go straight through. Even at a hundred paces, it's still likely to punch a hole in the armour."

"What about the pistols? They take the same shot. Are they just as effective?" Dan asked, watching Mat who was next in line to load and take a shot.

"They are for bloody show if you ask me. The barrel is too short. Anything more than ten paces and it will be down to luck if you hit anything." Froggy, his arms folded, watched intently as Mat used the rod to push the ball down the barrel. "Not so hard, otherwise it will stick," he warned.

"So at close range, it would still go a through a cuirass?" Dan asked, then added laughing, "I just want to be sure what to wear when Jack here gets hold of one again."

Jack shot him an evil look. "Carry on like that and you'll be inviting a shot in the arse."

"Well, before we finish with these, the Master suggested we gauge their effectiveness, so we will set them up against some armour and find out what they can do." Froggy received the weapon back from Mat who had just made two respectable shots and offered it to Andrew.

Froggy watched with dark beady eyes as Andrew efficiently loaded and primed the weapon. His first shot went wide of the mark, the lead shot scoring the bark from the tree trunk where the sheep was tied. The second shot went through the side of the dead ewe's head, taking with it most of its teeth and leaving an ugly gaping hole through the side of the jaw.

Andrew hefted the weapon in his hands before handing it back to Froggy. "There's a bit of kick from them when they fire."

Froggy said, smiling, "That's why you need to brace it against your shoulder. If you don't, it'll buck and the shot will go wild every time."

After an hour they had all hit the sheep, and Froggy was satisfied that all of them could safely load the muskets, prime them correctly and fire them safely. The shooting now moved to the straw target ranged further back.

They had varied degrees of success. Jack planted his first shot a hand's width from the centre, however his second went wide, the shot disappearing in the undergrowth – predictably he blamed the failure on the flintlock. Mat placed shots next to each other on the right side of the target, receiving praise from Froggy which delighted him and earned him a weary look from Jack.

Richard who had been watching the proceedings quietly, sitting on a fallen branch behind them, spoke then. "It will be a little hard to sell them unless we can make a good account of them, so when we are finished we will know exactly what they are capable of."

"Are you joining in?" Jack invited.

All of them had now taken their first few shots at the target.

Richard dropped from his perch lightly and held out his hand for the flintlock.

He loaded it smoothly and quickly. The shot when he made it was a good one, just to the left of the centre of the target. Loading a second ball he hoisted the flintlock to his shoulder. They all held their breath with him. The shot was near as made no difference through the middle of the target.

Froggy nodded with approval.

"And that, you lot, is what you will all be doing with a bit of practice," Froggy said, satisfied with his Master's performance.

Jack on the other hand wondered just when Richard had got some practice in. He very much suspected that his brother's performance was down to training and did not owe a lot to natural talent.

When the firing was finished, without asking, Scranton took the powder flask from Froggy's hands and poured some into his palm. Taking a pinch between his finger and thumb, he rolled it between them. "It's a little too coarse if you ask me for flintlocks," he said then. Dusting the powder from his fingers, he sniffed at the residue it had left. "And definitely not the best mix. If I may say so, someone has sold you poor powder and no doubt at a good price as well."

All the men heard the slight.

Richard seemed happy enough though and clapped Scranton on the arm. "Well, with your advice, sir, that will not happen again."

☦

Having used nearly all the shot, Froggy and Lizbet set out again the next day to make enough for a second practice session. There had been little left from the day before and certainly not enough for another round of training.

The breeze sent the stinging smoke straight into her eyes and she flinched, hands tipping the mould just as Froggy began pouring the lead from the ladle.

"For God's sake, woman, I've missed!" Froggy cursed pulling away from the fire.

Lizbet's eyes, watering, were closed tightly. She heard the lead spitting and crackling where it had been ignited by the embers.

Froggy rocked back on his heels. "It's a confounded task, and it's taking too long."

Lizbet wiped the back of her hand over her running nose and eyes and nodded in agreement.

"It needs to be on a skillet over the fire to hold it still, and if we had more than this one mould, we could set them all up next to each other and make a lot more and a sight quicker as well," Lizbet observed gloomily.

Froggy pulled the ladle from the fire and breathed heavily. "I've been thinking that all morning, lass. We can melt enough lead to fill fifty, even a hundred at a time, but it's the mould that's slowing us up." Froggy pulled his cap from his head, revealing a damp fringe stuck to his brow with sweat. "I'll go and see the Master. We need a new mould, or at least more of these. One just isn't going to be enough. It'll take some money and time to get it made, but in the long run it would be worth it."

Lizbet, busy removing the sprues from the top of the cooled balls, could not agree more. It was slow work for the results, and there were two burn holes in her dress she could have done without – spitting lead moved faster than she did, it seemed. So far, neither of them had sustained an injury, but the general feeling was that it would only be a matter of time.

Richard had the mould in his hand and turned it over as he examined it. "Tell me again."

"If we had something like this but longer, we could make ten in a strip, and if we had five or even more strips of them attached to each other then we could pour lead into the lot and it would make the task a much shorter one," Froggy supplied. "I was thinking we could make the mould in layers, and wire them all together, then when the lead has cooled, and that only takes a moment, we unwire it and separate the layers. I can't see why it wouldn't work."

"Neither can I." The Master was smiling, and Froggy, pleased, grinned back in return.

"The other thing is if we make it as a block then we can put it on a skillet or some such. No one needs to hold it and it'll make filling it a sight easier," Froggy said, then added, "It was Lizbet that gave me that idea."

"Indeed! I'd not have credited munitions manufacture amongst her skills." Richard handed the mould back to Froggy. "Get me some of the flintlock balls so I have the dimensions and I shall get you your mould."

†

Due to a lack of shot, the day was taken up with arms training instead. Pierre, Mat and Richard watched Jack and Andrew trade blows from where they lay on the grass in the shade. Mat was in a sour mood, having been told in no uncertain terms by the Master earlier, that training was a serious matter and under no circumstances was he to start laying wagers on the outcome of the bouts.

"Put more power in your wrist." Andrew held the pole level so Jack could properly see the hold he had on it. "Hold it like this and you can put more force behind the swing."

Jack, grinning, stepped back as the end of the pole whistled through the air and harmlessly past his face. He picked up his own staff from the ground again and held it up defensively. "Let's try that again, shall we?"

"Are you sure you want to?" Andrew asked.

The knuckles on Jack's hands were already grazed and bleeding where he had failed to keep them from Andrew's well aimed swings.

"Why wouldn't I?" Jack planted his feet firmly and readied himself for Andrew's attack that was not long in coming. This time though it was the older man who dropped his staff, clutching a bruised hand to his chest.

"I deserved that, I grant you," Andrew said, inspecting the damage and pulling away a flap of rent skin from the back of his hand. "I'll not make the same mistake a second time."

Jack lowered his staff and, planting it firmly down, leant heavily on it.

"Someone taught you well. You've all the basics covered. A little polish is all you need, that and a few tricks in your armoury as well," Andrew continued. "The Master tells me you were with Harry Fitzwarren?"

"I was a servant in his house, yes. As Richard likes to point out, it afforded me a wide range of opportunities," Jack replied sarcastically.

"I've seen your skill. He is right – you've had access to training at a level that not many can aspire to," Andrew chastised.

"Aye, I thank God daily for being so benevolent."

If Andrew heard the sarcasm in Jack's voice, he didn't acknowledge it. "We have to thank the Lord for all opportunities, even those which teach us difficult lessons. Life is a journey which will end when we kneel at his feet," Andrew pronounced.

"You missed your calling," Jack supplied, grinning.

"I didn't. I like this far too much." Without warning, Andrew swung his staff through the air neatly knocking Jack's staff away. His support removed, he staggered forward and a second neat swing to the back of the knees had him sprawling in the dirt.

Rolling to his back, Jack righted himself in a moment, hands dusting dirt from his knees. "Now I know where my brother gained his tactics from."

"It's a fine line the one that is drawn between fair play and foul," Andrew laughed, "and that might have crossed it. We just need to add a few tricks like that to the skills you already have and with your strength there will be few that will be able to best you."

"Looks like we have food," Jack said, still brushing leaves from his sleeves, as he spied Lizbet approaching, a basket slung over one arm.

"If this came out of the bake houses near the Thames, people would be asking for their money back, and the baker would be going out of business, I can tell you," complained Lizbet, banging down the basket containing five freshly baked solid brown loaves. "Look at it! Harder than a rock! It's good for fishing with and that's about it."

Jack tore one of the loaves in half. "Any cheese? Or is this it?"

"Just wait on, will you? Give me a chance!" Lizbet complained.

"Just hurry up, I'm starving," Jack said through a full mouthful and slapped Lizbet's backside, earning him a scowl as she unloaded more provisions from the basket.

Richard came and leant against the stone wall where Jack was standing. "She still not forgiven you then?" he asked, laughing and taking half the loaf from Jack's hands.

"The woman who weds me can scold me, but I'll not suffer it from a woman before then," Jack mused.

"You? Married?" Richard scoffed.

"I might," Jack replied, sounding hurt.

"Aye, and what would you marry for?" Richard asked.

"Money, what else," Jack replied bluntly.

Richard found himself choking on crumbs. "Let me know if you find a rich wench in the hay fields, will you? I'll have one as well."

Jack's face darkened, and he pulled himself up to his full height. "I'm not short of lassies."

"I know, the stupid kind who are fair taken in with your looks and kind smile. Even Lizbet has turned her back on you," Richard scoffed.

"Lizbet? What do you mean? She's not angry with me," Jack said. He quickly looked in her direction then back at Richard. "Is she?"

Richard just shrugged, saying nothing as Lizbet returned as promised with cheese and beer. She put them on the wall between the pair of them, popping a lump of cheese in her mouth before turning to go.

Jack caught her round the waist and pulled her close.

"Get off me." Lizbet pushed him away. "You stink. Keep your filthy hands to yourself." Pulling free, she turned her back on him and made her way to Froggy and Marc to dole out more bread and cheese.

"Did you put her up to that?" Jack said, looking murderously at Richard.

"Me? What's between your head is more solid than these loaves Lizbet keeps on complaining about," Richard replied, rapping his knuckles against the hard crust of the bread he held.

"What do you mean?" Jack sounded genuinely confused.

Richard shook his head. "Do I really need to tell you?" Then seeing the look on Jack's face, he realised he did. "Lizbet doesn't like sharing your affections."

Jack's eye's opened wide.

"Perhaps if you are looking for a wife…" Richard added grinning.

Jack visibly paled. "You don't think she's thinking I might wed her do you?"

"Who knows how a woman's mind works?" mused Richard. "You could do worse. She's excellent with a needle, knows how to strike a bargain, and she can put up with your temper, it could…"

"My God! You are not serious, are you?" Jack sounded worried. He cast a glance at Lizbet where she was pouring ale into Marc's cup. "Half the time she treats me like I'm wedded to her already with her nagging tongue."

"Well, there you are then, she's already treating you like a husband. All she's got to do now is get you drunk and make you into one," Richard agreed with him, then adopting a serious voice, "Be careful, Jack. We both know that drunk you'll agree to just about anything. And the law here is different."

"What do you mean, different?" Jack asked quickly.

"A pledge to wed, even a verbal one, is binding," Richard lied smoothly.

"No, really?" Jack gasped.

"Aye, it is. As long as she has a witness, it's as binding as if it was in a church. So be warned," Richard said managing to keep his face straight.

☦

Thomas Tresham, Grand Prior of the Knights Hospitallers of St John of Jerusalem, had been wondering exactly why he had received a visit from a Master Garrett now for several weeks. He'd known the name would be a false one, and the visitor had left little in the way of contact information either.

Master Garrett, it seemed, was an intermediary for a Master who wished to deal with the knights. The matter concerned an arms shipment, that much the man had divulged, along with the subject of the proposed deal which related to an unspecified number of flintlocks. Tresham, newly appointed to his post and eager to impress, had penned a quick message to his counterpart alerting them that a man wished to contact the Order regarding an arms shipment comprising a number of flintlocks.

Garrett had asked for leave to contact the Order and had asked Tresham to contact the Order's controller in Venice altering them of the possibility of a deal. Garrett's Master appeared to be aware of the Order's hierarchy and also its mechanisms for trade, and he knew that the controller in Venice would be the one who could strike a deal for the shipment if they were interested. He'd given them little more information. Only that he would be the contact once he reached Venice and hopefully by then the Order might be interested in opening negotiations.

Richard was well aware of the far reaching and far flung influence the Order had. He was relying on the fact that, with a few clues, they would rapidly find out that he might be the key to uncovering where the lost Italian cargo had gone. This quantity of missing arms would not have disappeared beneath the surface without leaving a lot of ripples, and ripples spread.

He relied also on their greed. If such a shipment was on the open market, it would be one they would very much like to acquire for themselves rather than any of the other European power houses taking advantage. It was highly unlikely they would want to return the shipment to the poor Italian armoury that had lost out so badly on the order Northumberland had placed.

Chapter 8
A Forgotten Lady

Miri it is while sumer i-last
With foulës song;
Oc now neghëth windës blast
And weder strong.
Ei, ei, what this night is long,
And Ich with wel michel wrong
Sorwe and murne and fast.

☦

    Whilst Mary had been in confinement, Elizabeth had been at Court. Catherine's life had become one of a simple servant at Durham Place. Now with the buds turning green on the willow branches outside the kitchen windows, Catherine was beginning to believe that this might be her situation for the rest of her life, an unpaid servant in a minor royal household.

    The basic maintenance staff were left to keep the manor in readiness for Elizabeth's return and one of these was Catherine De Bernay. When Elizabeth had left, the remaining servants had breathed a sight more easily; the tension that seemed to haunt Durham Place like a captive thunderstorm went with her. Kate Ashley, Elizabeth's governess and confidante, had selected those who were to attend Elizabeth and luckily Catherine had not been amongst them.

Spring moved into early summer and still Elizabeth had not returned, and more importantly, Catherine had heard nothing from Richard. He had promised to help her. When he had introduced her to Kate Ashley, his parting words had been reassurances that he would not forget her cause, or the debt that both himself and Jack owed to her.

His words had been solemnly spoken, and she had believed him; time though, had undermined that faith. Since that day, she had seen him for a moment when they had thought the house was on fire, but he had left her before she had the opportunity to say anything to him.

Kate Ashley had returned to the house a few weeks ago to supervise the removal of tapestries from Elizabeth's room that were to adorn the lady's bedchamber whilst she was at Court. Catherine had forced herself to beg leave to speak privately with her; the conversation had not gone well.

"That is a name you have been told not to speak aloud," Kate Ashley had said, taking hold of Catherine's arm in a tight grip and pulling her close.

Catherine tried to wrench her arm free, but Kate was not letting go. "He is a known traitor to the Crown and you will not, do you hear me, speak of treason while under the Lady Elizabeth's roof."

Kate had roughly released her and Catherine found herself rubbing her arm where Kate's nails had bitten through her sleeve.

So, after that, Catherine knew there was no way to find out what had happened, and if Richard was doing anything for her cause. Indeed after Kate's rough words, she wondered even if he had been caught and arrested. Something must have happened. She had risked everything to get Jack out of Marshalsea. Surely he would not forget her?

As the weeks and days passed and still no word came, she wondered if perhaps Jack had died. He had been so ill when they had redeemed him from the gaol, there was more than a good chance he had succumbed to the fever that had been upon him. It seemed to her that by the time summer came that the Fitzwarren brothers were either dead, or didn't care about her; whichever one it was, the outcome was very much the same.

Eventually though, Catherine's situation did change, and it was shortly before the return of Elizabeth to Durham Place that the incident happened.

Elizabeth had a spaniel and the creature was as disobedient as its mistress. The cosseted animal was marked as belonging to the princess with a collar picked out with pearls around its silky neck. Elizabeth's bedroom was empty now. Most of her furniture and her bed had been moved to Court, but the lady was about to return and her rooms were being cleaned.

Catherine, with a selection of cloths at her disposal, had the task of cleaning the window panes in the room and removing the band from the glass made by the spaniel as it pressed its pink wet nose to the glass and barked at those in the courtyard below.

Cleaning the panes down with water and then drying them to remove the smears, Catherine polished another and then adjusted her focus from the glass to beyond it. That was when she saw him.

There was a man in the courtyard, as fair as a May dance maiden, with hair like gilt straw. She knew only one man who had hair like that. Jack.

Cloths and cleaning abandoned, Catherine made it down the stairs on unsteady legs. It might not be just Jack, they might be both here. There might be news. At last, something. Finally they had come for her.

Catherine missed the last step, her knees buckling as she landed heavily. A hand on the wall saved her and she ran on towards a door that she knew opened onto the courtyard.

Her eyes had not lied to her. Standing by a sturdy chestnut mare that he had just dismounted, and passing the reins to a servant, was the man with the fair hair. His back was to her, but it didn't matter. Catherine sagged heavily against the stone door surround. That spare frame didn't belong to Jack, and neither did the thin reedy voice that was complaining about being kept waiting. Catherine didn't care who he was. He wasn't Jack.

Oh God – where was he?

Catherine tried to rub the tears away. They were too numerous to be cleared with a sweep of the back of her hand, and her nose was running. A sob caught in her throat. Catherine gave in. He must be dead. Jack wouldn't have left her if he'd been alive, she was sure of it. Jack was dead. He might not have been with her for a year, but his had been the name she thought of when she could not bear it anymore.

Jack wouldn't let them do that to her.
Jack would save her from this.
Jack would stop them.
Jack would take her home.

The sobs wouldn't stop, and she no longer cared. They came in gasps, shaking her body uncontrollably. Catherine didn't know if she was crying for herself or for Jack.

The following day she paid the price for the endless tears. Her eyes were so sore and swollen, it even hurt when she blinked, and her throat was painful from the sobbing. The other servants had nudged each other, but so far no one had asked. There was no point trying to disguise it, Catherine knew her red nose and puffy face told the world of her misery.

They would have been surprised to find out though that Catherine was feeling better. She'd known she supposed for a long time that Jack was dead, and she knew perfectly well that no one would be coming for her. Catherine had resolved during the night to stop waiting.

It was Richard's voice that had cut through her pain.

Part with sorrow, lady. Take a different path.

Richard had spoken those words to her what seemed like an age ago, when she first came to London with Jack. In her head she could still hear the serious edge to his voice and see his steel grey eyes holding hers. He was right. There must be a different path. Catherine accepted that she could not continue to wait. Her days and nights had been consumed with thinking of the moment when they would come and take her from Durham Place, when they would free her from this life, and she could return to Assingham. When she could go home. Catherine finally accepted that this was not going to happen, no matter how much she wished for it.

It was time to find a new path. She didn't know where it would lead, or indeed where it was going to start. If she looked hard enough, there would be an opportunity somewhere. That was what she resolved to focus on. An opportunity.

†

Christopher Morley was a man who believed always that the answer was in the detail. His current Master was William Cecil, and he although he was related by marriage to Thomas Parry, Elizabeth's household controller, he was Cecil's man.

Through Parry he had full list of everyone in Elizabeth's household; he knew who all of her servants were. How many grooms, stablehands, cooks, kitchen maids, ladies in waiting; he knew them all. Every one of them he had tracked down, speaking to each of them alone, looking for a link to Elizabeth.

Most were too stupid and too terrified to be of much use. Lilly Walters, a member of the kitchen staff, had been the most amenable to his suggestions as soon as "money" was mentioned. A selfish girl with ideas above her station, Lilly would do just about anything to pocket a few extra coins and she had willingly started to tell him anything he wanted to know. A few pointed questions though soon showed her words to be unfounded, not even half-truths; she simply repeated his questions, agreeing with him and eagerly hoping for some recompense.

He'd wanted to know if she ever had close contact with the Lady Elizabeth, and Lilly had started by saying she did see her in the gardens during the summer months, and when this hadn't seemed to satisfy him, she'd continued on until she had told him that on occasion, the lady liking her company so much, even invited her to join her while sewing the solar.

Morley had absently pressed a coin into Lilly's hand and left her. He doubted very much that the girl would be of much use to him. And he had also doubted very much that Eugenie, Kate Ashley's niece, would be of much use either, but every stone had to kicked over if he were to find the key he was looking for. And he was more than a little surprised when he found what he was looking for under this particular rock.

Durham Place was once again busy. While Elizabeth had been at Court, rooms had been cleaned, the lady's chattels polished, packed and stored. Little was left available for the chance thief. Elizabeth had been at Court during Mary's confinement and now that the Queen had returned to the world, flat-stomached Elizabeth had finally escaped Court and was about to return to her own house of Durham Place.

Catherine was arranging candlesticks on a dresser. The bases still had solidified lumps of wax on their shiny surfaces; they'd been carelessly cleaned. Using her nail, she pried the lumps free and rubbed the bases back to an even polish, removing her fingerprints. Using a hand, she swept the curling wax shards to the edge of the coffer lid to catch them in a hand when a voice behind her made her jump. Her hand dashed the wax to the floor as she whirled round to find the speaker.

"Well, that's the sign of guilt. What were you up to then?" It was Chistopher Morley. She'd never spoken to him before, but knew of him; he was related by marriage to Thomas Parry.

"Nothing, sir." Catherine bobbed an obedient curtsey. "I thought I was alone, that was all."

"Alone and doing what?" Morley smiled. His eyes noted that the girl's hands were shaking and that she rapidly picked up a cloth to hold to disguise the fact.

"Just cleaning the rooms, sir. These are to be used again soon and we are getting them ready. I just didn't hear you come in and you gave me a fright," Catherine replied, recovering from the shock.

Morley smiled. "I'm sorry. Next time I shall tread more loudly."

His smile was easy, and his manner relaxed and Catherine returned his smile.

"It is a lot of work, isn't it? Packing, unpacking, re-packing, it must be very tedious?" He had hitched himself up on a coffer and was idly examining a statue of Pandora that Catherine had previously unwrapped and set back its place. "I'm sure she resents being packed and re-packed."

"Quite apt really. If only we could put Pandora in one of these chests and pack her woes away with her, that would indeed make all our efforts worthwhile," Catherine said smiling.

"I hadn't realised it was Pandora," Morley said, then tapping the box the statue held in her shapely hands, said, "Of course."

"When I was younger, I used to try to imagine all the evils of the world fitting into something so very small. I thought that each must be no bigger than a grain of sand if they were all to fit inside." Catherine sounded wistful.

Morley set down the Greek statue of Pandora holding a symbolically part opened box, and for the first time gave her his full attention. This girl was no Lilly Walters.

"If only all our troubles were just like grains of sand," Morley said, then added, "It would make them a lot easier to swallow sometimes, wouldn't it, if they were so small."

"I agree. My mother always told me the longer you dwell on a problem then the bigger it becomes," Catherine replied.

"A sensible lady, and if only it were so easy to follow that sage advice." Morley's manner was friendly and the smile on his face seemed genuine.

"The older we get, the harder it becomes to see them as simple grains of sand," Catherine agreed as she folded the cloth she held into a square.

"You are too young to have such a serious outlook! It is old fools like myself who have turned our problems into elephants. You, my dear, have not had time yet to make a complication of your life." Morley reprimanded her and finished with a laugh.

"I wish that were true," Catherine replied, inadvisably. She saw Morley's eyes narrow and instantly wished she could take back her words.

"So what are your woes then that have outgrown Pandora's box?" Morley asked as he watched her carefully.

"Oh nothing, sir. They were just general words." Catherine's reply was a little too quick.

"I can see on your face that there is something. A boy perhaps?" Morley said, smiling.

Catherine blushed.

"Ah, so I have you, lass. It is a boy! Is it one you left behind in Cheshire or a new love you've found since you came to Durham Place?" Morley quizzed, still grinning.

Catherine realised where she had suddenly found herself, surrounded by traps, and one more ill-considered word and she would fall headlong into one.

"You are Eugenie, aren't you? Kate's niece?" Morley asked when she didn't reply.

"Yes sir." Catherine bobbed a quick curtsey, and cast her eyes towards the floor. Why did this man know who she was? How had he found out, and why had he wanted to know, more importantly?

Morley stood suddenly. "Mistress I am sorry. I can see you are busy and I am making your tasks even harder. If I wish to tarry away my own day, that is my business, but that doesn't mean I need to waste yours as well." Smiling, he left her watching his retreat from the room.

Catherine swallowed, and let out a long breath. She hadn't known it, but a grain of sand was about to become the size of a boulder. Though at the moment Catherine was blissfully unaware that Morley was set upon a course to find out as much as he could about Kate Ashley's niece.

†

William Cecil steadfastly knew which side of the fence to be on. When Northumberland had tried to take the throne from Mary and place Jane Grey on the throne, he was able to lay before Mary a detailed account of his own intrigue against Northumberland and his supporters. His place as one of Mary's advisors was secured and five decades of Cecil family intrigue surrounding the crown was about to begin. Religiously compliant, he was happy to conform wholeheartedly to the Catholic cause and show support for Mary and the Catholic reforms.

Gardener might have some direct control over Elizabeth's household, but it was Cecil who had pressed his contacts and who kept Mary informed of Elizabeth's activities. It had been Cecil who in the previous year had copies made of the annotations in Elizabeth's book of hours that had belonged to her mother. The book had passed between a besotted Henry and Anne Boleyn and their protestations of undying love to each other were written in their own hands in the book's margins.

Indeed Cecil still had copies himself of the late Monarch's notes to his mistress. Mary had fed the notes he had given her to the flames, but Cecil had thought it prudent to retain a set for himself. They did not implicate Elizabeth at all, but they had the effect of igniting Mary's Tudor temper and there was no knowing when that might come in useful.

Christopher Morley worked for Cecil. Exploiting his family link with Parry, he had been sent to find any likely channels of information that might come to them from the Lady's household. Morley had a detailed list of everyone at Durham Place and those who were currently with Elizabeth who would soon return.

"It is a game, Morley, you know that." Cecil pushed his glasses back up his nose. "Elizabeth knows perfectly well how closely her household is watched, and she knows it could never be otherwise. So what do you have for me?"

Morley stretched back in his chair and observed Cecil closely over the desk. "So far I have found that Simon Jessop, the head of her kitchen staff, has substantial debts; he has already hocked family assets at a moneylenders in Cheap Street. It seems his possessions are continually in and out of there."

"Gambling?" Cecil enquired a distasteful expression his face.

Morley nodded.

"The preserve of the stupid," Cecil said shaking his head.

"Well, his indebtedness could make him useful, and the other I have found is Kate Ashley's niece," Morley continued thoughtfully.

"Ashley's niece is not likely to be much use to us, is she?" Cecil's brow creased as he awaited Morley's reply.

"Well, you might think that, but I'm not so sure she is Kate's niece," Morley supplied. He now had Cecil's undivided attention. "The girl is supposed to be from Cheshire. Her accent is wrong, and come to that, her whole demeanour is wrong."

"Well, who do you think she is?"

"I don't know, yet."

The conversation was concluded rapidly. Cecil had little time for anything that was not valuable to him. As soon as Morley had imparted what little information he had, he found himself dismissed with directions to find out as much as he could about Kate Ashley's niece.

Chapter 9
A Fool's Regret

I saw myny bryddis setyn on a tre;
He tokyn here fleyt & flowyn away,
With ego dixi, haue good day.
Many qwyte federes hat the pye,
I may noon more syngyn, my lyppis arn so drye.
Many qwyte federes hat the swan,
The more that I drynke, the lesse good I can.
Ley stykkys on the fer, wyl mot is brenne;
Geue vs onys drynkyn, er we gon henne.

☨

Inside the inn, the conversation had been a difficult one for some minutes, and Andrew was looking very much like he would like to be elsewhere. He regretted turning the conversation towards Richard's time in Seymour's house and from there to the incident with Elizabeth.

Andrew brought the conversation to a hasty conclusion and prepared to leave. "God will judge our acts, and we cannot and should not be our own assessor. If there is a fault and a blame, it will be paid for on God's own terms. God will most assuredly address your father's wrong against you."

"God on this occasion is being a little tardy," Richard remarked coldly. He had no wish to discuss the past and made no effort to further the conversation. "Sit, please. I am sorry. The past is not a place I like to dwell and that it still rankles me is certainly not your fault."

Andrew dropped back into the chair and rubbed his hands over his face. "I want to help. It seems to me that the wheels were set against you years ago. I said before that I wished I could have saved you the pain. Elizabeth is her father's daughter alright. I could not believe that she would treat you so badly just to cover up her trysts with Seymour."

"What are you talking about?" Richard's hard gaze was upon him, and he spoke the words slowly.

"Seymour and Elizabeth," Andrew said, confused. "Surely you know now?"

"Know what?" Richard demanded, a cold feeling already starting to well from the pit of his stomach.

Andrew's face creased in pain. "Christ forgive me."

"Will you tell me, or do I need to get Jack to beat it out of you?" Richard spoke without humour.

"Elizabeth and Seymour were lovers. Catherine Parr had already found them together, and then you did as well in the garden."

"He was trying to rape her."

"Was he? Some women like a violent lover, especially one with a Tudor temperament," Andrew supplied. "I'd seen them before, him with his hands around her neck. God, the sin of it. You were a scapegoat for the pair of them, not just for Thomas."

The flat of Richard's hand banged down on the table. "This conversation ends now."

A moment later he had risen from the table and left the room.

Jack dropped down into the seat recently vacated by his brother. "So what did you say to him to send him to his room like a scolded child then?" The smile on Jack's face fell away when he saw that Andrew was in no mood for his levity.

"I tried to help. Sometimes words cause greater wounds than we realise," Andrew replied.

Jack's eyes narrowed. He was always interested in any details of Richard's past, and Andrew was a direct link to that.

Seeing the enquiring look on Jack's face, Andrew continued, "I have my own guilt. I should have tried to help your brother when he was at Seymour's house and I didn't. I regret that. I thought it was just a minor incident. I did not realise that Seymour and Elizabeth would make him a scapegoat and I didn't anticipate that his father would try and kill him, banish him and disinherit him either."

"Stop there! What did you just say? Seymour and Elizabeth?" Jack repeated.

"Yes, together they used him to cover up their own sinful love. Boleyn's brat is just the same as her mother…"

"You just told Richard that Seymour and Elizabeth were lovers?" Jack said slowly, his eyes wide.

"Yes, I thought he'd known for Christ's sake. Everyone else did," Andrew said, his hands thrown wide.

"If I were you, I'd stop out of his way for a few days, and I will be doing the same," Jack said darkly.

As soon as she entered the room, she became acutely aware that all of them were staring at her, and Lizbet, meeting their eyes, scowled back. It was Dan who came towards her carrying a tray that he held out for her to take.

"You know which is his room? Take this up," Dan said, holding the tray out for her to take.

Lizbet had little choice other than to take it from him, her eyes passing from one face to the next. "Why don't you take it?" she asked warily, wondering exactly what was going on.

It was Jack who answered her, from where he was seated playing dice with Mat and Andrew. "Simple. If we go, there is more than a good chance we will end up with a knife between our ribs for our pains and we are fairly sure he'd not do that to you."

Lizbet was alarmed. "Why? What's happened?"

"Nothing, lass. He's been drinking and Dan wants to make sure he's not permanently drowned his sorrows," Jack supplied, reaching out and picking up the bone dice from the table.

"Why don't you bloody go and find out yourself? What's it got to do with me?" Lizbet pushed the tray back toward Dan but he raised his hands and refused to take it.

"We'd rather you went, lass," Dan said, stepping back and leaving her standing alone holding the tray.

Lizbet's eyes flicked quickly between all their faces. "Are you all cowards?"

Jack laughed. "You have us, to a man."

"For God's sake!" Lizbet, clutching the tray, stomped off across the room towards the stairs, unaware that every one of them was watching her closely.

"She'll be running down those stairs screaming in no time at all," Mat said.

"Nah, I reckon he'll throw her down the stairs," Froggy chipped in.

"You reckon? So Mat says she'll be screaming, Froggy says thrown. I think she'll get that tray hurled back at her. So match my money, lads, and let's see who is right." Jack put two shillings on the table. "Dan, Andrew, are you in? What do you reckon?"

Dan gave Jack a sour look that Jack ignored.

"I'm in, and I'm with you." Andrew, grinning, rolled two coins across the table to join Jack's.

Lizbet put the tray down and knocked. No reply. She tried again, her knock this time a little louder. Still nothing.

"For God's sake!" she exclaimed to the empty corridor.

In her usual style, she pushed the door open with her rear and followed in with the tray.

Inside, the room was in darkness. The shutters were closed and what little light leaked around them showed an apparently empty and cold room. The fire was out, grey ash lying in the grate and the bed, although crumpled, was empty. Lizbet let the door swing closed with a bang behind her and put the tray on the table.

"So, whose idea was it to send you?"

"God's bones!" A hand to her chest, Lizbet wheeled round. Luckily, she had let go of the tray.

There, sat on the floor in the corner of the room, was Richard. He was wearing nothing but a creased linen shirt and hose. The room was cold and Lizbet, looking at him, thought he must be freezing.

Reading her thoughts, he said, "Get me another bottle of this to warm me through." There was an empty earthenware flask on the floor and he rolled it across the boards towards her, then added, "No, on second thoughts, get me two."

Lizbet ignored him. She picked up the tray. "There's dinner on here for you, and I'll get this room sorted while you have it."

Turning, she found him standing behind her. If he was as drunk as they had said he was, he didn't look it. Lizbet took two precautionary steps backwards.

Richard's eyes met hers. "Very wise." Scooping the earthenware flask from the floor, he deposited it on the tray. "Two more."

Lizbet's hands were shaking now. "I'll leave this." She put down the tray and, taking the empty flask from it, let herself back out of the door.

Five pairs of eyes watched her expectantly as she walked back down the stairs. She ignored them all and disappeared into the inn, returning a few moments later with two full flasks and headed back up the stairs.

Opening the door, she made to step into the room only to be met immediately by Richard who neatly relieved her of the two flasks. The door began to swing closed in her face and Lizbet was about to turn and leave when it was yanked roughly open and the tray she had carried up was ejected. Lizbet tried to grasp it, but it was too late. It tipped and the contents fell, bouncing off the floorboards.

"You bastard!" Lizbet exclaimed as the door slammed shut and she was left looking at the mess she'd now have to clean up. The bowl holding the pottage hadn't broken but the soup was all over the floor, mingling with the spilt ale.

Downstairs, laughing, Jack collected his winnings from the table.

It was another hour later when Dan pressed Lizbet to retrace her steps. "He didn't hit you last time, did he? And he might want more," Dan had reasoned.

Shoved none-too-gently in the back by Dan, she had made her way up the stairs. Opening the door cautiously this time, Lizbet remained sensibly on the threshold.

Silence.

Peering round the door into the cold gloomy room, she found the Master this time insensible, it seemed, and face down on the floor in the corner. Lizbet hadn't meant to let go of the door and it banged closed loudly, making her jump, but there was no movement at all from the man on the floor.

Standing near the door, Lizbet enquired tentatively, "Master?"

No reply.

Her eyes adjusting to the darkness saw the flasks on their sides next to him. Both with their stoppers removed and she presumed they were empty. Well, if he'd drunk that lot he had no right to rise again.

Moving across the room quietly, she looked down on him. He didn't look asleep, his body was in too much of an uncomfortable pose for that; he looked dead.

Nervously she kicked his foot, ready to back quickly away if there was a reaction. Nothing.

The second kick was harder. Still nothing.

Bloody hell. Had he killed himself?

There was one outstretched hand. The palm faced the floor and the fingers were curled. Lizbet trod on it hard, producing a groan from the man on the floor. Not dead then, just drunk.

Lizbet smiled down at the unconscious man; at least her employment hadn't come to an untimely end.

She'd had plenty of experience with drunk men before. When he woke, his head would be full of thunder and he'd not want to be reminded of how he got that way.

The counterpane from the bed lay in an untidy heap where it had slithered to the floor. Picking it up and shaking it out, Lizbet squared up the material and dropped it over the prone man. A pillow from the bed was delivered to the floor near an outstretched hand; he'd find it if he wanted it, she reasoned. When it landed, the draught sent an unfolded sheet of parchment sliding across the floor.

Lizbet eyed it for a moment. If it was the Master's, it was a fair bet it would be important. Retrieving the sheet, she folded it along the creases back into a neat square and tucked it inside her bodice. There was no knowing who would be in the room next so it was, she reasoned, safer with her. Another half an hour had the room put back to rights, the grey embers cleared from the grate and replaced with a steady, warming fire.

Descending the stairs again, she met five pairs of eyes watching her. "Lost your bloody bets this time, did you, you bleeding cowards." Lizbet marched up to Jack. There were indeed five coins still on the table before him. "I think they are mine." Before he could object, she'd slid the lot off the table and pocketed them.

"Hey, now, you can't just come in and steal that lot off the table," objected Mat who stood up suddenly, the bench behind him scraping back noisily against the floor.

"Why not? That's the price of sending me," Lizbet said, her hands firmly on her hips matching his angry stare.

Dan settled a hand on Mat's shoulder. "Lass has a point, and if it cost us a penny each, I think that is money well spent, don't you? Or do you want to go back to drawing straws for the privilege of seeing who it is that goes, eh?"

"Fair point," Froggy said. "Looks like it's your job now, lass."

"Bloody cowards, the lot of you," Lizbet said again.

"Aye, we are," Jack said. "When you've been on the wrong side of that drunken temper a time or two, you learn to keep well clear."

Lizbet had experienced his temper before but she had never seen him drunk. He'd been in his room for two days now. It made her wonder exactly what was written on the page she had tucked away in the folds of her dress; whatever it was, it probably wasn't good news for the reader.

†

If he'd spent two days insensible and half of that time laid in a heap on the floor, he didn't look it now. When Lizbet returned with a second tray bearing food and drink, she found the Master seated at the table, dressed and looking at her with dark, angry eyes when she came through his door unannounced.

"Since when did you stop knocking?" he asked, his voice angry.

Lizbet had assumed he would still be asleep on the floor and had dispensed with the formality. About to say something and hoping he would not send this second tray of food to the floor, she thought better of it, and instead simply said, "Sorry, Master." She laid the tray down quietly on the table and avoided meeting his eyes.

"Has anyone else been in here?" Richard's eyes held hers until she dropped her gaze to the floor.

"No one that I know of," Lizbet replied honestly.

He waved his hand in dismissal.

Lizbet pulled the white square from her dress and held it out. "Are you maybe worried about this?"

Richard didn't take it. He just stared at her, hard.

167

Lizbet, not knowing what to do when he didn't take it, put it down on the tray. "I'm sorry, Master. I'd thought maybe you'd not want just anyone reading it, so I took to looking after it for you." Then she added unnecessarily, "You know I can't read."

"Sometimes, I wish that I couldn't either," was all he said quietly.

Lizbet left him alone, closing the door quietly behind her and feeling very much like she had earned those five coins she had scooped from the table earlier.

It was a pale and shaking hand that reached for the letter Lizbet had put on the tray. Even that small movement sent his stomach into a spasm again, and he wondered why his body continued to try and vomit when there was nothing left within him. Punishment, he supposed, for being so bloody stupid. Waiting until his body stopped fighting him, he smoothed the letter flat before him again. He'd spilt aqua vitae on it and the bottom lines were smudged but still legible. It was a passionless recounting of the facts; the writer cared not for the reader at all. He had, after all, been pressed into service at knifepoint, so Richard could not really blame him.

It seemed that his brother, Robert, had indeed scoured London looking for him. Who could blame him after he'd been left naked and bleeding, robbed in the street. He had, it seemed, found the inn where they had lodged and it had not taken long once coin had been offered to find a man who had a tale to tell in exchange for it. Fendrel, brother of Roddy who owned the inn, had profited twice, it seemed. Paid well by Richard for his help and silence in depositing Colan and his dead cousin some distance from the inn, he had then taken Robert's coins and told of the help he had been forced to offer in disposing of the bodies.

So now a second warrant had been issued for the arrest of Richard and Jack and it seemed that even Lizbet had been named as complicit in the crime. The lines on the letter were well spaced. The penmanship would be that of Clement's able assistant Marcus. Richard was sure he could almost feel, emanating from the paper, the lawyer's smug satisfaction in knowing that it would now be wholly unlikely that Richard would be making his presence known anytime soon in London.

It was true. His support of Elizabeth had already marked him for a traitor's end if he were ever caught. Now it seemed he'd dragged his brother and Lizbet into the pit with him. For the moment, Robert Fitzwarren and Clement had a better hand than he had, that was for sure, but who knew what the next cut of the cards would bring. A new queen perhaps? Had his head not felt like it was about to split into two, he might have smiled.

†

While Richard sat at the table in the room above, head pillowed on his folded arms, downstairs Andrew was listening intently to Scranton's tale about the misfiring of a culverin which could all have been avoided if his advice had been taken.

"They packed the powder too tight. I told them it was only a matter of time before the gun failed, but they would not listen," Scranton continued. "Anyway this morning, Crill, the Sergeant I've already told you about, was on duty and supervising the firing of the culverin. He was a miserable cur who had no time for anyone who did not wear the King's uniform. When the gun fired, he was stood at the back and a huge piece of the barrel came out sideways and cut his arm off just above the elbow." Scranton shook his head in wonder. "It was as neat a cut as if it had been an axe. And a waste of ordnance."

Andrew smiled grimly. "It was a harsh lesson for Crill to learn, no doubt about that."

"My point, sir, and you seem to be a man of middling intelligence for a soldiering type."

Andrew raised his eyebrows but kept his counsel. Jack, sitting next to him, snorted beer back into his cup.

"Why is it that advice from outside the ranks is so hard to bear? It seems to me that there is a general failure in those of lower wit to recognise and heed the guidance of those at a higher level. It was the same when I was in Antwerp," Scranton complained.

"Perhaps the issue is that those with lower wit are such that they do not recognise their need for guidance in the first place," Jack pointed out unhelpfully.

Scranton cast him a sour sideways glance.

"I think what Master Scranton is trying to say is that there needs to be more respect for those with learning and skills," Andrew interjected.

Scranton beamed. "And status. A man is also marked by his rank."

"So on this scale of wit that you have devised," Jack said slowly, his eyes staring fixedly at Scranton, "you believe all those with rank have the wit and skills to guide the rest of us poor fools?"

Scranton returned his cold stare. "There are always exceptions to every rule. There are men who claim status and yet have not the wit to match their rank."

Jack did not miss the slur which he knew was aimed directly at him. What Scranton did miss, however, was the elbow jammed painfully in Jack's back from Dan who was sitting on the trestle behind him.

"I am sure your point is validly made," replied Jack calmly. "Cuiusvis hominis est errare, nullius nisi insipientis in errore persevarare."

Scranton stared at him. "A child can be taught to repeat words, that does not mean that it can comprehend their meaning, and…"

Jack cut off his words. "Fronti nuilla fides."

"I am inclined to disagree with you. Appearances, in your case, do not deceive," Master Scranton said bitingly.

Jack's cold stare never left Scranton's face as he rose and left the table.

"Master Scranton, you should have a care. Jack's a man with quite a temper on him," Andrew advised.

"He'd not dare to strike at me." Scranton sounded quite shocked at the very thought. "He knows his place very well. He's a bastard and they are a greedy and nasty breed by nature. It is an affront that he tries to emulate the Master."

"The Master has a care for him, that's true." Andrew was still watching Jack as he seated himself further down the table out of earshot with Dan and Mat.

"Sometimes charity is a weakness." Scranton was also still staring in Jack's direction.

Andrew nodded in agreement but didn't say anything. Lifting his cup, Scranton returned his attention to Andrew and fixed his beady eyes on him over the rim. "So what persuaded you from Antwerp? Thomas told me you had worked for Estinheer. He is a merchant with deep pockets. It seems like quite a step down for you to join such a small group."

Andrew smiled. "I needed little persuasion. I knew the Master when he was a lad and when I saw him again I was reminded of those days. Maybe I was reminded of my own lost youth as well."

Scranton eyed him closely. "You've a few years on the Master, but not that many, I would say."

"True. I was twenty when he was fourteen, and although that might not seem much of a difference now, back then it was. I provided much of his training and he was the best pupil I'd ever had, or ever would have, come to that," Andrew remarked. "Those were good days. Thomas Seymour was a man who did not stint when it came to his household. I've never seen a stable yet with horses

172

as good as the quality of those he kept. His men did not want for training or equipment and the gentleman's sons, like Richard, were well placed to learn their craft."

"I had not realised the Master had been a part of Thomas Seymour's household." Scranton sounded impressed. "His family must be well placed to have ties with the Seymour household."

"Surely you have heard of William Fitzwarren?" Andrew asked, slightly taken aback.

"William Fitzwarren, Henry's right hand? Of course I know who he is. So the Master is part of his family?"

"Not just a part, Richard is his son," Andrew provided and had the satisfaction of seeing Scranton's eyes pop from his head in surprise. "Aye, he's not the heir, that's Robert Fitzwarren, but Richard is his younger brother and Jack, who you've taken such a dislike to, is William's bastard as well."

"I am shocked. I would not expect to find such a lord's son embarked on an adventure such as this, with so few…" Scranton let the words trail off.

"The Master is set on a good course and I have faith in him," Andrew said firmly. "After he was banished from his father's door, there are many who would not fare as well, but the Master is in charge of his own destiny."

Scranton's whole attention was on Andrew's face. "Banished?" he repeated.

"I've said too much. It is not my place. The Master is his own man and runs this band on his own terms," Andrew said hastily.

Scranton, reminded about his own recent comments about status, was forced to agree and despite wanting to know more, allowed Andrew to change the subject back to black powder production.

Chapter 10
Forged in Fire

What more miraculous thing may be told,
That fire, which all things melts, should harden ice,
And ice, which is congeal'd with senseless cold,
Should kindle fire by wonderful device?
Such is the power of love in gentle mind,
That it can alter all the course of kind.

☦

 Jack felt the sweat trickling in tracks down his back, and his lips when he licked them tasted of salt. How men could work in here day in and day out in the stifling heat he had no idea. Richard had, he noticed, positioned himself near the door, and was benefiting from the breeze that lapped round the frame.
 "Come on, put your back into it," Richard goaded.
 Jack was about to say something unpleasant when the wooden handle he was holding that was attached to the kiln bellows dropped away suddenly from his grip as the man operating them with him drove them faster to feed the flames. It was back breaking and Jack knew very soon his already tired muscles would burn with pain.
 A steady pace was kept up until there came a signal from the kiln Master and then they needed to force air into the kiln, raise the flames and then soon the hot molten liquid would be taken from the

fire and poured into the mould waiting ready on the mud floor.

Growling against the pain in his arms and shoulders, Jack matched the pace; he'd not be beaten, and he certainly wasn't going to fail in front of his brother. Sweat dripped from his face, hair clung to his head in lank, dark clumps and his tortured muscles burned like the metal in the furnace before him.

At last the kiln Master held up his hand. Jack loosed the handle and letting out a final gasp he straightened and stepped away, allowing the kiln Master and his assistants to bring the liquid iron from the flames. As Jack watched, a black crust on the top of the crucible was deftly removed to reveal the bright hot orange iron underneath.

The mould was inside a sandbox, bound tight with wood and all held together with wire. Inside the sand was the mould and there were four points on the top for the molten iron to be poured into. It took three men, two to hold the crucible straight with long iron rods and a third to tip it just enough so the iron would pour into the mould. The sandbox sat on top of a wooden trestle and once the iron had been poured in and the crucible safely nestled in a holder, the men shook the trestle and, as Jack watched, smoke rose from each of the holes.

Wiping sweat from his brow, Jack backed to the door where the breeze could reach his hot skin. The relief was palpable.

"How long before they break it open and see if it has worked?" Jack asked his brother.

"About an hour. They'll take it outside soon. The trick apparently is not to let it cool too quickly. You could open it now and the metal will already be set, but it will cool too quickly and you risk cracks in the iron," Richard explained.

Two men carried the mould outside and the kiln Master, grinning, stopped in front of Richard. "He didn't do too badly there, for a beginner." Leaning over, he squeezed Jack's upper arm. "Still hurting, are they, lad? You did well. I've never seen anyone keep up like that before with Bron on the bellows."

Jack groaned, and shot a dark look at Richard, realising he had been set up. Richard grinned malevolently in return, his eyes sparkling in the half-light in the kiln room, and Jack realised the other two carrying the mould were also laughing.

"You bastard, you had a bet on me?" Jack exclaimed.

"And why not?" Richard replied innocently.

"You bloody well lost then, serves you right!" Jack retorted hotly.

"No, lad, he won and it'll be me and the lads that'll be paying for the beer while that cools itself," The kiln Master supplied laughing.

Jack, shaking his head, clapped Richard on the arm. "You are insufferable sometimes."

Richard winced and pulled his arm away.

"You be careful with him," the kiln Master said jovially. He inclined his head towards the kiln. "Old Nance there didn't take a liking to him the other day and he'll be wearing her displeasure for a week or two."

Quicker than his brother, Jack pulled up his brother's sleeve to reveal a long line of swollen blisters. "That's going to take more than a beer to heal. What happened?"

Richard roughly pulled his sleeve down. "I got too close," was all he said roughly.

"You need to get those burns dried out. When we used to brand the animals…"

Richard cut him off. "Does all your healing experience come from the woes of cattle and horses?"

"Not all. I've fixed up quite a lot of sheep." Then he added, "and the odd dog."

"It's all very reassuring," Richard said a little grumpily.

"And so it should be. Animals are often more valuable than men. Look at Corracha, ten men could toil their whole lives and never between them have enough to own him? So that makes him worth a damn sight more than they are."

"So an animal is worth more than a man," Richard summarised as they followed the kiln Master and his men towards the inn.

"Now don't go leading my words again. I didn't say an animal was better than a man, did I? And that was what you were about to accuse me of saying. Sit down there and let me look at those burns."

They had arrived at the tavern a short distance from the kiln. In the light Jack inspected the blisters for a second time before dropping the sleeve back over them.

"Well," Richard asked when Jack said nothing.

178

"I'm glad it's not my arm. Must sting like hell." Jack was intent on catching the eye of one of the serving women and, ale ordered, he returned his attention back to Richard. "I'll sort those blisters out for you later. You wouldn't like to put me off my food, would you?"

"Heaven forbid!"

☦

Jack grasped his brother's wrist and held his hand down on the table. Richard dearly wanted to pull away but he allowed Jack to keep his hold.

Assured that Richard was going to remain still, Jack let go. "Pull your sleeve up." Jack produced a long needle, the type he'd use for stitching leather with. Both men watched as Jack fed the tip to the flame until it blackened with candle soot. The point was sharp and the needle long enough for Jack to be able to hold it firmly. The line of blisters ran from elbow to wrist, the puffy skin bagged with the fluid trapped beneath it. Jack's right hand held the needle and the left a cloth. Piercing the bottom of each of the blisters, he rolled the cloth down the arm and pressed the blisters draining them.

"As you said earlier, it stings," Richard said through gritted teeth.

"A burn is the worst." Jack reapplied the cloth to the blisters above the wrist. "A bad one hurts as much days after as when you got it."

"That was an observation I could do without. It's on my arm – I'm well aware of how much it hurts," Richard replied bitingly.

Jack ignored him. Satisfied he put the cloth down and produced a small tub of brown grease.

"Dare I ask?" Richard looked at the unctuous contents of the earthenware jar.

"Goose fat mainly, with clove oil and lavender. Best thing you can put on a horse fly bite," Jack said, scooping out a fingerful.

"And you get a lot of horse fly bites, do you?" Richard said.

Jack looked at him levelly. "No I don't, but the horses do. Now hold still." Jack spread the sticky balm in a thick even layer over the blisters. "You can't bind a burn, it just makes it worse and it festers." Jack pressed home the stopper into the ointment pot and pushed the pot towards Richard. "Just keep an even layer of that on it."

The sarcastic reply died on his lips. The pain had dulled. Surprise showed openly on Richard's face. "Christ, that's taken the edge off it."

"Told you. I use that on Corracha, and if it can settle his evil temper when he's a fly bite under his saddle, it's a fair bet it will work on you." Jack was pleased. "Fitzwarren spent more on his horses and hounds than anything else. The Church says you can't use an animal's cure on a man; it goes against the law of the Church. From what I've seen, men and animals look pretty much the same on the inside. I know what I'd rather have when it comes down to cures as well. I'd rather someone tried to do something rather than leaving me and dropping to their knees in the hope that the Almighty might have time on his hands to save more than just my soul."

"Blasphemy Jack. But I'll agree." Richard was clenching his fist and the skin was not pulling as painfully as it had before Jack's ministrations.

"Now, tell me again. I want to hear about the flintlocks," Jack said rocking back in chair.

"You know the facts. Why do you need me to tell you again?" Richard asked, even though he knew exactly why Jack wanted to hear it all again. Burton had been a poor place, but it had been a good start. Its loss was still a knife in Jack's side, and when he thought about it, the blade twisted painfully. It had not been his, but there he'd had a place, and had run it, and run it well, in Richard's absence, until his brother had taken one risk too many and the whole house of cards had crumbled before his eyes, casting Jack once again out into the world, with little to his name and even less idea what he should do about it. He had, not through a fault of his own, ended in debtors' gaol, from where Richard had redeemed him.

Jack was happy to place his future in his brother's hands. Richard had resented this, but slowly he was coming to accept Jack's need to be led, and to accept that beneath the rough exterior was an unswerving loyalty, and a bond that, despite their differences, would take Jack to the grave should the need arise.

"You've told me how many, and how they ended up in England, and about the crossbows and how they are packaged. But you've never told me how you found them in the first place," Jack said.

"And I'll not tell you either. Just accept that as a fact. The man who has them is a friend, a good friend, and I'll not jeopardise him or his family."

"I'm hardly likely to tell anyone, am I?" Jack sounded hurt.

"Now, sat here, you can say that." Richard let the silence lengthen between them. "But if you were in England, in the Tower, where they have the rack that rips a man's muscles from his bones, could you still say that? Could you still honestly tell me that if they set your feet in the fire that you could still keep his name to yourself? If they set to hammer every bone in your hands flat, could you honestly say you could keep the name of a man you've never met to yourself?"

"You really know how to spoil an evening," Jack said gloomily.

"I only say it to keep a good man safe. It is not a slight on you." The look on Jack's face told Richard he needed to change the subject, the reference to the Tower was too much of a reminder of Jack's time in Marshalsea. Richard smiled. "This arm, it's putting me in a bad humour."

"How did you do it anyway?" Jack asked.

"The mould we made today was the second attempt. When they made the first, the sandbox blew up and I was standing a little close. My own fault," Richard supplied.

"Froggy will be pleased. His job will be a lot easier," Jack said absently.

"Not just Froggy's, Jack. At the moment every gunner has a mould. They can make three or four at a time, that's all. You've heard Froggy talk about the battle at Boulogne when the flintlocks became useless, when they ran out of both powder and musket balls. When we use this, it will be the first time that fifty can be made in one go. Froggy and Lizbet have been working for days and they can make about a hundred in a day. If they use this, they could make a thousand," Richard finished enthusiastically.

Jack looked confused. "But we are not going into battle, are we? Why do we need so many? Even for target practice and to become proficient with them, we hardly need that quantity, do we?"

"We are not just going to sell the flintlocks, we are going to sell a new way of using them," Richard said. "We can provide a new way to make the lead balls. No one has done that. And with Master Scranton, we can show how powder can be twice as effective. At the battle of Boulogne they had to stop using their powder munitions as they ran out of powder. If we could show how to make this go twice as far, imagine how much you'd pay to know that?"

"You really believe in the flintlocks, don't you? You've heard from Froggy how inaccurate they are, especially the pistols. Even if you have a few ranks of flintlocks, they are never going to replace men at arms, are they?" Jack argued. "And the men behind them are often some of the poorest skilled. It takes years to train to wield a sword with skill, and even Froggy said the flintlocks had been picked from the ranks where some had some of the lowest arms skills; they did not want to take skilled men from the ranks."

"That is probably the exact point why they are going to succeed. You don't need years of training. We've been practicing for a few weeks and everyone, even you, can hit a target. Name me another weapon where you can train for such a short period and get a result," Richard countered.

"Still, they are not very accurate, are they?" Jack was not going to accept his brother's argument.

"They don't really have to be. If there are enough musket balls in the air, they will still an advance," Richard replied.

"That's true if you can get them to fire at the same time. Even Froggy said that after the first round, it all starts to fall apart. The men can't reload at the same speed. Often there's so much smoke, they can't even see where they are firing. Froggy even told of an instance when the whole line broke into a retreat when they found themselves surrounded by their own fog and had no idea where the enemy were, so they ran."

"That's training though, and poor leadership. Any line of men will turn and run if they have not the stomach for the fight, no matter what weapon they have in their hands," Richard said.

"You'll not find me with one. I'll stick with edged blades," Jack said solidly.

"Its change you don't like really, isn't it?" Richard accurately pointed out.

"How can you say that?" Jack retorted hotly. "I've been through enough of it recently. One minute I'm right at the top of the dunghill and the next I'm back wallowing in the piss at the bottom again."

"So where are you now then?" Richard asked laughing.

"I'm not sure. Hopefully climbing back to the top where someone is going to give you a great deal of money for those damned flintlocks, then I will like them well enough," Jack provided.

"Let's just assume that I manage to secure a sale for these, and turn them into something eminently more transportable, then what shall we do?"

"I don't know!" Jack was exasperated, and it showed clearly on his face. He was still standing looking down at Richard. "I might not have your quick mind, but I'm learning, slowly. I am learning. It will matter not what I might think to do, before I have time to sit down on my backside you'll have announced some new scheme we will be involved in, or dragging me along with you to support your misplaced loyalties."

The last few words Richard did not appreciate, and they were cold eyes that lay on his brother. "If, is such a small word, isn't it?"

Jack huffed. "What are you on about now?"

"If," Richard repeated. "Small, insubstantial and often unreliable."

"Go on," Jack said wearily. "I'm listening."

"I dislike conjecture very much. Facts and the current situation are commodities I prefer to trade in. However it seems we need to consider what if."

Jack was paying close attention now. Experience had taught him that any difficult conversations Richard started like this one were usually going to be very poignant indeed. "Alright, go on, what if…?"

"...what if Mary dies," Richard provided.

Jack's shoulders dropped. This was hardly news. Everyone knew Mary was old at forty two, and it was unlikely now she would provide an heir for the throne. "Phillip," was all he said, then added, "She's tied England to Papist Spain, and they'll not let go easily."

"True, who else?" Richard accepted.

There was a long silence between them. "Elizabeth," Jack was forced to finally say. "It's always Elizabeth. You really think she will make to the throne? Christ, you are more a fool that I thought you were. If that's your 'if' it is indeed an unreliable one. She has small chance of settling her backside on the throne."

"I will thank you for keeping a civil tongue in your head," Richard warned.

Jack did not feel like being particularly careful. Unforgivably he said, "Remember that's a backside that I've had sat on my back."

Richard stood quickly and faced Jack. Had Lizbet not arrived at that moment, Jack would have been nursing a bleeding nose.

Lizbet looked between the pair, and then said, "You are not at the Master's throat again. It's fair tiresome, Jack."

"Why do I always get the blame?" Jack exclaimed, throwing his arms wide.

"Because I know what an argumentative pig-headed man you are, that's why," Lizbet said, then to Richard, "There's pies, cheese, cooked pork and that's about your lot, I'm afraid. What do you want me to bring?"

"Whatever you like I'll like the best," Richard said distractedly.

Lizbet nodded her satisfaction at the answer and turned to leave.

"And why is it that I don't get asked?" Jack complained at her retreating back.

"Because you ain't paying," she called back over her shoulder, laughing.

Jack returned his attention to his brother. "Alright, I should not have said that."

"Apology accepted," Richard replied, the tension leaving his body. Annoyed though that Jack, of all men, seemed to have the ability to ignite his temper.

"So go on then, tell me more about 'if'." Jack settled himself back in his chair.

"So, the question you need to consider is why do you think that Elizabeth could not succeed Mary?"

Jack didn't even hesitate before he delivered his reply. "The country will not stand for another woman on the throne."

"The country!" Richard sounded amused. "And who is the country?"

Jack looked confused. "England. I mean England will not stand for another woman at her head."

Richard considered this for a moment, and Jack felt unease welling from the pit of his stomach. He knew his brother was letting him wander off again down the wrong road and giving him an unhelpful shove as well.

"So the country, England, will not stand for another of Henry's daughters to sit on the throne." Jack just nodded. "And that's whose opinion then?

Yours? The men you drink with? The tavern crowd back in London, is that what they think?"

"It is," Jack said slowly. He knew he needed to tread carefully. He was a regular victim of the traps laid by his brother and he felt another was on the way.

"In one room, Jack, just one room, no bigger than the one you were playing cards in last night, you could place all of the people who can influence the succession. Your idea of popular feeling has nothing to do with it. Elizabeth offers a return to a Protestant England, and also one not under the yoke of Spain. There are powerful proponents of that, Jack. That the succession will be taken by a woman is a consideration well down the list. Those men want power, they don't want it diluted by Spanish overlords." Richard paused for a few moments to let Jack consider his words. "And if, Elizabeth takes the throne then, my errant brother, you just might find yourself at the top of the dunghill, and then what would you do?"

"I don't know what you mean," Jack said quietly.

"We cannot return to England now, but if Elizabeth was monarch, we could. There is also a good chance that the succession papers your father signed will be honoured then and you, my favoured sibling, would be Lord Fitzwarren. What, sire, would you do then?"

Jack's mouth was open.

"Our father, evil and predatory man that he is, sat fully for twenty years on the Privy Council. He was Henry's man to the core, enforcing his will, crushing those who rose against him, moulding and bending England to the shape he wanted it to be. Where would you be, My Lord?"

Jack had paled. "Richard, don't."

"If is such a small word. Would you take a place on the Council? Would you side with Protestant against Catholic? Would you steer a middle ground? Would you press for war against France would you…?"

Jack's fist banged down hard on the table and shouted, "For God's sake, stop."

"What would you do, Jack?" Richard pressed.

"Why are you doing this to me?" There was anguish in Jack's voice.

"Why not? You went to see Clement, did you not? You sought out your own inheritance, well face it, this is what it is." Richard drained his cup. "Or did you just think you could be like Robert and squander it on hunting and women? Care little for the position you've been appointed in society and ignore any form of responsibility?"

"Well that's all Robert does," Jack said defensively.

"Ah yes, Robert. Well, he luckily does not have me standing behind him to remind him of his responsibilities, does he? Whereas you do."

"This is not going to happen. You are being cruel. I've never, never, allowed myself to even think of this. If I dreamed when I was younger, it was of having enough to eat, of having a horse like those my Masters rode, and a dry bed to sleep in. What has happened is a cruel enough twist of fate and I do not need you making it worse." Jack's voice was hoarse.

"I've learnt my lesson well, brother. I have no desire to fight you again, or anytime in the future. So we are agreed?"

"Agreed?" Jack was now totally confused.

"I'll have the place on the Privy Council and you can spend your time and our father's money on horses and hawks?" Richard's words were meant to diffuse the tension, yet Jack still remained taught and serious.

"I know I could never take such a place if it was ever offered to me. I do not need you to remind me," Jack said sorrowfully.

"You are a good man. You have courage and conviction. Remember, terrible apart and even worse together. I'd not let you flounder," Richard replied.

Lizbet returned and saved Jack from having to reply. Her choice had been pies, and the platter she placed between them held two and was shortly followed by another with fresh bread.

"I know you too well. You'd let me flounder alright. You'd wait until I was on the brink of the pit and about to fall in before you'd offer a hand to pull me back," Jack said with grim humour.

"Suffering is good for the soul, and you have to know you've made a mistake before you can learn fully from it," Richard pronounced.

"And you'd enjoy my suffering," Jack said.

"I need to get something for myself from this! After all you'd get the title, the power and the money, so please allow me to gain a little amusement from the situation occasionally."

There was a silence between them for a few minutes. Jack, one of the pies in his hands, was forming a question in his mind, and Richard quite able to read his brother, waited patiently for it.

"Answer me this, I've met William. He is no man's fool. Surely he must feel shame to have Robert as his heir?" Jack replied.

Richard considered his reply carefully. "I agree. Our father, William, served on Henry's council for over twenty years. He was his monarch's friend, confidant and enforcer. Our father does not lack in wit or skill at all. However Robert is a lamentable fool. It must strike at our father's very heart that the bastard he reared in your place is a wastrel."

Jack tore the warm loaf in half and passed half to Richard. "Can't have irked him that much though, can it? You heard him. Not once did he think to undo what he had done."

"That's because he's bad tempered, impulsive and hates to admit he was wrong." Richard elbowed his brother in the arm. "Remind you of anyone?"

✝

Her arms carrying a woven basket stacked high with laundry, Lizbet could barely see where she was going, and was aware only of the obstacle when she banged into it. She cursed, clutching at the white linen about to topple from the basket.

"Stand still, lass. I've got it." The man she had walked into was Andrew and he had hold of the top layer that had rolled from the pile.

"Don't let it drop, for God's sake!" Lizbet exclaimed, trying to wrap her arm around her falling stack of linen.

"Where are you taking it? I've got a good hold. I'll not let it fall. My mother was a laundress and I know the tasks well enough to know you'd not want to do it all over again." Andrew smiled at her over the top of the folded shirts.

Lizbet didn't return his smile. "Thank you, sir. Just put it on the top for me. I would be grateful." Her tone was not quite at one with her words.

Adjusting his hold on the linen, he smiled. "I will carry it in for you, lass. Just don't tell the lads I've been helping you or I will never hear the last of it!" He grinned conspiratorially.

Lizbet forced a smile in return.

"So you came from England with the Master then, from London at a guess?" Andrew said as they walked side by side.

"Not London-born, my family. The miserable lot of them are in Kent," Lizbet said, punctuating the end of the sentence by spitting on the ground.

"Oh, not another one with family quarrels!" laughed Andrew.

"I've no quarrel with them. I'll as like never see them again and even that would be too soon," Lizbet replied.

"Have you been with the Master long then?" Andrew asked casually.

Lizbet's eyes narrowed. "A while," was the only answer she gave.

"I like London. Well, it's been a long time since I was there myself. Whereabouts in the city were you?" Andrew continued.

"Not too far from Smithfield," Lizbet answered carefully.

"I know it well. Were you lodging with the Master then?" he continued.

"I'll take that from you now, sir." They had arrived at the door at the back of the inn they were stopping at, and Lizbet nodded for him to deposit the linen he carried back on top of the folded stack she carried. Andrew hesitated for a moment before complying. As soon as he had loosened his hands from the damp white cloth, she turned and made a quick and neat escape.

†

Jack stretched his legs out in front of him and breathed deeply. Today had been a good day. His body no longer ached with the pain of use; now his muscles were again equal to the tasks and the day's work left him simply tired and hungry. Tomorrow was an early start and Jack, with his stomach full, was contemplating his bed when his brother joined him.

"It's Froggy's name day. Are you not joining them?" Richard asked.

"Not tonight. It's an early start and I don't want to begin the day with a sore head," Jack replied, then after considering what his brother had said he asked, "Saint Froggy or Saint Tate?"

Richard grinned. "Saint Eadfrith, it seems. I had to press him to tell me."

"Eadfrith! Christ! No wonder he kept that to himself. So who was Saint Eadfrith then?"

Richard shrugged. "No idea."

"It's just an excuse for Froggy to persuade everyone to pay for his evening's ale," Jack said.

"Surprises me then that you've not followed the tradition," Richard replied.

Jack shrugged. "Not even sure when I was born. I professed that my patron saint was Brigid of Ireland once and that earned me a beating when I was younger."

"And that surprised you?" Richard said, with his eyebrows raised. "She might be the patron saint of the illegitimate but that's not a subject the church likes to be reminded of. Just ask Scranton. Anyway, you were born on July 20th. It was in the documents our father signed. Your actual date of birth."

"July 20th," Jack repeated. "I didn't know that. I had an idea I was born in September, but I was never sure."

"That'll be when Robert was born, two months after you."

"And you? When were you born, then?" Jack asked.

"On the day of the Feast of the Holy Innocents," Richard supplied.

Jack snorted. "Hardly fitting, is it?"

Scranton chose that moment to join them. He was careful to pick a chair next to Richard, and studiously avoided even looking at Jack.

"Did I hear you say you were born on Holy Innocents' day?" he said, settling himself down.

Richard nodded. "I did. December 28th."

"A blessed feast day when we remember all those poor and innocent children massacred by Herod. They were the first true martyrs of the church. Mathew 2.18 tells us Rachel was weeping for the children, because they were no more." Scranton looked between Jack and Richard. "If you had children, sir, you would appreciate her loss. I have always thought Holy Innocents' day should be a sombre occasion and not an event for revelry and drunkenness."

"You would," said Jack under his breath, and thinking that the time had arrived to absent himself and make his way to bed, he added, "It's an early start tomorrow. If you'll excuse me, I'm going to bed. Be assured I shall pray to Saint Barbara before I rest, and ask her to look kindly on your endeavours tomorrow."

Scranton scowled.

Richard hid a smirk.

The Saint was not only invoked against the natural elements of thunder and lightning, but also against accidents arising from the explosions of gunpowder.

☦

They were fighting with wasters, wooden training swords capable of delivering bruises, and occasionally even broken bones, but not cut flesh. These were not merely wooden, to give them weight they had a central steel core so they weighed more or less the same as a real sword, and the weight leant to the swings an accuracy and force that required attention and skill to deflect. Jack had stripped to his shirt, but Andrew wore still a sensible padded jack that leant some protection to his upper body.

Andrew disengaged, shaking his head. "That was too high. You needed to block it lower otherwise your blade will slide off the wrong end and you'll not be able to push me back."

Jack, whose upper body was soaked in sweat, pushed wet hair out of his eyes, and readied himself for another of Andrew's attacks.

"Not very original," Richard replied, hitching himself up to sit on the top rail of the fence. "Hershey's defence?"

Jack breathing heavily, his hands on his knees, muttered, "Really? What's wrong with it?"

"Nothing. I just know your opponent too well, and I know that while he has your blade employed he's going to shift his weight, pull you off balance and either get you in the back of the knee or in your arse," Richard supplied.

Andrew spread his arms wide, a feigned injured expression on his face. "Would I do such a thing?"

The look on Richard's face was answer enough.

"Let's find out then shall we, especially now that I am forewarned." Jack had caught his breath.

Andrew too was grinning in anticipation.

"If you must," Richard stated resignedly.

The pair started again and this time when the blades engaged Jack had indeed got his a third of the way lower down Andrew's and pressed home his advantage, the hilts sliding together. The moment before the cross guards met and Jack had all his weight behind his blade, Andrew dropped his blade a foot or so and Jack staggered forward. Delight registered on Andrew's face and withdrawing his blade, he set it on a path that had it been a real blade would have ham strung his opponent.

Richard, about to state how predictable this was, opened his mouth to speak, but the next move stopped him. Jack, forced off balance, rolled his shoulders first over into the dirt, and in a second, with the agility of a court acrobat he was righted, blade in his hand, the point of it jabbed in Andrew's back.

"Forewarned," was all Jack said.

Richard added a slow round of applause for the performance from where he sat, and Andrew also seemed to be delighted by his defeat. "That's one you will have to teach me, lad."

†

Richard in the company of his brother later asked, "Andrew Kineer, what do you think?" Richard was watching Jack closely.

"Knows what he's talking about, and he's backed by a lot of experience, and he likes Scranton about as much as I do."

"Well that at least should recommend him to you then," Richard said, and then, a serious note in his voice, he added, "I learnt much from him, and I am grateful he agreed to join us."

"He's told me about the time he saved you a whipping when you thought it a good idea to pour oil onto Seymour's fish ponds and set light to it, killing all the fish," Jack grinned, "and about the time when you put beach nuts under the horse Master's saddle after he boxed your ears when he found you in the hayloft with one of the kitchen girls. And then there was the time…"

"Enough," Richard said quickly. "I shall have to have words with Master Kineer, before he shares all my childhood transgressions with you! There are a few stories I would prefer to remain untold."

"Those are the only stories he shared, and only after I pressed him for them," Jack replied smiling. "I'm pleased to know there are more. I shall get him drunk soon enough and find them out."

Richard laughed. "They were good years. I miss them sometimes. When you get him drunk, get him to tell you about the time when he was shooting at the weather vane on the top of the stables."

Jack did indeed ask Andrew about the weather vane the following day.

"Oh Christ! I had forgotten about that!" Andrew said, his eyes widening. "We were shooting arrows at the target and Richard and another lad bet I couldn't hit the cock on the weather vane on the top of the stable." He leant across the table to Jack. "It was a good distance, about from here to the where that tree is over there, and I remember the weather vane was about the size of a pheasant, so not an easy shot."

"Go on," pressed Jack.

"I missed twice, and the lads were laughing. So I shouted at them to take their shots, and they both took two and missed as well. I took a third and I hit it hard and the vane was spinning like a dolly wheel." Andrew was shaking his head and laughing. "What we didn't know was that three of the arrows we had fired that had missed found their marks in two of Seymour's prize cattle on the other side of the stable block. One was dead, shot through the eye and the second, shot twice in the rump had crashed through the fence and was headed for the kitchen gardens." Andrew stopped, wiping tears of mirth from his eyes.

"What did you do?"

"I did nothing. It was the Master, thinking quicker than any of the rest of us, shouted poachers and raised the alarm. Within five minutes there were twenty men combing the fields looking for the bowmen who had shot at Seymour's cattle. Needless to say none were ever found."

"That sounds like Richard. I don't think he's changed much," Jack said, laughing as well at the story.

"He always keeps one step ahead of trouble," Andrew agreed.

Chapter 11
A Warning Ignored

†

Lizbet and Froggy had the fire set by the time Richard arrived. The flames had receded and in the centre there was a glowing pit of orange and red shifting colours fanned by the breeze. Lizbet pushed a stray strand of hair behind her ear, cheeks glowing pink with the heat. Richard knelt down next to Froggy and watched. The small ladle they had used to melt the lead had been replaced now with an iron bowl that Froggy had nestled into the coals. To fill the mould that Richard had made would take more than the small ladle they had used before.

"It's not ideal," said Froggy, beginning to add lead strips to the bowl. "We can ladle out so much from the bowl, but we'll never get to the bottom of it, so we have to melt more than we need."

"I'll have to think about that." Richard's hand pinched his chin in thought. "Let's see how we do anyway."

Lizbet dropped the iron skillet they had brought over the hot embers. The framework was high enough to hold the freshly made mould over the flames to warm it without it getting too hot. Too hot and the lead would not cool properly, too cold and they risked fracturing the mould as the molten metal was poured in.

Froggy poured the lead into the mould and three pairs of eyes watched his steady practised hand tip the smoking silver stream into the mould.

They ran out before the final row was filled. Richard held up his hand to stop Froggy from melting more.

"It's enough. We can see how well it has worked. There's no need to melt more. We can work out the quantities later."

Froggy, using the thick hide gloves he had purchased from a blacksmith, pulled the skillet away from the fire and they waited for the mould to cool.

None of them had foreseen that the huge iron mould would remain searing hot for quite so long, and it was some time before Froggy, still gloved, undid the retaining wires that held all the sections together.

Lizbet clapped her hands together as the first freshly formed musket balls fell from the mould. "They are just as good as the ones we made with the proper mould."

"You sound surprised." There was a slight acid note in his voice, as, with a stick, Richard rolled one towards him. She was right, once the sprue was snipped away, the ball was as good as any Lizbet and Froggy had been making.

"I just think that the men who made the guns would have had more of a notion about how to make musket balls than you would, that was all I meant." Lizbet edged one of the still warm lead spheres towards herself, a look of approval on her face.

"Your confidence is ever heartening," Richard said sitting back on his heels.

"What's he mean?" Lizbet said to Froggy, shooting him a confused look.

"No idea, lass. Get them clippers and let's get these cleaned up," Froggy said and they set to work, snipping the sprues away and putting the unwanted lead back into the bowl for the next time it went into the fire.

"That's a damn sight quicker." Froggy was holding up one of the musket balls in front of his face and rolling it between his thumb and forefinger.

"So how many do you think you could make in a day?" Richard put the question seriously.

Froggy looked thoughtful for a moment, and then said, "If we had enough lead to keep going, we could easily fill that ten times, even given the long time it takes to cool. And each time we fill it, we get…" Froggy's brow furrowed as he looked at the mould and began to count the entry points the lead was poured into.

"You're brain is fuddled, Froggy. There's twenty five," Lizbet cut in.

"Quite right, and if we used it ten times…"

Lizbet cut him off. "I'm not stupid, you know. Two hundred and fifty if Froggy here has melted enough to fill it each time. And if he hasn't, then it'll be a few less."

Richard threw one of the balls up in the air and then caught it as it dropped back to earth. For once he looked happy.

†

Lizbet used a vinegar scrub on the rings and thin strips of read mace. Pushing the thin rasping strands through the gold fretwork, she cleaned the dirt from the gold until the rings shone bright.

Happily she held one up for inspection. They were heavy rings and all of them bore some deep scratches of wear. The dirt embedded in them had made them dull, but now, cleaned, the scratches were no longer noticeable dark lines; the rings looked new. There was no one around and Lizbet slid them onto her hand. Far too big, they hung on her fingers, but still Lizbet thought her hands would look nice with a line of rings upon them.

Sliding them back into her palm, she set off to take them back to the Master in his room.

Lizbet knocked before pressing the handle and opening the door, jumping involuntarily when she found it wasn't the Master on the other side of the door. It was Andrew and he seemed equally unhappy to see her.

"What are you doing in here?" Andrew said, his eyes narrowing

Lizbet's hand closed defensively around the three rings she'd cleaned, unwilling to leave them now the Master was not here. "Master had work for me, and you?" was all she said.

"I was just looking for the Master." Andrew lay unfriendly eyes on her.

"Aye, well he's not here right now," Lizbet relied coldly. She did not drop her gaze from his. Behind Andrew, a book lay open and she was sure she'd seen him looking through the pages when she opened the door.

"I'll bid you good day." Andrew pushed past her, leaving her standing watching the door swing closed and wondering.

†

They needed more supplies and made the decision to take the cart the five miles to the main town of Bendanaburg to collect what they needed. Lizbet wanted to come and rode her mare at the back of the group next to Mat.

The rain from the previous week had been so heavy that the stream they were to cross was still a foaming torrent. The fording point, with raised stones in the riverbed was knee deep, and the fast racing current was strong enough to take a man's legs from underneath him.

"The horses can make it, and the wagon is high enough so the water won't reach the bed," Dan reported as he returned from the river.

"I'll ride across. Sometimes it's worse towards the middle," Jack replied. Shortening his reins, he set the mare towards the river and helped her pick her way carefully across. Beneath the water the streambed was cobbled, worn smooth with the passing of the water and pressured by the current. The passage was treacherous. His mare took two steps into the water, then, ears flat and feeling the force of the water on her legs, she stopped. Jack's legs pushed her on, heels persuasively making her step forward, and the mare, eyes still wide, obeyed the rider and moved further into the racing stream.

From the safety of the bank they watched his passage, and in a few more steps the horse began to free herself from the water, and picking her feet up bounded quickly up on to the opposite bank.

"Come on. If Jack can make it, we all can," Dan declared.

Froggy took the wagon over next. The spoked wheels offered little resistance to the water and the passage across was an easy one, the yoked horse straining to pull the wagon clear of the water to join Jack.

Richard and then Dan rode across and then Mat, a firm hand on the bridle on Lizbet's horse, began to lead her over as well.

Jack saw it going wrong before Mat and Lizbet's horses were even hock deep in the water, shouting a warning that the wind whipped away.

Scranton, waiting impatiently behind, had pushed his horse forward and it had edged itself between Mat and Lizbet's horses. It was forcing the small mare that Mat was leading to stumble away from the shallow area of the ford and it stepped straight into the deeper water.

Jack shouted again and Richard, seeing the same danger, added his warning as well. Mat saw their concerned faces, but he could not hear their warning, and when he realised what was happening it was too late. Scranton's horse pushed between them, and the bridle he had hold of was pulled from his grasp. Lizbet's mare took two more steps and plunged into the deep water. The vicious current pressed now up to its belly, pulling its legs from beneath it. The horse and rider fell sideways into the river.

Lizbet had been warned before crossing to loosen her feet from the stirrups and as the horse fell, she landed in the river. The mare, thrashing, rolled over next to her, the hooves flailing in the air uselessly as it sought to right itself. Lizbet was borne up for a moment by her skirts until the water wrapped its fingers around her dress and the sodden drapery weighed on her like iron pulling her under.

Clawing and fighting for breath, her head surfaced once more for a futile moment before disappearing beneath the foaming water. The water rolled her over, forced her down and she felt her face being grazed against the riverbed. Her head banged with more sound than pain against a submerged boulder and her struggles ended.

The hand that found her wrapped her unfurled hair around a wrist and dragged her from the riverbed. Once at the surface Jack hauled her through the water towards the bank. Away from the centre of the river, he put his feet down and thankfully felt the rocky streambed beneath him. Coughing, water streaming from him, Jack staggered as he reached the bank, Lizbet's sodden weight heavy in his arms now she was clear of the water.

A quagmire of mud and cow dung, pock marked with bovine footprints was the bank Jack dropped Lizbet on. Her eyes were closed, brown hair tangled across her face, blood running from a cut above her eye, and her cheek was raised and raw from the impact with the streambed.

"Lass? Lizbet? Lizbet?" Jack's muddy hand pushed the hair from her face.

The girl's body convulsed.

"Thank God." Jack rolled her onto her side and held her as she retched, her body bent only on ridding itself of a stomach full of river water. Her hair clotted with mud, body shaking, face pressed to the wet riverbank, Lizbet could do little to help herself.

Jack heard them crashing through the woods before he saw them, and his shout brought them to him. The rain was still pouring from the heavens and there was little they could do other than load Lizbet into the wagon underneath the tarpaulin on the back and keep going. Lizbet's mare was lost, and Jack, soaked, bruised and frozen to the core, rode on in silence. Scranton had returned to his position next to Richard in the lead and Jack could do little other than stare contemptuously at his back.

It was a solemn group that returned from the town early that evening. With an insistence that was natural, Richard secured the services of one of the inn serving girls and had a warming tub filled with water set in a room at the inn.

Scranton sat next to Richard, and Dan watched him, wondering how long it would be before his temper snapped. Scranton had taken no responsibility for the accident that had sent Lizbet and Jack into the river and had lost the group a horse as well. He was sitting now next to Richard complaining, which was something he excelled at.

"The food is tasteless and dry. I wouldn't pay for it. If I was paying, the landlord would be getting none of my money for such poor fayre. And the rooms are cramped. I'd not thought we would be stopping so long in such a poor a place as this. It is not what I am used to, sir," Scranton finished.

"Consider yourself fortunate, Master Scranton," Richard said, regarding him with cold grey eyes, "that I am not my brother."

Richard had noted that the passage of the serving girl carrying warmed wine to Lizbet's room had been delayed. She was now sat on Jack's knee. A hand to her mouth, she was stifling a laugh at whatever suggestions he was quietly making in her ear. The tray sat abandoned on the end of the table. Leaving his seat next to Scranton Richard pressed his hand to the earthenware jug holding the wine; it was still warm.

He knew which room it was and knocked. Hearing the noise from within, Richard pushed the door open with his free hand, the tray balanced on the other. He heard the noise of shifting water and saw Lizbet immersed in warm water in front of the fire. Setting the tray on a table, he poured a cup of wine.

Lizbet sniffed loudly. She'd not heard him approach.

"Wine, mistress?" he asked in a voice she'd be forgiven for not recognising

"Put it on the table," snapped Lizbet, lowering herself protectively below the folds of the warm water. A moment later an arm stretched over her shoulder and a cup of wine was held out for her to take. Lizbet was about to let loose a list of choice words when her eyes fastened on the hand holding the cup. The firelight played in the jewels on the three rings on the hand, rings she recognised. Christ! The Master! Lizbet swirled in the tub and an amount of water cascaded over the side to the floor.

"There's no need to soak me, woman!" he said still holding out the wine, then he added, "It's spiced and warm. Take it."

"What are you doing in here?" was all she could manage.

"Just take it before I change my mind and drink it myself. Scranton is testing my temper and Jack is being insufferable and I'm not sure if I can listen to his tale one more time."

"Jack is always insufferable," Lizbet said accepting the offered cup. "You should know that by now."

Richard dropped to the floor, his back propped against the tub. "I should, you are right. He has the natural gift of the storyteller. Who am I to spoil his night? I am sure you are in agreement that he has earned the right to boast a little."

"I cannot ever thank him enough," Lizbet said, her voice hoarse and strained with fatigue.

"Oh I am sure by the time he has reminded you of it for a few weeks you'll be feeling quite differently." Richard raised the jug and drank from it. The wine was warm, heavily spiced and sweet with honey. Even when he'd swallowed it, his mouth was still full of the rich heavy flavour. "I'll leave the jug on the floor for you, and if Jack will set his hands from the serving wench then I shall send her up to help you."

Lizbet twisted in the tub. Richard heard the displaced water slap against the sides.

"You're not going to soak me again, are you?"

Lizbet's voice was quiet, unsure, and he heard the nervous edge. "I don't mean to talk out of turn, Master, but you know you asked me to clean your rings?"

Richard looked down at his hand. "I have them all back, so this isn't a confession of theft. Go on."

"I took them back to your room, and…" Lizbet swallowed hard, and hesitated.

"Just tell me. It's something you think I need to know. I'll not hold you to account," Richard said.

"When I went in, Andrew was there. He'd been looking at one of your books," Lizbet said quickly.

"You were right to tell me," Richard replied.

After a long while, he added, "Lizbet?" over his shoulder.

There came no reply.

"Lizbet?" Richard said again. When she didn't reply, he swivelled his head round. The cup he had given her was floating in the water spreading a red stain across the surface. Her hand, open, hung next to it, and Lizbet's head, eyes closed, serene in sleep, rested against the side of the tub just above the water.

"Lizbet! Come on, woman, you can't stop there like that." Richard added a shake to a naked shoulder which regrettably settled her face even closer to the water.

"Damn you, woman!" Richard muttered realising he couldn't leave her where she was.

Water sluiced from her body for the second time that day as he picked her up from the tub. The bed had been turned back ready, Richard laid her on it and flipped the cover over her wet body.

Returning to the inn downstairs, he retook his seat next to Jack.

Jack, his knee occupied, looked past its occupant and at his brother. "What happened to you? Raining outside, is it?"

Dan didn't comment at all and hid his look of disapproval.

Chapter 12
An Unavoidable Trap

✝

The spaniel's nose, black and endlessly inquisitive, had left another level line of smears along the glass where it had chased along the window seat, nose pressed to the panes, barking pointlessly at anything that moved in the courtyard below. Catherine, a wet cloth in one hand, set to remove the marks, knowing full well that the spaniel would ensure that by nightfall all of the nose marks would be replaced.

"Now that's why I won't allow dogs in any part of my house but the hall," Christopher Morley said, striding into the room. "Good day to you, Mistress Eugenie. I was looking for Kate Ashley."

"I am afraid she has not yet returned, sir. They are due later today. Lotty and some of the other ladies have arrived and they brought Elizabeth's spaniel with them," Catherine supplied cautiously, hoping he would bid her good day and turn on his heel.

Morley knew very well that Kate had returned, and Catherine would have paled had she known that he had come in search of her and not Elizabeth's governess and confidante.

"I have been misinformed. It was not an important matter. I will find her later on no doubt," Morley said. "I'm sure you'll be pleased to see your Aunt again."

Catherine made a move to return her attention to the spaniel's nose marks but Morley was regarding her closely and she couldn't really turn her back on him. "It will be good to have everyone back again at Durham Place. It is a large house, and a lonely place when there are so few of us here."

"Ah, I have found you out! You are lonely, so it was a love you have lost that you would not tell me about last time?" he laughed, his manner easy and warm. He was older than Jack by a good few years, but still he reminded her of him, and she returned his generous smile. "So how did you lose him then? Has he gone to Court with the Lady Elizabeth or did you leave the lad in Cheshire?"

Catherine's face clouded; she had, she supposed, lost someone, and she was very lost herself.

"I've done it again! I've made you sad. I'm such an insensitive clod!" Morley sounded rather upset himself. "I've no right to ask. I am sorry, mistress. I think everyone in London suffers as I do. My family are from Lincolnshire and I miss my wife Anne, and our children very much. I do not get to return to them as often as I would like."

Catherine had been to Lincoln, and nearly said as much but stopped herself just in time. "It is sad to be parted from your family. How many children do you have?"

Morley brightened. "I have two boys, Jacob and John, and two girls, Margaret and Nan. She's called Anne for her mother, but we've always called her Nan."

"How old are they, sir?" Catherine asked.

"Well, Jacob and John are twins and they are fourteen now, big lads and I am proud of them both. Their sister Margaret is twelve and my little Nan is nine. I'm hoping to bring the boys to London with me next time I go back home. I've found places for them in good houses. I would have brought them last year but Anne said she would miss them so much and begged me let her keep them for one last year," Morley said.

"Twins? Do they look alike?" Catherine said. It was rare for twins to live. The babies were often small and weakly and not well prepared for the fight for life that all children must make.

"They are alike in looks but not at all in temperament. Which is lucky, otherwise we would not be able to tell them apart. John is bookish, and a harder working, more studious lad you would have to look hard to find, and his brother Jacob…" Morley smiled, "… wherever he is, there will be mischief. He's not a bad boy but always seems to getting into trouble. He rarely thinks before he acts."

Catherine smiled as well. "I used to know someone like that as well, and you cannot help but like them."

"I know that well. I have to talk sternly to Jacob, but it is hard to keep from laughing. Our cook used to get Jacob to bring the eggs into the kitchen for her. He had to get up early, the coops were a short walk, but he'd decided he didn't want to do it anymore, especially in the snow. So the cook came down to open the kitchens up and found Jacob had brought the birds to the kitchens. He'd meant for them to stay in small storeroom, but the clod left the door open. There were chickens pecking their way through the grain, roosting on top of the cupboards, even trying to nest in the cook's pots." Morley was laughing and Catherine couldn't help joining in. "The dogs came bounding down into the kitchens to chase the birds. There were feathers flying everywhere, the cook and kitchen maids trying to round these birds up and keep the merry dogs at bay…" Morley paused to laugh at the memory of it.

"I can imagine!" Catherine said, laughing herself, then asked, "and where was Jacob?"

"In his bed! He'd no need to get up early had he as he'd brought his work home with him and so he was fast asleep while my kitchens were ransacked by his feathery marauders. Do you have any brothers? If you do then you'd know what young boys can be like."

"I don't, sir, but I can imagine," Catherine replied, still laughing.

"I do miss home, and I miss the open countryside. London is not such an easy a place to live, especially when you do not have your family around you," Morley said, a sad note in his voice. "I believe you are from Chester. I have family from that way myself. It is such a lovely city. Do you not miss it?"

"London is becoming my favourite city," Catherine said cautiously.

Morley shook his head from side to side as if weighing the options. "We have to be careful to not let London define us, I think. When I am at home I find there is a peace to life, here I always seem to be

215

at someone's beck and call. There always seems to be much undone that I need to attend to. Just trying to get across London on some days can be a trial in itself. The roads are so bad. To get from my house to Lincoln it is so easy. I can ride a horse across the fields or down the North road. I'm not going to get endlessly held up by wagons, processions, floods, markets stalls blocking the way, crowds gathered around preachers."

"I agree. When I first came to London, I remember being so surprised that there wasn't a middle. I'd expected an open green, something to mark the fact you were in the centre of the city, but it just went on and on," Catherine said, remembering that first journey to London when Jack had reluctantly brought her to the town house Richard had been gifted by Mary.

Morely laughed. "I agree. London had much the same effect on me when I came here the first time when I was a boy. Even Chester where you are from, although a large city, still has the Cathedral in the centre and the marketplace."

Catherine wisely chose not to comment on Chester but nodded and diverted him back to his own family. "Have you ever brought Anne to London, sir?"

"I've not brought Anne. I think I will when the girls are grown and wed. Her family are from Lincoln and I don't think she would like the city and its ways."

†

He left her shortly after this, Catherine still smiling and thinking of the chickens having an early visit to the pot. It had been good to laugh, and when she saw him later in a corridor beckoning to her, she smiled and followed him into the room. Morley closed the door with a quiet click behind her and Catherine saw that he no longer had his accustomed smile on his face.

"Sit down," he commanded, pointing to a stool at the wooden table.

Catherine seated herself and waited, her heart hammering in her chest.

What was coming? What had she done?

"Let's not waste too much time. I know perfectly well that you are not Kate Ashley's niece," Morley said conversationally.

Catherine didn't reply. Morley watched with some satisfaction as her face went white.

"So, if you are not Eugenie, then who are you?" Morley asked, then added, "Think carefully before you speak, mistress, and do not tie yourself up in lies you will not be able to escape."

What was she going to do? He'd obviously discovered she was not Eugenie, but what to tell him?

"The truth sometimes," Morley said, turning his back on her for a moment, and almost reading her mind, "is often not as evil as you have come to think it is."

Could she tell him the truth? Where she was now could hardly be seen as her fault, could it? From the moment she had hidden in the hayloft while her mother was murdered, her life had been directed by others. The choices had not been hers to make.

"Well then? Have you anything to tell me?" Morley said, taking the stool opposite her, his face serious now, not unfriendly, but the eyes that regarded her closely across the table warning her not to lie.

"My name is Catherine De Bernay," she sniffed and wiped a running nose on her sleeve.

"I'm pleased to meet you, Catherine. Now, can you tell me how you come to be in Elizabeth's household?" Morley said promoting her to continue. De Bernay – that was a name he recognised.

This was a gamble. Was Morley Elizabeth's man? She didn't know. Her father had been an ardent supporter of Mary, and had lost his life supporting her cause. But whose side was Morley on?

"I'm not asking you to trust me, that would be foolish, but you know you will have to tell me, so who, Catherine, are you?" Morley asked again.

Another sniff.

"Do you want me to report that there is a spy within Elizabeth's household? Do you want to be arrested?" he said. "Can you really be that foolish? They will certainly find out who you are and where you came from, in circumstances that I can promise you will not be as comfortable as this room is now. So tell me now, and perhaps, only perhaps, those discomforts might not occur."

Her eyes flicked up and met his. She'd seen Jack in debtors' gaol, and had no wish to imperil herself like that.

"So you do know where you'll end up?" Morley said, reading her expression.

"My name is Catherine De Bernay. My father died fighting for Her Majesty two and half years ago, my mother was killed and my household lost to me."

Catherine told her tale, and Morley listened in silence. She ended with the probable death of Jack and with Richard's deposit of her in Elizabeth's household.

"Well, when I asked for the truth, I certainly got it." Morley let out a long breath, his cheeks puffing.

Catherine sat in silence, wondering what he would make of it, and what was going to happen to her next.

Morley pushed himself up from the table. "I will speak with you tomorrow. Do not think of taking flight into the streets of London. We would find you, and the outcome would then be most wholly unfortunate for yourself." The threat was clear. "Take consolation in this, I am Her Majesty's sworn servant, but that does not mean we can condone your actions of being uninvited within the Lady Elizabeth's household."

He left her shortly after this and Catherine was forced to return to domestic duties that she had no enthusiasm for. Work was followed by a long night, most of which she spent awake.

†

"How did this happen?" stormed Cecil when Morley had finished recounting the story of how the

De Bernay girl had come to be a part of Elizabeth's household.

"By accident it would seem," Morley said.

"By design. We thought Richard Fitzwarren was dead. It seems he escaped last year. He spirited away papers Gardiner had on Elizabeth and they have never been seen or heard of since. Does she know where he is now?"

"No, she's not seen him since he took her to Durham Place and she joined Elizabeth's staff." Morley supplied.

"And you believe her?" Cecil asked.

"She's a young girl, Cecil. I know what you are thinking, that he is using as her an informant to pass messages to and from Elizabeth, and if that is the case we will soon know. I have already arranged to have her closely watched. Her story, what happened to her family, does indeed ring true. I've checked and Peter De Bernay was indeed killed in fighting before Her Majesty took her rightful throne," Morley said.

"Had it occurred to you that she could be an imposter?" Cecil said, pulling on his beard.

"It did, especially after she herself told me that she was presumed dead in the fighting to take her father's manor at Assingham. And I agree, we cannot be completely sure, however my gut feeling is she has been used by the Fitzwarrens. She told me Robert Fitzwarren took her to his house hoping to secure Assingham for himself, and I believe Richard may have deposited her in Elizabeth's household for safekeeping, perhaps believing that he too could lay a claim to the lady's property when times are more…" Morley paused while he selected the right words, he could hardly say when Mary was dead, "favourable towards him."

"Mmmm…" Cecil continued to think. "Do you think we can use her?"

"Possibly. That does depend on what reports I have back. A false task to prove her worth might be the best cause of action," Morley suggested.

"See to it. Maybe we can use her to trap Richard Fitzwarren after Renard's failure last year." Cecil waved Morley from his presence and settled back in his chair to contemplate this recent twist. Richard Fitzwarren was a known supporter of Elizabeth and he'd allegedly stolen papers from Gardiner. Reaching for a pen, he pulled over a sheet of paper, calling loudly as he wrote. "Crake get in here, will you?"

Crake arrived silently from a door to Cecil's left, one of his three trusted staff, and he handed him the sheet of paper. "Bring me everything we have, and there should be a record from last year," Cecil said, handing over the paper with the name Richard Fitzwarren written on it in Cecil's neat economic writing.

There was more than he had expected. He'd heard the name, and it had been Sir Ayscough in Lincoln who had dealt with the treasonous whelp. Prior to his death he had purloined papers that the Archbishop had relating to Elizabeth. These had never surfaced again and, Fitzwarren, badly injured after the fight, had been presumed dead.

It was news indeed that Richard Fitzwarren had been closely linked with Elizabeth when she was under the guardianship of Catherine Parr and Thomas Seymour. The papers held a signed statement by Kate Ashley attesting to his assault on the princess.

Cecil put the statement to one side and tapped his fingers on the desk. Was this man for or against Elizabeth? Who was he working for, that was the question, but the answer to that question he did not find as he shuffled through the remaining pages in the file.

If this man were still alive, and it was more than probable that he was, not only did he have these papers, but he also had, it seemed, access to Elizabeth, and if not directly to her, then via Kate Ashley. Cecil wrote another note. This time he sealed it and sent it to Morley – he needed to know everything there was to know about this man, and more importantly where he was now.

†

"The Master is not so well these days, you understand," Edwin said to Morley as he directed him to a room to wait while he informed his Master, William Fitzwarren, that he had a visitor. "I will go and tell him you are here, sir."

"Who?" William boomed, after Edwin told him that there was a man requesting to see him.

"His name is Christopher Morley, my lord, and he says he comes from Cecil," Edwin explained again.

"Well, bring him in," William said, waving Edwin to the door. "Go on, get on with it."

Edwin, relieved, backed to the door and hastened along the corridor to the waiting Christopher Morley.

"Lord William will see you. If you would be so kind as to follow me, I shall take you in," Edwin said, leading Morley to William's rooms.

"My lord," Edwin announced, opening the door, "Christopher Morley to see you."

"Get the man a chair," William barked.

Edwin dutifully brought one over and set it down.

"Not there, you bloody idiot, here – otherwise how am I going to hear him?" William glared at Edwin who moved to the chair to the spot where William's gnarled finger pointed. Edwin quickly brought an extra glass for Morley and filling it, set it on the table that was now between them.

"Now get out, go on…" William scowled at Edwin.

Morley had taken the offered chair and was smiling amiably at William. "My lord, it is very good of you to see me, especially when you are unwell."

William cast his assessing gaze over the man. He was well dressed, but there was little to mark him out, the cloth good but with little in the way of embellishments, and the man wore only one simple ring, a wedding ring. This was a man who did not want to be remembered, thought William.

"So why do you want to see me?" William demanded, a crooked finger pushing his glasses up his nose. He wished to miss nothing.

"My lord, I work for Master Cecil, legal advisor to the privy council. About a year ago, your son, Richard, was involved in a crime in Lincoln, a murder, from which he seems to have escaped punishment and made his way to London," Morley provided.

"Why have you come to me? I'm sure your Masters will be very well aware of the shame he has brought on my name and this house. He is no son of mine," William spat.

"I am aware, my lord, however we are most anxious to trace him…"

"I am sure you are," William cut him off, "and you think I can help, do you?"

"I am trying to locate him, yes." Morley reached for his wine.

"Why? What's that treasonous dog done now?" William barked.

"I'm not at liberty to say, my lord, but my Masters would like him to answer for the crimes he has already committed, and we would like to know if you have heard from him."

William considered this for some minutes. He could lie, but then he was housebound and had no idea if Morley and his lackies had seen Richard enter his house. If he gave them what little he had, would it bring the cur to heel? It might, he supposed, although the risk was that Robert would find out, and that he could damn well do without.

Morley seemed in no rush, and enjoyed the wine while William contemplated the possibilities.

"If I help you, I have a condition," William voiced at last.

"Perhaps I can help, let me know," Morley replied pleasantly.

"My son, Robert, he gets to know nothing of this. There is a great enmity between him and Richard, and it is a wound I would not reopen," William said.

Morley nodded. "Anything you tell me, my lord, I shall not repeat to Robert, you have my word."

Those few words told William that Robert was also on Morley's list of people to question.

"Aye, he came here a few weeks back, intent on theft, threatened to murder me where I sat," William supplied.

"Did he say anything about where he was going, what he was doing?" Morley asked.

"No, he just had his eyes fixed on my gold that was all he was after," William said.

"I am sorry this happened. Did you not think to report it?" Morley asked.

"And bring more shame on my name, that my son robbed me, an old man. Look." William held out his hand where Richard's knife had incised the flesh at the base of his thumb. The cut had festered and was healing badly.

"I can understand, my lord. Sometimes it is better to keep things within the family."

"Well if you find him, you are welcome to him," William said.

"Do you have any idea where we might look? Did he mention any places or names, my lord?" Morley pressed.

William was silent for a moment. He didn't want to mention Christian Carter. If he did, Morley might find out that he had sent a message to summon Richard and the whole sorry story about Eleanor's son might come back to haunt him. It was enough that someone like Morley was looking for Richard. They would find him – and God help him when they did.

"None. He will have spent my money and be back in a gutter somewhere, I have not doubt," William growled.

☦

It was three days before Morley found Catherine again. Indeed she had begun to think he had forgotten about her and the terror she had felt was beginning to lessen, especially in the face of the mundane household tasks that were her life now that Durham Place was once more occupied.

He found her in the garden cutting rue and tying it into bundles.

"Mistress De Bernay," he announced, for there were no others within earshot.

Catherine nodded and dropped the bundle she had just finished tying into the basket.

"So I hope today finds you well," Morley smiled. "It seems that my Masters would like to find Richard Fitzwarren as well. Is this something you can help me with?"

"I told you, I have not seen him since he left me here. He just left me, that was a long time ago. He promised to come back and he didn't, and I don't think he will," Catherine said.

"That may be so, but there must be something you can give me that I can take to my Masters. Where was he stopping in London?" Morley asked.

Catherine didn't reply straight away and then she remembered Morley's words – 'think before you lie'. They were going to find out anyway, she had been there herself, had stopped there before Richard had brought her to Durham Place. It was not likely that he was there now, she supposed.

"An inn, the name of it I don't know, but I know where it is," Catherine said slowly.

Morley smiled. "Good lass. That probably won't be necessary. If you can give me a good description I can probably find it. Now I want you to come and tell me everything, and I mean everything you know about Richard Fitzwarren."

Catherine went white.

"Child, he left you, did he not? If not for him, your family very well might still be alive? He is a traitor, a murderer and a thief, it seems. Do not stand on the same shore as this man. Now come with me."

Morley took her inside and there, in the same room he had taken her to before, waited a second man, a scribe, ready to record the details of their conversation.

"Don't mind him, my dear, my memory plagues me these days. It is the way I suppose and age makes me forgetful. So Crake will record the details my frail mind may forget. Now then let's start with where you think this inn is, shall we?"

Catherine told them where she thought it was. He asked her so many questions, sometimes a question relating to the recent past then a question relating to her time when she was still at Assingham, then forward again to how she had come to be in London, then back again to when she had been at Burton.

"So how did you get from London to Burton? You told me Fitzwarren brought you to London while he alleged he would try to contact your family, but after this how did you get back to Burton?"

"Jack took me..." Catherine stopped. She'd not meant to mention Jack. He was dead anyway, he didn't matter, but she'd tried to reconstruct the past for Morley without him, and it hadn't worked.

"Jack?" Morley asked slowly, the look on the girl's face telling him she'd said more than she had meant to. There was a long silence, then he said, "You haven't lied to me yet. Let's not change that, Catherine. Now tell me, who is Jack?"

"Jack's..." Catherine couldn't help it and the tears came like rain in a thunderstorm. "Jack's dead."

Morley patiently waited. It eventually took the rest of the afternoon and Morley had to admit that his own head was pounding by the end of it. William Fitzwarren, it seemed, might have been keeping a little something from him. It seemed he had a bastard son as well who was with Richard.

From her description he knew where the inn was and resolved to find out if he was right the following day. Catherine he left, dazed, confused and feeling sick with the sense of betrayal.

Chapter 13
A Hunter's Folly

✝

Froggy and Lizbet departed early into the woods to set up a fire to produce the musket balls. Richard had told them Scranton would be coming to watch them, a fact that pleased neither of them.

Lizbet, returning to the clearing her arms full of dry firewood, found Richard and Scranton already crouched down next to Froggy who was feeding the fire with a steady supply of wood. Avoiding Scranton's unpleasant stare, she dropped the firewood next to Froggy and sat herself down near the fire.

Eventually happy with the fire, Froggy added the charcoal and covered it with another layer of dry wood. The fire soon lit the charcoal and the character of the flames changed, the wood smoke lessened and the charcoal began to give off white wisps as it burnt. Lizbet felt the heat from the blaze on her cheeks, and she knew the fire was ready.

"Right then," Froggy announced, giving the fire an experimental prod with a stick, "I think we are ready."

The lead went onto the charcoal and they all watched as it began to liquefy, turning into a bright molten silver. Lizbet put the skillet over the fire. Scranton scowled at her, but she ignored his disapproving looks. Froggy checked the securing wires on the mould and settled it on the skillet, satisfying himself that skillet and mould were both level. Lizbet and Froggy worked together and with practised skill filled the mould and lifted it away from the fire to cool. Scranton had observed the whole process with nothing short of contempt on his face.

Froggy handled the still hot mould with the blacksmith's leather gloves and unwound the retaining wires to let the freshly made lead balls tumble from the mould. If Scranton was at all impressed that Froggy and Lizbet had just made more ammunition in one go than a flintlocker could make on his own in two days, he didn't show it. Using a stick he rolled one of the lead pellets towards him and cast a disdainful look over it.

"The sprues are a little thick. It'll make them uneven and effect their flight, I should think," he finally pronounced.

Lizbet looked at her feet. Froggy's hands balled into fists inside the leather gloves but he said nothing. It was Richard who spoke.

"We are grateful for your expertise," he said. The lead balls were sufficiently cooled and he picked one up. "We might be able to adjust the mould to change that. We'll use these later and you can judge the results."

Scranton's pinched face wore a thin smile as he received Richard's praise.

Shortly after, Richard and Scranton, with the latter talking constantly, left. Froggy and Lizbet watched them retreat from the clearing.

"Why does the Master put up with him?" Lizbet said once they were out of earshot.

"Lord knows," Froggy said in agreement. "Master will have his reasons you can be sure."

†

The noise was the first alert that they had. Twenty horses at least stamped and rattled their way into the yard at the inn. It was a group of mercenaries, and it became very soon apparent that their captain was letting his troop rest for the night with express orders to enjoy themselves. Half a dozen of them were already in the taproom, and with ample coin they were on a determined and dedicated path to get insensible as soon as possible. Two extra staff had already been deployed by the enterprising inn owner to make sure as much ale as possible was exchanged for coin. A card game between another group was taking up all of one of the larger tables, and serving staff carrying platters of cooked meat and pies were elbowing their way as best they could through the packed room.

Jack's face had already soured when the blonde lass he had been seen with seemed to have scented a profit and was attached to the knee of one of the mercenaries playing cards at the table.

Richard leant his head close to Jack's. "Double the guard on the wagon, and let Lizbet sleep in your room tonight."

Jack inclined his head in acknowledgement but his eyes were on his lost conquest who was laughing and helping to refill her new man's cup.

"Please don't tell me a romp in an inn has finally made you sentimental?" Richard asked, following his brother's gaze to where they rested on the girl.

Jack took his eyes from the girl and turned his cold blue stare on his brother. "I'll make sure the guard is doubled," was all he said as Richard, rising from the table, left him alone with Andrew.

Lizbet put down a large bowl of pottage on the table between Jack and Andrew and, placing out bowls, began to serve. She missed nothing and nudging him with an elbow asked, "and where's your new lass tonight then?"

Jack, ignoring her comments, pulled his bowl towards him and dipped an exploratory spoon into the grey stew. Jack's eyes met Andrew's.

Andrew smiled. "It's poor fair for a man," he said.

"Woman, I've still got teeth. I've a mind to use them occasionally." Jack, already in a bad mood, discarded the spoon in the bowl and pushed it away. The thin liquid slopped over the rim.

"It's all they have. It's not my fault. That lot over there bought all the meat there was to be had," complained Lizbet as she moved to serve Andrew.

Andrew put his hand over the top of the bowl to stop her.

"Not you as well," Lizbet grumbled, dropping the serving spoon loudly back into the pot.

"Didn't you spot some pheasant as we rode into the village?" Andrew said to Jack.

"I did," Jack said, nodding in agreement.

"Well then?" Andrew said, and leaning forward he grinned conspiratorially. "Have you got a bow?"

Jack hesitated, then pushing the bowl away, he said, "Lizbet get a pot and I'll get something to fill it with." Jack stood suddenly and turned his blue sapphire gaze on Andrew. "Shall we?"

Andrew rose smoothly from his seat returning Jack's smile.

†

Jack had a short hunting bow, made from yew and strung tightly with twisted gut. The six arrows he carried with it were steel tipped hazel shafts all fletched with goose feather. The arrowheads were of the bodkin type, narrow and pointed and designed to penetrate mail but also ideally suited for bringing down pheasant without obliterating the bird. And pheasant was the quarry Jack had in mind. He had seen a field next to the forest full of them as they approached the village. He knew that as dusk fell, the birds would appear in the field to feed on insects in the long grass. In that special hour before nightfall, Jack would be able to shoot enough to fill the bag Andrew was carrying.

Andrew accompanied him and after the shot arrows had met their marks he went to collect the lifeless birds. There were four in the bag and they took them back to the inn where Lizbet dutifully gutted them and had them cooked.

Their meal would have been less pleasurable had Jack known that his shooting exploits had already been reported as poaching and men had been dispatched to arrest him. Jack was about to find out that poaching laws were the same here as in England.

†

The door to the room open with a slam, banging back round against the wall. Lizbet jumped.

"Hey Alex, there's one in 'ere and there's no one with her," the man swaying in the doorway announced to his companion who appeared at his shoulder.

"Well she's got someone with her now," Alex said, pushing his way into the room.

Lizbet was on her feet in an instant.

"Out you bloody well get. This isn't a brothel. Get out," Lizbet shouted.

"Come on, lass," Alex said. "You've no one with you. Col an' me have coin."

"Get out, now." Lizbet was wearing a shift with a shawl tight around her shoulders and she pulled it tighter as they moved across the room towards her.

"Don't you go complaining. We'll not keep you long," Alex announced. Grabbing an end of the shawl, he yanked it from her shoulders, leaving her standing before him in her linen shift.

Alex leered at her. "Come on, get the rest off. Let's take a look at what I'm paying for."

Alex had his hand on the front of her shift trying to pull it from her. Lizbet, both hands on his chest, was trying to keep him away from her, and she heard the stitching complaining as he continued to try and pull the material from her body.

235

"Col, give us a hand here," Alex called to his companion.

Lizbet shrieked and her nails left a parallel set of scrapes across Col's face as he attempted to lift her shift up and over her head.

"You bitch!" The back of Col's hand connected with Lizbet's face and she was sent across the room, fetching up painfully against the bed frame.

"Aye, lass, get your backside on that bed," Col growled. He took hold of her, pushing her down onto the bed, his body on top of her. Lizbet, dug her heels in the bed, and tried to push away but a painful hold on one arm and another hand around her throat prevented her escape. The pressure on her neck increased, then panicking she realised her vision was dimming and knew she was about to black out. Lizbet tried to scream but the noise wouldn't pass the hold around her throat. She'd been here before and knew that if she fought on, it was just going to make it worse. She stopped struggling.

"That's right, you just bloody lie still." Lizbet heard his words in her ears and then his laughter. They were drunk, they probably wouldn't take long.

Lizbet cursed Jack. Where the hell was he?

Col was too preoccupied with his own feral grunting to hear the noise behind him of Alex being neatly felled and landing face down on the floor. His attention however rapidly changed focus when the blade of a lethally sharp poniard was stabbed into his exposed straining backside. Col screamed, convulsed and rolled off the bed.

Lizbet, flat on her back, shifted round her waist and found herself staring up at Richard. Col was rolling on the floor cursing loudly. A boot heel to the back of the head silenced him.

Richard extended a hand that she took and he pulled her up from the bed; he looked less than impressed.

"Sorry!" Lizbet wailed.

"Come on, you can't stop in here. The bloody door is off its hinges." He pulled her after him.

Lizbet grabbed her shawl from where Alex had thrown it and, barefooted, she followed Richard out of the room to the one he was occupying opposite.

Lizbet pulled him to a halt. "I can't just leave them two in there. Jack's belongings are in there. They'll bloody wake up and take the lot."

"I would say that might serve him right," Richard replied, and then relented. "Get them, and bring them in here." Richard opened his own room door and left it ajar.

Two minutes later Lizbet returned, her arms full, and dropped everything on the floor. Setting the latch back, she secured the door.

Lizbet sniffed loudly, and looked round. The fire wasn't lit, but the room was still pleasantly warm. Grabbing Jack's cloak, she made to settle herself down near it. She had barely had time to lay herself down when the door to Richard's room crashed open, the latch popping from the frame as the big man pushed hard on the door.

Dan was speaking before he was in the room.

"They've taken Jack. We couldn't stop them," Dan blurted.

"Who? Where've they taken him?"

"He was poaching pheasants by all accounts," Dan said.

Lizbet was on her feet in a moment. Dan's eyes widened at the sight of her.

"Pheasants? I plucked them for him."

"Where did he get them?" Richard demanded, already sitting on the edge of the bed and pulling his boots on.

"I didn't ask." Lizbet was biting her lip.

"When Jack brought the pheasants back, had he been hunting alone?"

"No," said Lizbet. "It was Andrew who was with him. Andrew goaded him into going in the first place."

"Andrew's more sense than to do that. Jack though, would lead a saint astray. For God's sake! It's like being in charge of a nursery!" Richard said though clenched teeth.

Everyone suffered that night and wished fervently they were elsewhere. Dan was dispatched quickly back to the camp and the men flung on jackets, saddled unwilling horses and rode with Richard to retrieve his brother.

The castle at Bertradaburg had as its overlord, or Freiherr, Henlyn Gelfrat, an imperial knight owing fealty as part of the Holy Roman Empire directly to Charles V. The legal system was fragmented and the Empire did not have the court system that England possessed. Cases were decided in the adhoc courts set up by Gelfrat and justice was dispensed as he saw fit. The main market was set for the first Saturday in the month, and Gelfrat and his advisors would hear cases brought before them, similar in many ways to the assize courts in England. However justice was dispensed a sight quicker and those found guilty of serious offences would find themselves treading the boards to the gallows before noon.

It was to Bertradaburg to seek a meeting with Henlyn Gelfrat that Richard rode in stony silence with his men equally quiet behind him.

Two hours later Marc saw the Master ride back into the yard and dismount. Pierre hurried forwards and caught the reins that were thrown at him, and Richard strode off into the inn leaving them staring at his retreating back.

"Well?" was all Dan said, staring up at Jack where he still sat on his horse.

"Well, what?" Jack spat back as he dropped from the saddle, the look on his face murderous. Turning his back on them, he led his horse from the yard.

Lizbet jumped so hard when the door was banged with a fist on the outside she pricked herself with the needle she was sewing with. Dropping the sewing, she hastily made her way across the room and lifted the latch.

Richard pushed past, ignoring her.

Lizbet swallowed hard. As quietly as she could, she pressed the door shut and lowered the latch back into place. There were two loud bangs as Richard threw his boots at the wall before dropping to lie on the bed, knees raised, hands over his face.

Lizbet, still standing, froze. Well acquainted with his temper she had no intention of being on the receiving end of it again. Barefoot still, she stepped carefully, praying the boards beneath her feet stayed silent. She nearly made it back to the corner where she had been sat sewing and where Jack's cloak lay spread on the floor.

"Do you know how much I have just had to pay for four bloody pheasants?"

Lizbet froze, the voice was taught with anger.

"I'm sorry, Master." Lizbet's words were quietly spoken.

Richard breathed in noisily, a hand still covering his face.

Lizbet swallowed hard, caught like a rabbit in the open between the door and the corner of the room where she'd set herself to sleep. The door was the more desirable option, but noisier so Lizbet crept instead towards the corner.

"You are wise enough to know he'd not bought them. Next time tell me," Richard said, then when she did not reply, he lifted his hand from his face, and raised his head, grey eyes holding hers in an unblinking stare.

"Yes, Master, I will. I'm sorry," Lizbet said on a quiet breath. With relief she watched as he dropped his head back to the bed and stared up at the ceiling.

"You know what Cicero said about fools?" Richard said sadly, the anger gone from his voice.

Lizbet shook her head, even though she knew he couldn't see her.

"It is the quality of a fool to perceive the faults of others and to forget his own," Richard supplied when she didn't answer him. "I'm angry at myself. I'm Cicero's fool."

The following day Scranton wore a triumphant smile. Jack's exploits the night before and his extraction by his brother had confirmed Scranton's opinions of Richard's bastard sibling. Rising early and preparing for a day with Andrew overseeing the building of a powder store, he found Richard already awake and sat alone in the inn. The whore was predictably there as well serving the Master. Scranton scowled at her as he seated himself opposite Richard and she returned his look in equal measure.

After some minutes he said, "I hear you had a troubled night?"

"Master Scranton," Richard raised his eyes from where they had been regarding the table before him and looked at Scranton coldly, "my brother's shortcomings are my business, I would thank you for remembering that." Scranton paled, Richard continued. "I would also add that if we encounter trouble on this route the safest place for you to be would be behind my brother. You might want to remember that."

Lizbet still close enough behind Scranton to hear every word, had to bite her lip to stifle a laugh.

Chapter 14
The Alaunt

†

Lizbet had her back to the door, sleeves rolled up, pounding linen shirts in the communal wash tub and singing in time to the rhythmic noise of the wooden clothes paddle. For white linen the best thing to use was black soap, but Lizbet was having to make do with a lye she had made from wood ash and urine.

Richard stood outside and his nose wrinkled as it caught the scent coming from the tub. "I hope my shirts aren't going to smell of that when you've finished?"

Lizbet, her arms still in the soggy mix of shirts, lye and urine, laughed. "They didn't smell that good when I started. I can't see that anything I could do would make them any worse."

"I have something for you." Richard sounded curiously excited.

Lizbet dropped the paddle in the tub, rinsed her hands in a bucket of water and turned, smiling. The smile fell from her face. Lizbet shrieked. The dog that Richard was holding on a lead barked, and Lizbet retreated. "God's bones, get that beast from me."

Richard laughed and loosed the lead a little. The dog strained forward towards Lizbet, who grabbed the clothes paddle and waved it at the dog. "Don't let it go. Stop it!"

Richard let the lead slip a bit more and Lizbet backed into the corner. "It's not funny. Stop it."

"Put the paddle down." Richard's voice was serious. "You can't let him know you are scared of him."

"But I am!" Lizbet exclaimed but lowered the paddle anyway. "Why did you bring him in here to scare me anyway?"

For a moment, though she could not be sure, she thought she read disappointment on his face, but if it had been there it was quickly replaced by a hard look.

"I bought him for you. He's an Alaunt hound, loyal and fierce. He's called Kells and he'll not let anyone near his Mistress." Richard unwound the lead from his hand and held it out.

Lizbet swallowed hard. "Why?"

"Just take him, woman. I might not be there next time, he will." Richard was sounding impatient now.

Lizbet reached out nervously and took the lead. Turning on his heel, Richard left.

Lizbet eyed the dog nervously.

Froggy Tate appeared not a moment too soon. Smiling, he took the lead from her and dropped to his haunches next to the dog. "Master said you might be needing some help." Froggy let the dog lick him, and clamping one of his big hands on the dog's head, he scratched him behind the ears. The dog was almost completely black, apart from a white blaze on his chest. His short fur shone over the muscled body.

"He is a fine dog. Bred for hunting boar, they are. They've the speed of a greyhound and the heart of a lion. He's quite a prize, lass. You just need to make him yours."

"How do I do that?" Lizbet sounded relieved that Froggy had hold of the dog.

"Finish what you were doing and I'll help you," Froggy replied and took Kells.

The Alaunt was indeed friendly, and it seemed well trained. Froggy had some meat scraps and let Lizbet feed it, and she was surprised as how gently the big dog took the small morsels from her hand. Holding it on the lead, it didn't pull but remained obediently at her side.

Froggy ruffled the dog's ears. "We'll take him with us when we go to the wood this morning, and I'll show you what good company a dog can be."

"Good company?" Lizbet did not sound convinced. "Any dog I ever came across was nothing more than a scavenging mongrel good for the pot."

Froggy laughed and leant close to Lizbet. "Kells is too good for the pot. I'd reckon it cost the Master quite a bit to buy him."

"Really?"

"I'm sure he did. He's an Alaunt," Froggy explained, then seeing the baffled expression on her face continued. "He's a hunting dog, lass."

Lizbet's eyes were open wide. "Really? And I thought he'd saddled me with some cur he'd found in the street to teach me a lesson."

Froggy wound his hand around the dog's lead. "No, he's a fine dog, one to be proud of. I'll take him down to the camp with me while you finish here, show him to the lads."

Lizbet, pushing her sleeves back up, prepared to return to her laundry. "I won't be long."

She had just about finished pegging out the linen shirts, her hands and forearms reddened from the lye, when she became acutely aware of a pair of eyes upon her.

Turning, she found Jack regarding her with one of his most winning smiles. Lizbet scowled at him.

"Fix that, will you?" He was wearing only a linen shirt, holding out his doublet to her.

Lizbet raised her eyebrows, hands on hips, and stared at him. "I've a long list of repairs already before I can get to yours. You might as well keep it for the moment. I'll not get it done for a few days."

"Why not? It only needs a button and this tear sewing." Jack turned the garment over to show her the offending rent in the material properly.

Lizbet snatched the doublet from him and held it up to observe the tear. "I've got hose to re-stitch and clean for Froggy, and Marc has given me a pile of linen to wash that'll have me scrubbing for hours if he ever wants to see it white again."

"Since when did you start doing Marc and Froggy's washing?" Jack exclaimed.

"Since they started paying me." Lizbet's eyes narrowed in a challenge.

"I'll pay you. Just fix this." Jack gestured to the doublet she was still holding, his eyes bright and the smile now gone from his face.

Lizbet, still bent on punishing him for what had happened the previous night and for also exploring the charms of one of the inns more alluring serving girls, told him with finality. "There's a queue, and you'll be at the back of it. There's a laundress in the village. Get her to take it in for you."

Jack's blue eyes blazed. "Oh, come on, Lizbet. You are only doing this because you are angry with me!"

"Angry with you?" Lizbet pressed the doublet back into his hands. "Why would I be angry with you?"

"Because you don't like the new company I've been keeping," Jack pointed out accurately, although that was only half of the reason for her anger. It suddenly occurred to Lizbet that Jack probably had no idea what had happened to her the night before, and her mouth set in an even harder line.

"Come on, Lizbet." The smile returned to Jack's face again.

If Lizbet had been angry before, now she was fuming. "See this…" She pulled her linen shift away from her shoulder to show him the purple bruises and scrapes from the mercenary's nails where he had held her down as he tried to rape her. "That's your fault." Lizbet's anger was fully ignited now.

"How? I've not touched you." Jack sounded genuinely confused.

"No, but while you were away last night, those bloody drunk soldiers took to throwing me across your room."

"So why is that my fault?"

"If you had not been out thinking of your stomach as usual, it wouldn't have happened, and the Master would not have had to get up to go and retrieve you in the middle of the night either," Lizbet blazed.

"The fault of that is yours woman, not mine. If you'd found me some decent food, I'd not have had to go and find my own, would I?" Jack had already had the errors of his ways outlined in painful detail by his brother the night before, but he'd not been told by Lizbet that the fault of it was his own.

Without saying a word, she angrily pulled the doublet back from him and carefully examined the tear along the seam that he wanted her to sew.

Jack's manner eased, thinking he had won her over, and he forced a smile back to his face. "I'll pay you as well. Just see if you can do it tonight."

In a quick movement, she balled the doublet up and threw it in his face. "Like I said, I'm busy. Get your whore to stitch it for you!"

While Jack was fighting to free himself from the jacket that had landed over his head, Lizbet had turned on her heel and left him, determined to have the last word.

†

The routine at the camp continued for the next few weeks. Froggy's training sessions and those devised by Andrew filled the days, which were long and hard. Jack, falling into bed at the end of each of them, had little time to think, and the incident with the pheasant was now well sunk to the back of his mind.

His brother was providing lessons on tactics and strategy. He had groaned inwardly before the first one, but had found himself genuinely engaged in the discussion. Richard knew more than he had given him credit for. Andrew had a provided a detailed training programme and Jack had to admit that under the man's tutelage he was attaining a skill level he had never before known.

They were now painfully short of powder despite Froggy's frugal measures. Richard, with Scranton in tow, had been away for two days to source more and negotiate a price, their destination the town of Haltenberg. When they returned, his brother was in less than good humour, but informed them that he had sourced what Froggy needed. Scranton had vouched, eventually, for the quality, and it just required that they take the cart and pick it up.

Richard had been prepared to pay for it and carry it back in hessian sacks but Scranton had caused such an incredible fuss and insisted that the only safe way to transport it was in kegs, properly secured and fastened to a wagon.

✝

Andrew was on his knees next to the wagon when Marc arrived, a half-eaten chicken leg in one hand.

"What's the matter," Marc said through a mouthful of food.

"It's just the brake. The pin keeps coming loose. I've told the Master," Andrew grunted as the palm of his hand pushed home the securing peg. "There it's back in." Standing, he dusted the earth from his knees. "Well, I think I've fixed that so at least it'll not be rolling away down the hill."

Marc finished tearing the meat from the bone with his teeth and threw the remains on the grass, rubbing his greasy fingers down the front of his hose. Then he took hold of the wagon and pulled himself up. "Froggy's refused to drive it, says he has spent more than his fair share of time up here having his bones shaken apart."

"I'd rather a ride a horse any day than be up there," Andrew agreed, and then added, "It's not a long journey. Couple of hours either way should see you there and back. Who is going with you?"

"Jack's coming and Scranton. I just hope he's not riding next to me!" Marc raised his eyes to the heavens.

Andrew smiled. "I am sure Master Scranton's tales will pass the journey away."

"I don't know about the journey, but it will be making me want to pass away if I have to listen to him all the way there and all the way back," Marc shot back, laughing.

"Well, just don't you forget to check that brake when you get there and make sure it's not come loose again, and I'll go and mention it to the Master as well."

✝

"Why do I have to go?" Jack complained loudly.

"Because I've just had two days of his company and if I have to suffer one more then it will be his last," Richard said through gritted teeth.

"Patience, you told me. Remember?" Jack replied. "So you trust me not to have the weasel by the throat by the time the day is out?"

"Right now I care not if you decide to beat him within an inch of his life," Richard snapped. "Just as long as I don't have to spend another minute with him."

"Humour him, you said. He's an expert, you told me. We need his experience… Do you recall any of those conversations?" Jack's voice was incredulous.

"That was before I had to listen to two days of his prattle on how to store and transport powder. It can't be too hot, it can't be too cold, it can only be packed by Master Scranton, it can only be inspected by Master Scranton, only Master bloody Scranton has sufficient experience to handle it in these quantities."

"I did warn you." Jack sounded amused.

"You can return with him and collect it. Think of it as a penance," Richard replied acidly.

"Penance for what?" Jack accused.

"Oh, there will be something. Don't make me have to turn over the past to find a reason," Richard replied bitingly.

An image of a bag with four dead pheasants in it sailed into Jack's mind and he decided not to press his complaint any further, conceding defeat.

"Alright, I shall take him with me." Then he asked, "Do we really still need him?"

"I'm afraid so. He has the knowledge to be able to refine the powder to make culverins fire at an additional third of their normal distance, and that's the piece of the puzzle I need to find out. Then as you rightly point out, Master Scranton will cease to be useful," Richard replied.

"Bit hard to find out really. Last time I checked, heavy ordnance was not amongst our assets."

Richard smiled and then added, "Don't drop it off the back of the cart, please."

"Good God. Really? Well, if there is a chance that Scranton might blow himself into the hereafter, I will be willing to put up with him for the day." Jack's eyes were bright. "So what exactly have you bought?"

"You'll find out when you collect the powder," was the unsatisfactory reply.

"Now I am going to have to be passingly pleasant to him as well." Jack sounded morose, realising the trap he had fallen into.

"Exactly. As I said, see it as a penance." Richard had an evil smile on his face.

A half hour later, Jack led his horse towards the cart where Marc and Scranton were waiting for him. He met Andrew on his way to one of Froggy's training sessions.

"I don't suppose you'd like to come with me, would you?" Jack asked hopefully.

Andrew, grinning, read Jack's mind. "Scranton is not that bad. It is often the case with men of learning, that they sometimes do not know…"

"…when to shut up," Jack interrupted.

"I wasn't going to put it quite that bluntly, but yes. You'll have an easy day, Jack. I for one would rather spend the day on an easy ride than have to spend an afternoon in the tilt yard in this weather," Andrew explained.

Jack acknowledged his point. Apart from the prospect of having to share his day with Master Scranton, it was going to be a fairly easy one, and it would probably be punctuated by a pause at an ale house on the return journey from Haltenberg. His grounds for complaint were not particularly valid. "You have a point," he said. "So beware, after I've had a day's rest, I'll be paying you back for that beating I got yesterday."

"You think so, do you?" Andrew's voice was full of mirth, then he added before Jack could speak. "Just watch out for the brake on the cart, lad. It keeps coming loose. I fixed it this morning and I've told Marc to keep an eye on it as well. Master knows and we should take it to the wheelwright when you get back and have it repaired."

"I will, and you make sure you give Mat what he has coming to him today as well," Jack replied, putting a foot into one of the stirrups and rising into the mare's saddle.

Andrew waved a hand in the air in a gesture of farewell and Jack turned his horse towards Marc and Scranton.

Chapter 15
A Narrow Escape

✝

Jack, eyeing the small cannon his brother had bought, had to admit he was not as impressed as he had hoped he would be. He had expected something larger, and the stubby bombarde was no more than two feet long with a large muzzle opening just over a hand's width across. To add to his disappointment, the piece was old, mounted on a very worn and rickety wooden frame and it was filthy and blackened.

It was, however, heavy, and it had taken four of them, all staggering under the weight to lift it from the back of the wagon.

Scranton had watched them heave it from the cart from the comfort of the back of his horse. As they had laboured to bring it safely to the ground, he had offered a continual stream of unhelpful comments. Once it was on the ground, the little man slithered from his saddle, cast the reins in Marc's face without even looking at him and advanced on the bombarde.

"I will need it cleaned, and all this framework here…" Master Scranton pointed at the aged wooden mount, "will need replacing as well."

The men just looked at him and it was Andrew, stepping forward, who spoke first. "I am sure we can get that organised. Pierre helped build the tilt yard and he's some skill with wood. I am sure we can make a sturdier framework to house it in."

"Good. I shall supervise, and make sure you build it to my specifications. I shall have the drawings to you in the morning," Scranton provided.

Pierre shot Andrew a filthy look, the thought of having to work with Master Scranton appealing not at all.

Then Scranton, looking directly at Froggy, added, "And I want it cleaned, inside and out, top and bottom."

"Aye, sir," Froggy acknowledged.

Scranton walked around the antique, his fingers tugging at his chin thoughtfully. "On second thoughts, leave it until I return tomorrow. I would rather make sure you do it right."

Froggy was standing behind Scranton. He swore silently and looked skyward.

Pierre turned his head away hiding a smirk.

"First we need to build a secure place to keep the powder," Scranton decreed.

Scranton fussed over the powder endlessly. Richard gave him Froggy, and Marc to labour for him to build the store he wanted, and Pierre to build the framework for the bombarde.

Powder was not only a volatile commodity, it was also highly valuable, and Scranton insisted that a guard was kept on it at all times. Andrew was in complete agreement with this and a roster was devised to keep a guard on the store, day and night. For reasons of safety, it was located some distance from the main camp but remained within sight.

Scranton's design necessitated building a store that was part underground to keep the powder cool. The ground was dry and hard and the work backbreaking as they took it in turns to dig out the pit which would form the store. When the square was as deep as a man's waist, much to their relief, Scranton declared it to be deep enough. After that a framework of hazel was erected and the whole top covered with cut turf, the thickness of the turfs keeping the interior cool from the sun.

"It's not to scale!" Pierre complained for the third time. "Look at that cross brace there…" his stubby fingers jabbed at the drawing Master Scranton had given him for the framework he wanted making for the bombarde, "it's the same length at this one across the front."

Dan took hold of the drawing and turned it to view the tangle of lines and measurements that Scranton had provided for Pierre. "Which is the top?"

"Give it back here, you've no clue what you are looking at either!" Pierre snatched the plan back.

"Make whatever it is he wants. If it works then it will be his triumph and if it doesn't…"

"… yes I know, it will be my fault," Pierre interjected moodily.

"Master knows what Scranton's like. He'll not hold you to account over it," Dan tried to placate Pierre. The son of a Master carpenter, he had more than enough skills to produce what was needed to hold the bombarde, however Scranton's treatment of him had been little better than if he had been a stray dog in the street and Pierre's professional pride was somewhat dented.

"Aye, well you've got the Master's ear. Let him know what I think of the damned plan, will you?" Some of the anger had left Pierre's voice.

"I will, don't worry about that," Dan laid his hand reassuringly on Pierre's shoulder.

Jack finally found Richard. He was sitting in close conversation with Froggy over the mould they had made, and they were re-examining some of the latest shot it had produced. He was forced to wait until they had finished, and Froggy, mould under his arm, left.

"I can see from the look on your face something is not pleasing you," Richard enquired.

"How much did you pay for it?" Jack asked, dropping into the seat just vacated by Froggy.

"For what?"

"You know what I'm talking about," Jack shot back quickly.

"Oh, the bombarde?"

"Yes. How much?" Jack put the question again.

"Does it matter? We need it to test Scranton's worth."

"So it was expensive then." Jack didn't like at all that their joint worth had been reduced to buy something that was as antiquated as the bombarde.

"It's all relative, and if Scranton's theories are shown to work it will have been well worth it," Richard replied in a manner aimed to calm his brother.

"And if it doesn't?" Jack asked.

"Then I was wrong, and I've wasted our money. That is what you want me to say, isn't it?" Richard replied wearily.

"I just wished I'd known that was what you were buying. I think Scranton's old but for God's sake, Richard, that bombarde is ancient enough to have been at Agincourt!"

Richard grinned. "It probably was, I agree. I know it is not perhaps as impressive a piece as you might have hoped, but Scranton is sure it will serve his purposes and he will be able to show us just how much more effective his powder process is than the conventional method."

"I'll just make sure I'm stood behind him when he lights it." Jack did not sound amused.

†

As it turned out, Scranton refused to light it. That, he argued, was too lowly a task for such a man as himself, plus the bombarde on the new wooden framework crafted by Pierre was far too low for him to reach with his aged back.

There had ensued a swift argument between the men, none of them wanting to be standing too close to the aged cannon when it was fired. Lizbet, sitting on the grass someway distant, the Alaunt's head in her lap, was enjoying the discord. The Master and Jack were standing on opposite sides of the cannon and from the looks on their faces they were not as amused by the situation as she was. Eventually Froggy, losing his temper, snatched the glowing taper from Marc's hand.

"Get out of the way. The lot of you are cowards to a man." And he advanced on the bombarde and reached down to press the lit taper to the fuse.

The others took several steps back to safety. If Froggy had anticipated that the fuse would give him a little time to retreat, he was wrong. As soon as he had straightened from his task, the powder charge ignited and Froggy disappeared from view in a cloud of smoke.

There was a fairly strong breeze and the grey smoke from the powder was quickly whipped away to reveal a shocked Froggy looking down at the remains of the wooden framework. The carriage that had held it was splintered and the cast iron of the cannon was buried in the soft earth with only a foot's length showing above the grass, residual smoke still rolling from the muzzle.

Jack quickly caught his brother's eyes where he stood on the opposite side of the bombarde.

"Master Scranton, a word if I may," the Master announced loudly before turning to leave, an equally shocked elderly powder manufacturer stepping quickly after him.

†

After the morning's mishap with the bombarde, Froggy was happy to return to the training he was providing with the flintlock, and was glad he was no part of the group busy under Scranton's direction repairing the carriage for the cannon. His afternoon group had already assembled and were waiting for him when he arrived. Over his shoulder he carried a hessian bag containing the flintlock they would train with. His group that day consisted of Andrew, Thomas, Jack and Marc. Pierre should have been with them but his services as carpenter were in demand elsewhere. The smaller groups were working well. It meant each had more time with the weapons, and their aim was improving consistently. Loading the flintlocks was not quite second nature but their actions were becoming smoother and quicker the more they practised.

"I hope you lot will be better than the lot I had yesterday. Pierre must have had a quantity of ale. His hands were shaking like a leaf in a gale. I thought he was aiming for the pigeons not the target." Froggy swung the bag from his back onto a trestle table that he had set up near the practice range.

"Pierre's hands always shake," Marc laughed. "It's your fault, Froggy, you make him nervous."

"I'll make you nervous in a minute," Froggy chortled as he laid out the flintlock, powder and lead balls.

Lizbet, a water jug on her hip, and cups in her hand, walked over and joined the group, Kells trailing close behind. "It's a hot afternoon. I thought you might like a drink."

"I hope that's ale you've got in there." Jack leant to sniff the jug.

"If it is, Lizbet, you can take it back again. I'm having none of this lot taking shots with fuddled brains." Froggy admonished.

"It's well water, cold and fresh," she advised, dropping the jug onto Froggy's table. The weight made the table tip and Froggy's row of neatly lined up musket balls began to roll towards the edge.

"Shift that, woman." Froggy began to quickly round them up before they rolled off to be lost in the grass. "You know yourself how long it takes to make the damn things."

Lizbet retrieved the jug and balanced it on her hip again.

"Right then, who's first?" Froggy announced, satisfied that he had everything laid out on the table again to his liking.

Nearest to the table and the flintlock was Thomas, and he reached automatically for it.

It was Andrew who stopped him, saying, "Let Jack go first. He's itching to show us how much he's improved."

"When you are that bad to start with, it's not hard to show an improvement," laughed Froggy.

Jack reached for one of the cups Lizbet had brought and held it out for her to fill. "I'll let someone else set the standard today. Go on, Marc, you go first. Let's see if you can hit the target today."

Marc, of all of them, had the worst aim it had seemed. Froggy suspected his eyesight was not as good as it could be but Marc argued hotly that he could see just as well as the rest of them, which had led to him being presented constantly with a series of eyesight challenges which he invariably failed.

Marc, grumbling, pushed past Thomas and began to load the flintlock under Froggy's watchful gaze.

"I'll stand behind you. I think that will be the safest place," Jack jibed.

"Take no notice of Jack." Lizbet moved round to stand a few paces from Marc. "He just can't stand Froggy telling him what to do."

Marc, intent on his tasks, ignored them all. The ball rammed home, he laid the rod on the table and hoisted the flintlock to his shoulder. Screwing his eyes up and holding his breath, he levelled the barrel towards the target. Marc pulled the trigger, and the gun misfired.

Marc was enveloped in a cloud of smoke as the powder flashed back. Screaming, he dropped the flintlock.

The powder had burnt the right side of his face and his right hand as well was scorched.

"Lizbet, the water," Jack shouted at her.

Lizbet didn't move.

"Woman, the water, pass it here!"

Jack turning towards her saw why she didn't move. Part of the shattered wooden stock was impaled in her left arm. Blood poured from the wound and her face was the colour of flour.

☦

Lizbet, her face white, clutched the bleeding arm to her chest and shook her head.

"Lizbet, please, just drink this," Jack tried again, holding the cup to her lips.

Lizbet twisted her head away. "No, not that, please. I saw what it did to Colan."

Jack sat back down heavily. Mat watched from behind Lizbet but kept his mouth shut.

"Alright then," Jack reassured, his voice still calm and even, "just let me look, lass, please. One of us needs to see what needs doing, you know that, don't you?"

Lizbet sniffed loudly but didn't move.

"It'll be alright, Lizbet, I promise you," Jack smiled. On the table already was a bowl and cloths. "I will get rid of all of this lot." Jack put them down the other end of the table. "Now all I want to do is look, Lizbet, that's all. I won't touch you, I promise. Look, I've got my hands on my knees. Now just put your arm on the table, lass, and let's have a look. It might be it's not that bad at all, a bit of blood always makes things look ten times worse."

Jack was still smiling, his voice gentle, calming.

Lizbet relented. Letting go of her arm, shakily she laid it on the table.

"Well done, lass. Now then, you don't need to look it. That's right, you look over there at the fire. You just keep your eyes on the flames."

What Jack saw was not as bad as he had first feared. The powder had flashed back and burnt the material of her sleeve to her skin, and when the stock of the flintlock had exploded it had embedded two shards of wood in her arm. They hadn't gone in too far and the material, although burnt, had shielded the skin from the worst of the powder burn.

"Good lass, Lizbet, you keep looking at the fire." Jack raised his eyes quickly and looked at Mat stood behind her. Mat knew what Jack wanted him to do, and he quietly stood ready.

There was a nod from Jack and Mat had firm hands on her, one hand on her wrist pinning it to the table and another on her waist holding her fast. She screamed and pulled against his hold but couldn't free herself and was left sobbing and breathless.

Jack, a knife in his hand, appearing unconcerned by the noise from his patient and, completely absorbed in his task, began to carefully cut away the material, and piece by piece peel it away from the cut.

"Lizbet, please lass, have a drink of this. It will make it so much easier for you." Jack picked up the cup again but Lizbet's mouth was firmly closed and the eyes that held his were full of fear. "I'll be as kind as I can."

When Richard and Dan entered the room, Lizbet's protests had stopped and her head lolled against Mat's shoulder.

Jack was still talking to her quietly, his voice level, and his tone didn't change when he spoke to Richard. "Just keep the noise down. I'll be all done here soon. Right then, Lizbet, that's the last piece out." There were two cuts that had closed now the shards of wood had been removed. Jack squeezed the cuts together. Lizbet flinched, and Jack's brow furrowed. "I don't think I need to stitch those, they'll close by themselves. You've been lucky, lass."

There was a mumbled reply, that Jack couldn't make out, however Mat's ear closer to Lizbet's mouth picked up the words, and he grinned. "Lizbet doesn't feel she's been that lucky," he supplied.

The burn though from her wrist to her elbow he knew would probably be more painful than the cuts. Jack applied the same balm he had used on his brother and sat back. "Mat, you can let the lass go. Lizbet, can you hear me?"

Mat released her and she slid from his hold face down on the table. It was Jack who picked her up and carried her to the bed in his brother's room. Laying her on the bed, he looked at her face. Her closed eyes were swollen from crying, her cheeks tear-streaked and still spattered with her own blood. An exchange of coin secured the services of Emile, the landlord's daughter, to sit with her during the night.

Emile felt sorry for the girl, and quickly had Lizbet stripped to a shift and bundled beneath the covers. She made sure Lizbet finished the drink which the man who had carried her in had provided. He assured the girl in the bed that it was only aqua vitae, and soon after drinking it she was soundly asleep.

Jack ran his bloodstained hands through his hair and resolved very much that he needed a drink. Walking into the inn proper, he found Froggy Tate at a table, the split and tattered remains of the flintlock on the table in front of him, and helping him dissect and analyse the damaged gun were Andrew, Thomas and Scranton.

"What a day." Jack dropped heavily onto the trestle next to Andrew.

"The lass, is she alright and Marc?" Andrew asked quickly, concern in his voice.

"Lizbet will be fine. She's asleep in Richard's room. The cuts are not deep, but the burn she has will hurt for days. Marc's lost half his beard! I think he is suffering more from that than the burn he got. What the hell happened, Froggy?"

The little man shook his head. "I don't know. Look here, the pan and the frizzen have been blown off the side and half the wood from the stock has been torn apart."

Andrew reached over and pulled the remains of the gun towards him. "Maybe Marc rammed the musket ball in too firmly and then when it fired it blocked the barrel?"

"I watched him and what he was doing was fine." Froggy sounded puzzled.

"Were you using the musket balls from the new mould?" It was Scranton who chimed in now. Froggy nodded. "I told you they were misshapen. The sprues were too large. Chances are the ball got stuck in the barrel."

"That's what's worrying me," Froggy's said, lines creasing his brow. "I've never seen anything like this happen before."

Andrew leaned over the table and clasped Froggy's arm. "It's not your fault. We can do some tests with the other flintlocks and the new musket balls and find out if that's the case, but you mustn't blame yourself."

Froggy smiled half-heartedly at Andrew. "Easier said than done. I've a liking for the lass, and I'm sorry for what has happened."

"Good God!" exclaimed Scranton. "Look, look!" Scranton, his eyes wide, was holding up the end of the flintlock. Although part of the stock had been blown apart, the butt remained intact and there, in the metal engraving at the end was a clearly hammered cross.

Jack ripped it from Scranton's hand, his mouth open in disbelief. "Christ! How did this one end up in use? It's one of the ones Richard said had been taken apart and were never to be fired."

Jack found Richard descending the stairs from his own room where Lizbet was now in his bed watched over by Emile.

"I've seen it. It's as plain as day. The flintlock that exploded is marked, like the ones you showed us." Jack, already three steps up, stopped his brother's progress.

For a moment only, Richard looked confused. "Those ones are locked away. It can't be."

"Well then, show me them," Jack demanded, taking another step up the stairs.

"They are locked in the coffer in my room." Richard quickly turned retracing his steps. "Be quiet though, Lizbet is in there."

Both men entered the room and under the disapproving gaze of Emile, Richard produced a key and unlocked the coffer. Inside wrapped in cloth was the pistol and the flintlock.

"I told you, they are both locked in here," Richard said under his breath.

Jack, not satisfied, lifted the flintlock out and unrolled it from the cloth wrapping, exposing the stock. Where there should have been a neatly hammered cross, there was none.

"How the hell did you mix them up?" Jack blurted loudly.

"Please, some quiet for the girl?" Emile had a disapproving look on her face.

Richard took the gun from Jack, and stared at the stock. His eyes met Jack's, his voice serious. "I don't know. They have not been out of here since the night I showed them to you all."

"That's not true though, is it? One of them is in pieces downstairs after it blew up in Marc's face!" Jack's voice was angry.

"Please! Some quiet," Emile chastened them again from the chair where she was seated, and Kells, laid across the bottom of the bed, his head on Lizbet's feet, emitted a threatening growl.

"Come on, out of here." Richard took the flintlock, dropping it back none too gently into the coffer and locking the lid. Then taking Jack's elbow, he propelled him from the room.

†

Andrew and Richard were at Froggy's range. The table was still there. The musket balls had all rolled into the grass when Lizbet had dropped the jug onto the table. A dried bloody handprint showed where she had leaned on the boards for support.

"It's a terrible thing what has happened, and I know you are suffering for it," Andrew said quietly, coming to stand close to Richard.

"I don't know how it happened," was all Richard said in reply. "The coffer is locked, I have the key, and they have never left it since the night I showed them to you all. Never."

Andrew sounded sad when he spoke. "Sometimes what can seem impossible becomes very probable. Did you ever lend anyone else the key perhaps?"

Richard shook his head.

"The woman, Lizbet… she is often in your room. Could she have had access to them?" Andrew continued to question.

"It wasn't Lizbet." Richard sounded distracted.

Andrew laid a hand on Richard's arm. "Leave this with me, please. I will find out who has had their hands on them and switched them over. One of them will turn out to be the son of a locksmith. We will find out how this happened."

Andrew's diligent enquiries however took him only to a host of dead ends. There was only one person who had access to them, and that was the man who held the key to the coffer – Richard.

Chapter 16
A Bond is Cut

†

The mood was sombre. Word it seemed had travelled swiftly amongst them that one of the marked flintlocks had been used in error. Andrew had asked each of them searching questions about whether they'd had access to those guns. With Lizbet absent, none of them wanted to play cards and they were a drunken and melancholy group that evening, especially Jack who had drunk far more than was usual and wanted no company, despite Andrew's best efforts to get him to join the others.

Work was rapidly completed the following day on the second carriage for the bombarde. Pierre when questioned by Richard had admitted that the wood he had used had simply not been thick enough to take the force of the explosion from the barrel. It was, he had pleaded, not his fault. Building gun carriages was not something he had ever done before and he had adhered to Master Scranton's plan. The Master had accepted his apology and Pierre had set to making a second on a much larger scale, the wood supports on this one being four times as thick. Also Pierre's design included far fewer joints so there were a vastly reduced number of weak points in the whole structure.

A day later the mood lightened a little. Lizbet was up and although pale as fresh linen she had accepted their kind comments with a smile and not one of them pressed her with tasks. She was again seated on the grass, perhaps this time a little further back from the bombarde, with Kells laid at her side, watching Scranton reload the cannon.

This time there was no debate about who would light the fuse, and Froggy, a smoking taper in his hand, stepped forward and pressed the hot end to the fuse. As before the bombarde exploded almost immediately, however this time when the cloud of smoke dispersed, the barrel was still firmly in place on Pierre's re-crafted wooden mount.

Pierre's relief was palpable. "Thank the Lord for that!" He advanced towards the smoking gun intent on seeing if any of the joints had suffered on the framework.

Even Master Scranton looked relieved. "A good result. Now we can test it with shot," he announced, turning to regard Richard with a smile.

The bombarde was cleared, and under Scranton's supervision it was reloaded and this time on top of the packed powder was a stone shot.

Scranton talked all the time. "Please, Master Fitzwarren come closer, I wish you to see how this is packed so you know that the same process will be used with the second type of shot I have developed."

Richard moved closer, and Scranton without even asking, grasped Froggy's arm and used it as a support to lower himself down onto his creaking knees. "This is a conventional sized charge. The shot we have here are the same size." Scranton indicated the two stone balls waiting to be loaded next to the cannon. Richard nodded, and Scranton continued. "I wish you to see that I am going to prepare both charges in exactly the same way, the only difference between them will be the type of shot used."

Scranton finished and waved his right arm in the air. Froggy, his face set in a grim expression, obliged and lifted the little man neatly back up.

"Right, that is all set." Scranton backed away several paces as did Richard, and Froggy moved forward and lit the charge in the barrel.

The explosion this time was of a different order. This time the charge was not just igniting, it was also propelling the shot from the barrel and the ground around them shook with the force of it. Froggy jumped and Kells howled.

Scranton was talking before the smoke had cleared. "Go on, find it," he commanded.

It didn't take long. Both of the shot balls had been treated to a coat of limewash to whiten them and make them easier to find. It was Dan, shouting from the field, who signalled that he had located the first cannon ball laid in its own small crater in the field. The spot was marked and Scranton, watched closely by Richard, prepared the bombarde again.

"This is the type of black powder we will use this time." Opening a cloth bag, he showed the black pellets to Richard.

"Looks like rabbit shit to me," Jack, standing and looking over Richard's shoulder, observed unhelpfully.

The two kneeling men ignored him.

"I am using two thirds of the quantity I used last time. Do you agree?" Scranton asked.

"I agree. Yes, there is less," Richard affirmed.

"Good, now watch," Scranton instructed, completing the loading process.

Froggy hauled Scranton back to his feet and again advanced with the taper to fire the bombarde.

It was Dan again who found the second shot, and he was standing a good thirty paces further away than where a stick pushed into the earth marked spot where the first stone ball landed.

Richard's eyebrows raised. He advanced and flung an arm around the little man's shoulders. "It seems, Master Scranton, that you need to come and tell me all about this. I am wholly convinced."

Jack, looking at Scranton, thought bitterly that he had never seen the little weasel look happier than at that moment.

"Come on, hand it over, boys." Mat's mouth behind his scraggy beard had split into a wide, satisfied grin as he cast his eyes over his companions. He did not realise the error of his words until his eyes met those of the Master who was not smiling at all.

Lizbet, who missed very little, saw the brief exchange and winced. This was a bet Mat was going to regret placing.

†

"He has a punishment coming and he knows it." There was concern in Andrew's voice.

Richard did not reply, but the look on his face told the other he knew what he said was true.

"He was fairly warned last week. Men like Mat will sin again and again if it goes unchecked," Andrew pressed.

"I know," Richard accepted. "I live in simple hope that my words will be listened to."

"And after what Jack did, Mat had plenty of reasons to expect to avoid punishment for his actions," Andrew added.

Richard's eyes narrowed. He had never entertained the thought of publicly punishing Jack for poaching.

"You should let me do it. You are his brother. His discipline you can delegate, the men would accept that, and so would he," Andrew suggested. "William Marshall said it is never a kindness to defer discipline, and he was right."

"Was he ever wrong?" Richard replied drily, and, picking up a whip, set his feet toward the yard where all the men were assembled waiting for him.

Lizbet was pushed inside so she missed the first part of the tongue lashing Mat received, however after hurtling up the stairs followed by an excited Kells and running into the Master's room, she had a good view of the proceedings taking place in the yard. There was no need to worry about the Master finding her there as he was currently in the yard, sitting on the edge of the back of the cart, legs swinging in the air, while a very penitent Mat knelt on the ground before him wearing shirt and hose only.

The rest of the men, silent and watchful, were arranged around the yard. Lizbet knew it had all gone too far now for Mat to be able to leave without a beating, that was for sure. The Master had promised punishment if his rules were flouted and Mat, a habitual gambler, had crossed the line once too often by betting on the Master's endeavours. She had little sympathy for him either. Froggy had told him the Master gave him fair warning a week ago when he had placed bets on the outcome of a training bout between Andrew and Jack. Froggy was of the opinion the Master had been too lenient at the time.

As she watched, the verbal punishment ended, and Mat stood and shrugged his shirt off over his head, laying it on the top of a barrel in the yard before kneeling once again.

The whip cracked, Kells' ears pricked up and he pushed his head past his Mistress. Lizbet, a firm hand holding him by the scruff of his neck, stopped him from jumping up at the window. A second lash. Lizbet, stood to one side of the window, seeing the livid red line appear across Mat's back. Mat, kneeling, took the lash, his body jerking to the pain of it, but he remained kneeling, waiting for the next.

Lizbet grimaced when the leather impacted on flesh for a third and then a fourth time. The whip spoke one more time. Mat lost his balance and found himself falling forward and, holding himself up on shaking arms, he vomited between his hands, saliva and bile running in sticky tendrils from his beard.

Richard. without a backward glance. threw the whip in the cart bed, turned his back on the assembled men and without another word left.

Lizbet, loosening her hold on Kells, let out a long breath. At least it was over. Already turning to leave, aware that the Master might return to his room, she stopped when she heard Andrew's command from below.

"Hold him still, lads!"

Hands on the window frame she stared down into the yard. What was happening?

Jack, his shirt ripped to his waist, was on his knees and Thomas and Froggy had hold of an arm each, pinning him there. From the angle she could not see Jack's face.

"The lads are going to let go, and I expect you to take this like a man, like Mat did." Andrew's voice sounded like it belonged in a pulpit.

Lizbet couldn't hear what Jack said, but a moment later both Froggy and Thomas released his arms and head bowed, he knelt in the yard as Mat had done and waited for the lash.

Andrew wasted no time, and the strokes, hard and deliberate, were laid on at a pace Richard had not used. Jack had no time to recover from one stroke before the whip was reversed and laid on his back again. Lizbet had her fist in her mouth. She counted seven strokes, then an eighth was delivered and Jack fell forwards and lay sprawled on his front in the yard. The lash had broken the skin on one of the strokes and blood ran from his back.

Nine.

Another stroke was delivered.

Christ! He's not stopping.

"Enough!" she screamed from the open window. Lizbet, eyes blazing, turned to run from the room and cannoned into Richard coming through the door.

If he was going to ask her what she was doing, she did not stop to give him the opportunity, pushing past him, one hand on Kells' collar, and dragging the dog with her, she took the stairs two at a time and ran for the yard.

"Stop!" Lizbet screamed, "Stop now!"

Andrew turned, the whip coiled in his hand, his face set and hard. "I do not like what I have had to do. I am pained as much as Jack is, but the Master will have discipline." Then casting his eyes over the rest of the men. "Do you hear me? The Master will not tolerate breaches of the rules, not even from his own flesh and blood. So let this be a lesson, and heed it well," Andrew pronounced, and then to Marc and Pierre, "Get him inside and get his woman to see to him."

Richard, shaking hands on the window frame, heard the final pronouncement from the yard below and closed his eyes against the scene below him.

☦

"Lie still, will you?" Lizbet scolded.

"I am lying still. If the devil himself was in the room now I couldn't move to get away," Jack mumbled, his face in the pillow.

Jack had been rolled onto his back when Froggy and Pierre had tried to help get him from the yard and back inside, and there was mud, and worse, stuck to the blood on his back.

"Jesus!" Jack groaned. He pushed himself up on his right elbow, grasped the cup from the table near the bed and emptied it for the third time. "Fill it again." The empty cup rattled noisily back on the wood.

Lizbet had a flask and unstoppering it, she refilled the cup with aqua vitae. Jack emptied it straight away and the flask still in her hand, she refilled it.

"Just be careful you don't make yourself sick," Lizbet warned.

Jack emptied it again and dropped back flat on the bed.

Lizbet shook the flask. He'd had most of it. She refilled the cup for him and resolved to wait a while before she started to clean his back again until the aqua vitae took a proper hold.

She was sitting on the edge of the bed trying to judge whether he was asleep or awake when the door opened, and Richard, unannounced, stood in the room.

Lizbet was on her feet between them in a moment, a cloth stained red held out in front of her. "You'll not come near him, you hear!"

"Get out!" Jack's words were still clearly spoken despite the ministrations of the alcohol.

Richard looked between them for a moment, then turning on his heel, he left, slamming the door in the frame behind him.

†

"Did I say whip him?" Richard growled.

Andrew's eyes were wide. "God forgive me! I misunderstood. I thought you meant for me to take his punishment upon myself. I hated it, but I did it. Jack's a good man and I will seek his forgiveness."

"I didn't say punish him, did I?" Richard's voice was incredulous.

Andrew laid his hand on Richard's arm. "You told me you agreed with William Marshall's words. I thought you had meant to discipline him." Then when Richard looked at him blankly. "Poaching those birds could have brought your venture to an end. He needs to recognise that and accept his punishment."

Richard was shaking his head. "I didn't say …"

Andrew's grip on his arm tightened. "It's done. The men will respect you for it. Jack will as well, in time. Marshall told us the lessons we learn painfully are the most important."

Richard wrenched his arm free. "Damn William Marshall!"

Chapter 17 An Inevitable Ending

Whan the turuf is thy tour,
And thy pit is thy bour,
Thy fel and thy whitë throtë
Shullen wormës to notë.
What helpëth thee thennë
Al the worildë wennë?

✝

They did not see Jack for a day. And when he returned he was pale and wore only a loose shirt. Only one of the track marks had broken the skin, the others had just left flat sore brands across his back. When Lizbet cleaned away the blood and dirt, the damage, although painful, was not as bad as she first feared. The real damage though was to Jack's relationship with his brother; that he had suffered such a brutal and public humiliation from Richard, even if the delivery had been made indirectly, was tearing at his soul. Jack's mood was dark, and his temper sore.

As soon as Andrew heard that Jack had been seen outside his room, he had gone in search of him.

"I told the Master I would seek your forgiveness for what he made me do, and I hope I shall, in time, gain it." Andrew delivered the words seriously. Andrew dropped to his knees before Jack, his head bowed. "I humble myself before you, and any penance you see fitting I shall accept."

Jack, for once, was stuck for words. Any anger he had felt towards Andrew dissipated in his confusion.

"For God's sake, get up," Jack implored. "It's not you I have an argument with. It's my brother."

†

Mat heard it before he saw it. The sound was like thunder and his eyes moved automatically to look at the clouds above him. That though, was not where the sound had come from. As he lowered his gaze back to the lane before him, he saw what was making the booming drumming sound. The cart, untethered from the horses and still laden with the wood cut for building a new firing range, was heading down the narrow lane towards him. The cartwheels fast in the ruts kept it on a downward track and the steep banks at either side left Mat little room for escape.

He threw himself to one side and hoped the cart would pass him, but as it did the rut nearest him deepened, the cart dipped towards him, and the side struck him squarely on the temple, felling him instantly.

The cart continued to rumble on until the road levelled out and, losing momentum, it rolled to a halt as the lane began to rise again.

Mat lay in a pool of spreading blood on the road; his body was still by the time they reached him.

"Mat!" Richard dropped to his knees next to the crumpled heap of the man at the side of the road.

Mat's eyes looked towards the voice, unfocused, his lips parted. Richard, his head close to Mat's ears, spoke softly, the words he said too quiet to be heard by the men behind him. A ringed hand swept gently across Mat's face and closed his unseeing eyes, whose final sight had been the clouds racing across the sky above.

The first noise was the skittering of pebbles and the sound of boots on the road as Andrew came running down the hill to fetch up next to Marc and Pierre who stood holding their horses.

"What's happened? I saw the wagon rolling down the hill. There was nothing I could do," Andrew exclaimed.

Richard, still knelt, said nothing, his head bent and one hand resting lightly on the dead man's arm.

"It's Mat," Pierre managed. "I think he's dead."

Andrew looked around the group, and took charge. "Pierre, take the Master's horse back to the inn and fetch the rest of the men, then get the cart and put Mat on it. Now go."

Marc and Pierre were galvanised into action by Andrew's quick words of command.

Andrew spoke quietly. "It was an accident. Let me see to him, Master." When he didn't get an answer, Andrew laid a gentle hand on Richard's shoulder. If he was shocked by the reaction it provoked, it did not show on Andrew's face.

Richard pulled from the touch as if burnt and was on his feet facing Andrew. Turning, Richard set off to walk back up the hill, leaving Andrew alone with Mat's cooling body.

†

"I do not want company." Richard's words were quiet, and upon hearing them, Dan nodded and heeded the warning leaving the Master alone at the table.

Lizbet, followed by the Alaunt, moved through the tables and brought a fresh flask and a cup and put them down silently before him. Pulling the stopper from the earthenware flask, she filled the cup and set it near to where his hand rested on the table. Richard didn't look up, his fingers stretched for it and took it into his keeping. A moment later it was once more on the table, empty. Lizbet filled it again, slowly.

A cat, the inn mouser and chief rat catcher, chose that moment to stroll into the room, proprietary, tail high and eyes observant. The Alaunt saw the cat first. Tail windmilling, paws spread, it barked at its feline foe, hackles raised and running the length of the black fury body.

"Shut it up, Lizbet, or I'll cut its damned throat!" Richard growled through clenched teeth.

Lizbet, two hands on Kells' collar, swearing under her breath, dragged the excited and barking dog from the room. Moments later, Richard and the jar of aqua vitae had also disappeared.

†

Froggy sought out Dan's company, finding him in the stables, a cloth in one hand, grease in the other, cleaning his mare's saddle. The big man was quiet. Deep lines furrowing his brow, he acknowledged Froggy who hitched himself up on the end of a saddle rack.

"I can't sit in there with them any longer," Froggy said eventually.

Dan met his eyes. "I know. It's no way to behave on the day of a man's death. I've known Mat a lot of years and a bit of respect is what's needed."

In the inn, primarily fuelled by Thomas and Scranton, a heated and drunken debate was in progress about how the wagon had ended up rolling down the hill towards Mat. They might not be naming the Master as being wholly to blame for Mat's death but that was the unspoken conclusion. Scranton and Thomas were raking the facts over and over until Froggy felt his temper rise and he'd left.

"Andrew's taking it badly as well," Froggy added.

"Is he? Why's that then?" The tone in Dan's voice told that he was not overly concerned with Andrew's suffering.

"He feels he is to blame. He'd tried to fix the brake. If he'd done a better job of it then the accident might not have happened," Froggy supplied, leaning his chin on folded arms and regarding Dan from under his bushy eyebrows.

"Well, he is probably right then. He should have repaired it properly," Dan answered roughly.

Dan was the Master's man, and Froggy knew he would never hear a word said against him; the tone in his voice told Froggy that he considered the line of conversation closed.

☦

Lizbet's hands were clamped over her mouth. The scream she had made had Froggy running across the yard in a moment. Lizbet, seeing him, flung herself against him and Froggy closed his arms around her.

"Lass, what's happened?"

Lizbet couldn't speak; she was sobbing loudly and pointed to the wood pile.

Froggy pushed her behind him, and with a knife in his hand, he advanced on the wood pile. What he found on the other side though needed no knife. Lizbet's Alaunt, Kells, lay in a pool of congealed blood, its throat sliced through. Froggy turned back and folded his arms around the crying girl and led her from the yard.

"What is it?" Jack was on the doorstep as Froggy, Lizbet still clamped to him, entered.

Froggy said not a word but the movement of his head sent Jack across the yard to where the Alaunt lay.

Jack knelt down and looked into the glassy eyes of the hound. He slid his hands across the dog's body, cold, but still soft, and underneath, between the dog and the ground, he could still feel the last of dog's warmth. He'd not been dead long then, less than half an hour at the most.

Picking the Alaunt up, Jack carried him the short distance and lay his body in the folds of green bracken near the edge of the wood. The carrion would have him now, and he'd be gone in a few days. He felt little for the dog, but for Lizbet, at that moment he would have killed anyone.

Striding back to the inn, he found her still with Froggy.

"Lass, come here." Jack put his arms around her and pulled her into a quiet, silent embrace. Lizbet felt numb. Her head against his chest, she wrapped her arms around him and wept.

☦

Jack finally found his brother sitting alone in the churchyard, his back to a stone marking the final resting place of a long dead member of the village. Jack dropped to sit opposite him, his legs crossed on the grass. It was the first time they had spoken since Andrew had applied the lash to him in the yard.

Jack expected Richard to say something when he found him, and when he didn't, he said bluntly, "You do know they all think you killed the dog?"

Richard, with his knees drawn up, forearms resting on them, looked at Jack levelly. "I didn't kill the dog."

"I know," Jack accepted. "Sometimes your own words are a little too accurate."

"Which ones?" Richard asked bleakly.

"Remember you told me we need to suffer for our mistakes if we are ever to learn from them?" Jack replied.

Richard raised his head and met Jack's blue level gaze. "I did not mean you to suffer. I…"

Jack cut him off. "I don't care what you meant, 'tis done. I have learnt my lesson well, make no mistake about that."

Richard dropped his head back to his knees; there was little he could say to appease his brother's anger with him. Anything he could say would sound nothing but a poor excuse, and it was too late. Jack had suffered the humiliation in front of the men. They knew now just how much esteem he held his brother in and there was nothing, nothing at all he could do about that.

"It was the break on the cart that was at fault. Why didn't you listen to Andrew? If you'd bloody well had it fixed, this wouldn't have happened." Jack wanted his brother to very much know where the blame for Mat's death lay.

"I checked it, Jack. I swear I did. It wasn't loose." Richard sounded anguished.

Jack saw the pain in his brother's eyes and ignored it. "Andrew said it kept coming loose. He's taking it badly as well. He's blaming himself for not having checked it again, or for having fixed it badly last time."

"It's certainly not Andrew's fault. I will talk to him," Richard replied.

"Good, it's not right for him to have to shoulder the responsibility for this. He's a good man, and bless him, God fearing." Jack stood smoothly and looked down at his brother. He suppressed the urge to extend an arm to pull his brother to his feet – those days were gone. Instead he said, "Come on, you need to face the men, and Andrew."

"Why did you come to find me?" Richard asked suddenly.

"I wasn't going to. Then Andrew was about to set himself to look for you. He feels Mat's death is his own doing and I'd not let you accept that from him. The fault was yours. That you don't have Pierre's and Lizbet's blood on your hands as well from that gun that exploded is only by sheer luck," Jack said bitterly.

Richard looked up at him from where he still sat on the ground. "And of course my own treatment of you has not helped my case either, has it?"

Jack took in a deep breath. "Next time you want to teach me a lesson, use your own hands and not those of another. What you did was bad enough, but to mire Andrew in it was shameful."

Richard rested his head back against the gravestone, his eyes closed. "Answer me one more question?"

"I might," was the reply from Jack.

"Do you think I killed it?" Richard opened his eyes and regarded Jack closely.

"You have to ask?" Jack's cold blue eyes met his brother's.

"After what I've done, yes I do."

Jack didn't hear his words, he had already begun to walk back to the camp.

☦

Mat was buried with little ceremony in the churchyard. Richard paid for the service and the church dues and the internment was quickly and efficiently performed. It was summer, the temperatures hot, and everyone was aware that Mat would be better under the soil as soon as possible.

By the end of the funeral service, they wanted little more than to move to the inn and remember Mat in words that were not mumbled in Latin and punctuated with the heady smell of incense.

As they emerged into the light from the church, Andrew turned to Richard, a hand on his arm, and said, "Let me say a word, if I may?"

Richard, left with little choice, nodded his assent.

"Lads, the Master has provided coin for food and ale, and it would be a credit to a good man's memory to spend an afternoon in remembrance of Mat. Let's give him a proper send off, and remember him as he would wish to be remembered."

There was a general nodding of heads, and Andrew, throwing an arm around Marc and Froggy's shoulders, announced, "Then we shall lead the way, and Mat, should his soul still tarry, will be heartened by our thoughts and words of him this day." With that, he headed the march that led them all from the church back to the inn.

The long tables had been pulled together and food and ale had been laid along the length for them when they returned to the inn. They all took seats apart from Richard who seated himself apart from the rest. He knew this day they would want to talk of Mat, of what had happened, and if he sat at the table with them he would stilt their conversation.

Richard was seated far enough away from him that Thomas knew he could not hear their words. "It could have been avoided. The man shouldn't have died," Thomas stated bluntly.

Andrew raised his hand. "Men die, it is the nature of things, and we are in the business of war so it is…"

Thomas interrupted. "I accept that, but this was not a death brought about on the battlefield, was it? This was brought about by carelessness. You warned him often enough about the wagon break; if he had heeded your words then Mat would still be alive."

"Now Thomas, that's a rash statement and we cannot know for sure. I'm sure the Master did check it, and I wish I had done a better job of the repair." Andrew's voice was full of pain.

Thomas reached over and laid a hand on his shoulder. "You cannot blame yourself."

It was Dan who spoke next. "It was an accident. I'm sure the Master checked it."

"He's a temper on him and there was no need to take it out on the lass's dog either." Thomas was adamant that every one of them should see where the blame squarely fell.

Marc and Pierre remained silent, but exchanged uneasy looks. Jack had said little, but they noticed he did not move to defend his brother; he seemed intent only on emptying the cup before him and then the jug as quickly and methodically as possible. The mood was sombre and expectant. Something was about to happen.

Lizbet, sitting next to Froggy, saw the flask one of the tavern girls placed in front of Richard. It wasn't full of ale, and she knew no good would come of him drinking it either. Making a quick decision, she took one of the ale jugs from their table and took it to him.

Lizbet's eyes were reddened and sore; even she did not know who she'd shed the most tears for, Mat or Kells. When she put the ale jug on the table before him, she avoided his gaze.

Reaching out, he wrapped his hand around her wrist. "Lizbet, I am sorry."

She nodded and as he looked he saw her eyes fill up again, tears threatening to run down her cheeks. "I've never had anything someone didn't try and take from me." Pulling her hand from his, she made a quick move to take the flask containing the aqua vitae, but quicker than her he grabbed it, shaking his head at her. Lizbet, a look of resignation on her face, released her hold on it and returned to her place next to Froggy.

Richard sat immobile, elbows planted on the table, head resting in his hands. Jack, sitting next to Dan, watched him closely.

When he spoke, the hushed conversation stopped immediately.

"My father…" Richard's eyes looked at each of them in turn. "…would tup anything, however it is said that we should not be held to account for the sins of our fathers."

Jack felt his stomach twist; he had not expected this. The men knew he was Richard's bastard brother but no more. Was this going to be some sort of public apology? He bloody well hoped not.

Richard stood and walked between the trestle tables they sat at.

"We are not in England, but the law there is well defined. If a man, or his family, acknowledges a bastard, then they can take their family name."

The men glanced at Jack. They knew he was the Master's bastard brother, so where was this going? Jack's throat was tight; he didn't know either.

"My father is not here, but I am. My name is Richard Fitzwarren, and it pleases me now to sit in the company of my sister." Richard's hand was outstretched towards Lizbet.

Dan choked on his ale.

The cup fell from Jack's hand, spilling the contents across the table.

Jack's eyes glanced blindly between the pair, and Lizbet, staring at the outstretched hand, realised she had no other choice but to place hers within its cool firm hold. As she did, a half smile played on his face, and leading her to the table, he sat her next to him. Lizbet, her face pale, sank onto the chair, her hands shaking in her lap. Richard resumed his seat and dropped his head back into his hands.

Jack swallowed hard, and was not sure if it was relief for himself or for Lizbet.

Lizbet sat, her back straight, her trembling hands held tight her lap, and her gaze fastened on the table. She felt the eyes of all of the men on her and dared not turn and look at them.

☦

Jack's anger at his brother was fuelled now by drink and Mat's death. Richard tried to push past him, but Jack caught him by the shoulders and pushed him hard against the wall of the corridor.

Jack's words were quiet, and meant for his brother's ears only. "Do you know what you have done?" With his hands still on Richard's shoulders, Jack rammed him hard against the wall again. "Do you?"

Richard made no move to free himself from the hold. "Why? What have I done?"

Jack moved his face even closer to his brother's. "Because of you I am a murderer. I have committed treason. Twice. I have been involved in burglary and traded in stolen goods. And now…" Jack took a deep breath. "…and now, not satisfied with humiliating me at Andrew's hands, you have just added incest to the list." Jack felt Richard's shoulders shake beneath his hands, and realised he was laughing silently.

Jack's hands dug into into his brother's shoulders and he pulled him forward before banging him back hard against the wood panelling.

"Why is that funny?" he demanded.

"You should thank me. Just think how dull your life was before you met me. I'll make sure you can add blasphemy and heresy to the list before we are done." Richard, quicker than Jack and not quite as drunk as he had appeared, knocked his brother's hands away, breaking the hold.

"She can be your Hera then, can't she?" Richard said as he nimbly ducked under Jack's arm, opened the door behind them in a smooth movement and slammed it, leaving Jack alone in the corridor.

"Damn you!" Jack turned on his heel and stalked off back the way he had come.

†

"I'm not going," Lizbet said for the third time.

"Yes you are." Dan took her by the shoulders, turned her around and with a good push in the small of her back, sent her towards the stairs. Grumbling under her breath, Lizbet mounted the wooden stairs and made her way reluctantly to the Master's room.

Lizbet had no idea what was going on. Richard's drunken pronouncement had left them staring at her and she had refused to comment. If it was some kind of twisted drunken joke from the Master, it had not been a very funny one, leaving her shamefaced with her cheeks burning.

Reaching the door, Lizbet paused. She'd done this once before and ended up regretting it. She took a steadying deep breath and tapped firmly on the door. No reply. Lizbet tapped again.

For Lord's sake woman stop being a fool.

Lizbet firmly pressed the door open and stepped inside. Quickly she scanned the room. The occupant was, it appeared, out cold, sitting at the table, arms outstretched across the wood, cheek against the cold surface, eyes closed. A cup lay on its side, the spilt aqua vitae still wet on the table, the smell stale and acrid.

Tentatively she lay the back of her hand on his cheek; he didn't acknowledge her touch and the skin was cold. Pulling the counterpane from the bed, she draped it over the sleeping form and set to clearing the grate and setting a new fire. The kindling lit and the logs set to catch the flames. She rose, rubbing her hands down the front of her dress and turned.

Lizbet yelped. "Jesus, God and Mary! You scared the life out of me."

Richard was standing behind her, the counterpane wrapped close around him, his body shaking uncontrollably.

"Ah, so I look that bad," was all he said.

Lizbet's relief that he wasn't about to lose his temper with her showed plainly on her face. "Come here." She dragged a chair as close as she could get it to the fire and guided him into it. Dropping to her knees again, she set more wood to burn. "That'll start to warm you soon enough."

Richard had pulled the blanket tightly around himself, but still he continued to shake, and the hands holding tight onto the counterpane trembled. His bare feet were white with cold on the wood floor. Lizbet, still kneeling, reached out a hand and pressed it to one frozen foot.

"God love us, you do like to bloody suffer, don't you?" she announced, standing, and then unnecessarily added, "Wait here, I'll get something else to warm you through."

She was back soon enough, with a warm brick from the bread oven on a tray, wrapped in sack cloth, and on the other end bread and ale.

Lizbet fussed about, and when she was satisfied the hot brick was securely wrapped, she put it under his feet. "There, now don't fidget, if you do and your feet touch the brick, it'll have the skin burnt off them in a moment."

Richard remained quiet, but let her push the wrapped warm brick under his feet.

He placed his palms on the chair arms and slowly pushed himself from the chair, the counterpane slithering from his shoulders.

"Can you juggle?" he asked Lizbet without looking at her.

Lizbet's brow wrinkled in confusion. "It's a child's trick. Of course I can."

On the table sat an earthenware bowl full of musket balls. He took three and threw them in the air, effortlessly passing them through his hands. "A child's trick, as you say."

Lizbet watched nervously, but kept her counsel.

Richard took another lead ball and added it to those all in the air already, and then another. Now five flew up in the air in front of his face. "And I'm not a child anymore, so more should be easy." He fished out two more and now there were seven musket balls going round and around, his hands moving quicker to keep them in flight. Judging his moment, he added another two to the spinning circuit.

Lizbet held her breath as he took two more from the bowl, adding them to those already in the air. Now there were eleven, so close and moving so fast. Lizbet couldn't help herself and her hands involuntarily shot out to catch them, it was too many to keep going; the speed needed was not one a tired man would be able to keep up for much longer.

Suddenly he pulled his hands away, dropped back into the chair and the lead balls bounced off the table. Two landed on the edge of the earthenware bowl, breaking it in half, and the heavy round spheres, released, rolled across the table.

Lizbet yelped, threw her arms around the escaping bullets and managed to stop most of them falling to the floor.

"It's not so easy," Richard said quietly.

"I can see that." Lizbet was still trying to round up the musket balls. "You should have stopped at ten."

Richard looked up at her, "…ten. Yes, probably."

Lizbet swept the rolling lead into a trap between two books on the table and prevented their escape using the upturned broken bowl. Scooping up a handful that had fallen to the floor, she added them to the rest, her hands grey from the lead.

"I don't want you falling on them and making yourself even worse," she said, rounding up the last one, still rolling it between her thumb and forefinger. Holding it out between them, she met his eyes and dropped it in with the rest. "Sometimes you are better fighting one thing at a time. I might look simple, but I did know what you were trying to say. It would have been a sight easier if you'd used words rather than breaking the pots."

Richard couldn't help himself and smiled wearily.

Lizbet picked another lead ball from the floor and standing again, let it roll around her palm. Her eyes on it, she asked, "Why did you say what you did? Did you feel so much that I was one of your burdens?"

There was a lengthy pause.

"Sorry, Master." Lizbet dropped the ball into the pile with the others, and rubbing her hands down her apron, she made to leave.

"No... wait..." It was only his voice that arrested her. Then he added, "Sit, please."

Lizbet slowly pulled another chair near to the table and sat down carefully.

"Words spoken cannot be undone, nor do I wish them to be. The declaration I made will give you a future, a place, and I... we... owe you much."

Lizbet's temper finally snapped Tears welled in her eyes. "Now what do I do? They are treating me like a bloody harridan." She took hold of one of the musket balls and threw it at him. "I don't want you to owe me anything."

Richard pressed his hands to his face. "For God's sake, woman, get out!"

Lizbet slammed the door.

Richard swept the books from the desk, releasing the lead ammunition which rolled ponderously across the table until they fell to the floor with thunderous clatter.

Chapter 18
A New Master

†

Morley had been right about where he thought the inn was – it was on the corner of Stonegate. Catherine's description had told him it was near where the water sellers gathered and by the apple market, and that had narrowed it down. Arriving with three men, he soon found the landlord, Roddy, in the taproom, who seemed not at all surprised that yet another person had arrived asking about his recently departed tenant.

"Has he been found then?" Roddy asked when Morley mentioned Fitzwarren. Roddy hadn't known him by that name but it had been shortly after he had left that Robert had found the inn, and it seemed Roddy had profited handsomely telling the tale of how he had been forced to find help for Richard and Jack shift the bodies of Colan and his cousin from the upstairs rooms to an alley some way distant from the inn. It had not been long after that that the pair, along with a whore called Lizbet, had disappeared.

Roddy didn't know where they had gone; the man's rent had been paid up, and Roddy couldn't say for sure when he had left. The first he had known for sure that he had gone was when Robert Fitzwarren had turned up and he had been forced to go upstairs in the inn to show him which rooms he had leased to Richard. The door had been locked, and despite Roddy's protests, Robert had ordered one of his men to shoulder it open. Once the door opened on its splintered hinges, it became quite apparent that whoever had occupied the room had left.

Roddy could add little to the narrative Morley already had from Catherine, but he did now know that William's other son Robert had also tried to track down this man he sought. He obviously bore him ill will, for as a result of his actions, warrants had been issued for both Richard's and Jack's arrest for the murder of Colan and his cousin. Morley shook his head; this man was leaving quite a trail of destruction behind him.

†

Catherine saw Morley approaching her again on the day Elizabeth was due back from Court. He seemed to move about the place unheeded and she could only assume that Travers was well aware of him and left him to his own devices. Whether he would retreat into the background when Elizabeth returned would remain to be seen; Catherine deeply hoped so.

Morley smiled.

Catherine scowled.

"Can we both not be on good terms? What needs to be done will be done, and neither you, nor I, for that matter, can change this," Morley said, coming to stand near where Catherine had been busy beating the dust from a selection of rugs.

Casting her eyes about her, she noted that what servants there had been in the vicinity had, as usual, melted away.

"It's a skill," he agreed, taking up a position upwind and away from the dust still emanating from the suspended rug.

Catherine continued to apply the beater to the tightly woven threads with renewed vigour. She wondered if he would tell her if he had found Richard; she was certainly not going to ask.

Morley seemed content to watch her, and arms folded, he applied himself to the wall while she continued to exercise her temper on the rug. He spoke only when, smiling, he saw her arm beginning to tire. "I feel a lot safer now."

Catherine gave the rug two more extra hard belts releasing another plume of fine grey dust.

Morley laughed. "I have a task for you. It seems your placement here at Durham Place pleases my Master and he seems willing to overlook how it is that you came to be here, if you would perform a small service for him."

Catherine looked at him closely. "What small service?"

"A very simple one. It should not be beyond your wit." Morley reached inside his doublet and produced some folded cream sheets. "I just wish you to place these in Mistress Kate's rooms, perhaps not on open display, somewhere where they will be hidden from the lady."

Morley held them out, but Catherine did not take them. "Good God, girl! They won't bite."

Catherine took the sheets and opened them. Neatly printed in black ink were two leaflets detailing Knox's latest writings.

"Dear God!" gasped Catherine, looking up from the sheets to meet Morley's calm face.

"It will be an indication of your trustworthiness. You will be allowed to stay at Durham Place and in time my Master may look into the issue of your lost inheritance for you," Morley said.

Catherine folded the sheets and pushed them into a pocket in her dress. "Do I have a choice?" she asked, knowing already what the answer would be.

Morley inclined his head. "Not really," he said. Smiling to himself, he left her.

Catherine easily found somewhere to put them. Folding the sheets in half, she pressed them behind a painting hanging from the wall in Kate Ashley's room. She'd no liking for Kate but sill her conscience pained her. She had no doubt as to what the outcome for Mistress Ashley was likely to be if, or rather when, they were found.

It was three days before they were found. Catherine was working in the kitchens and only got to hear about what had happened second hand. There had been a great commotion. Travers had been instructed to search Mistress Kate's rooms and there seditious writings had been found. Kate had been immediately arrested and within hours had been confined to Fleet Prison. Catherine felt her throat tighten, and it was hard to swallow. She consoled herself with the thought that at least Kate was not in the Tower.

Chapter 19
The Day of The Innocents

Why have ye no routhe on my child?
Have routhe on me ful of mourning;
Tak doun o rode my derworth child,
Or prik me o rode with my derling!
More pine ne may me ben y-don
Than lete me live in sorwe and shame;
As love me bindëth to my sone,
So let us deyen bothe y-same.

✝

Lizbet tapped rapidly on the door, but there was no reply. She repeated the knock and then knocked again, louder and longer.

The door was pulled open and Lizbet jumped.

"What is it?" Jack's voice was hushed and angry.

Lizbet looked past him, saw a pair of white naked feet on the bed behind him, and she scowled at him. "I need to talk to you."

"Not now." Jack made to close the door and Lizbet rammed a foot forwards to stop it closing.

"It's important. I need to talk to you," Lizbet hissed.

"Later, not now." Jack shoved the door hard and her foot began to slide backwards as the door started to close.

"Well, when you're finished then. Say in about five minutes? I'll be downstairs." Then loud enough for the girl in the room to hear, she added, "He'll not take much of your time, love. He's faster than a greased pig at a fair. Just make sure he pays you full price even if he doesn't take long."

Lizbet smiled maliciously at Jack, and before he could reply, she'd pulled her foot away from the bottom of the door and it slammed shut. Laughing loud enough for both of the room's occupants to hear, she set off downstairs to wait for him.

She did not have long to wait. Within minutes, with a face like thunder, Jack dropped heavily down the steps, looking for her. Quickly, she grabbed his arm and steered him towards the yard.

"Where are we going?" Jack said angrily, pulling his arm from her grasp.

"I'll not keep you long. Come on, I want to talk to you, but not in there." Lizbet said, hurrying on in front of him.

"This had better be important," Jack growled back, striding after her.

"Stop complaining. The lass'll wait for you, unless you've been stupid enough and paid her already," Lizbet shot back at him.

"Where are we going?" Jack said, catching up with her.

"Here. This'll do." They had reached the back of the communal wash house at the back of the inn, and were standing behind it, out of sight and engulfed in the dark shadow it cast.

"Well?" Jack demanded. With his arms folded, he glared down at her.

"Something is happening," Lizbet said quickly.

"Well, I can tell you about something that isn't happening," Jack growled at her.

"For God's sake, Jack! Can you think about nothing other than your cock tonight?" Lizbet thumped him in the chest with the flat of her hand.

Chastened, his expression softened. "Go on then, tell me."

"Everything is wrong. Everything. The Master doesn't make mistakes, not like this," Lizbet said.

"Well, he's made a pile of them recently," Jack said.

"I don't think he has. I can't believe he'd mix those guns up, or overlook the brake on the wagon. And Froggy has just told me that he had left the wagon on the flat, so how did it make it to the edge of the hill? And Kells…" Lizbet's chin trembled. "Who killed him? It wasn't your brother."

"Are you so sure? He was drunk. You know what a temper he has on him when he has been drinking. A week ago I would have agreed with you, but not anymore, not after what he had Andrew do to me," Jack said slowly.

"I don't think he meant for that to happen. I've spoken to him and he's suffering for this," Lizbet said quickly.

"He's suffering!" Jack's voice was incredulous. "Have you dragged me out here to discuss the state of my brother's soul? I hope he suffers from now until eternity, and may that be a very, very long time."

"Jack, please. I think someone is playing games with you."

Jack was turning to leave but her words stopped him. "So someone else switched the guns, someone else pushed the cart down the hill, and Kells had his throat cut by the same person at a guess? Is that what you think?" Jack snarled and, grabbing her arm, he forced her round to face the yard behind them. "And did that someone else force me to my knees over there and whip me until I passed out in the mud?"

"Yes! Andrew did that, not the Master," Lizbet wailed. The hold he had on her arm was hurting.

"He made Andrew do it. It was no different than if he had held the whip himself." Jack's voice was cold, and then he added, "Andrew told me that Richard watched from the window and that he'd told him to deliver to me twice the lashes he gave to Mat. You didn't know that, did you?"

"It wasn't like that. I was in the Master's room. He didn't see what was happening until after I'd shouted for Andrew to stop." Lizbet twisted and tried to pull her arm free from his hold. "Andrew's lying to you."

Jack suddenly released her. "God, I wish that could be true. I could have forgiven him anything, but not this."

"Please Jack, think…"

But it was too late. Jack was striding away from her, back towards the inn, leaving her alone to rub her bruised arm.

✝

"Jack, lad, are you alright?" It was Andrew's voice calling across the tap room, then turning to his seated companions, he said, "Let me out, lads. I'll just have a quick word with Jack and I'll be right back."

Thomas and Marc moved and Andrew squeezed between them and headed for Jack.

"You've a troubled look on your face, lad. Come and join us," Andrew said, laying a hand on Jack's arm.

Jack ran his hands through his untidy tangle of blond hair. "Troubled? Yes I am," he conceded.

"Your brother? Am I right?" Andrew said, and seeing the expression on Jack's face, he knew he was right. "These are difficult days, but ones we will get through."

"I will be glad when they are all well behind me," Jack agreed, smiling weakly.

"Have you spoken to your brother yet?" Andrew asked, his voice serious.

"Not about what he did, no," Jack said, and then with his eyes on Andrew's face, he continued, "When you told me he stood and watched you lay every one of those strokes on my back from his window, I could not bring myself to speak him."

"I understand, I do," Andrew said. "I had looked to him and hoped he might bid me stop, but he didn't. I am sorry."

"And he told you twice as many strokes as he delivered to Mat," Jack continued, "and then he just stood and watched?"

Andrew nodded. "It was a harsh punishment, Jack, I agree, and I wish I had not been the one he picked to deliver it."

"Aye, well what's done is done," Jack said, concluding the brief exchange and, placing a hand on the bannister, set his feet back to the steps to the rooms above and the waiting Angelique.

Andrew intercepted Lizbet outside the inn and propelled her quickly into one the empty stables.

"And what have you been saying to Jack, my lovely?" Andrew had a tight hold on Lizbet's wrist and pulled her towards him.

Lizbet felt his fingers digging into her skin and the eyes that were staring at her were unfriendly.

"Nothing!" Lizbet tried to pull her hand free, but his hold was a firm one.

"Why do I not believe you, my pretty little whore?" Andrew was smiling, but there was nothing pleasant in it. "Maybe there is something of Richard in your face? Same dark hair, same high cheek bones and same tight arse." Andrew's other arm reached around her and pulled her against him. He buried his face in her hair for a moment. "You'll tell no one, and even if you did, they'd not believe you anyway." Andrew laughed as he pushed her round and forced her over a saddle stand. Ripping her skirts over her head, he groaned in delight at the sight of her white skin in the gloom. "And it's not your arse I'm thinking of right now." Andrew, a hand on the small of her back, held her immobile as he forced himself upon her. "Ah God! There's been more than a time I've wanted to humble him on my cock, but taking his sister, that's almost as good."

He was finished with her quickly and sent her sprawling across the dark stable when he was done, discarded.

Wiping the blood from the corner of her mouth where he had hit her, she listened to the sound of his laughter.

☦

The explosion sent a shockwave through the inn. The wooden structure heaved against the blast and had barely recovered when a second one, greater in ferocity, assaulted the slatted walls. The end of the nave of the church was gone. Stonework was littered across the road. When it had fallen, the masonry had crushed the houses, but worse, it had set them on fire. The wooden thatched houses of the villagers were now nothing more than a long line of smashed kindling and flames licked along the row of collapsed dwellings.

The camp was closer to the village than the inn was and by the time Richard arrived, with Jack hard on his heels, his men were already there. Froggy and Marc heaved at a wagon frame that had been blown against the doorway to one of the flaming homes.

"There are people in here! Help us!" Pierre screamed.

Smoke rolled from the doorway when, cleared of the wagon, they could pull it open. The screaming from within had changed to choking gasps as the smoke robbed air from their lungs. Richard was first in, ducking beneath the burning lintel. In the suffocating fumes he found first one child and then another. Passing them through the doorway to Froggy, he dived back in again. Suddenly the interior flared as the roof gave way and the flames within fed on fresh air.

Marc grabbed the Master's arm. "Get out! The roof will be on our heads in a moment!"

Above them, the remaining thatch crackled and sparked and the supporting trusses were all now well alight.

Richard pulled against his hold. The next step he took saved the life of the woman on the floor who had collapsed where she had succumbed to the fumes from the burning thatch. In the dark, they found her arms and dragged her to the safety of the night air beyond the remains of her home.

Four people had died, eight homes were completely destroyed and the Church no longer had a nave. It was a night the village would never forget.

Jack, his face blackened, hair crisped and with a searing burn over his right eye, stood transfixed and watched as his brother was arrested. His hands were tied and as the perpetrator of the night's carnage, he was dragged none too carefully from the village.

"Jesus! How did this happen?" It was Jack who spoke as Andrew, looking equally kissed by the flames, appeared from between two of the houses.

"Everyone is out. There's no one else we can help. If there are any left inside, it will be God alone who can save their souls now." Andrew looked back at the tightly packed row of houses. They didn't even resemble houses anymore, just a long line of faggots stacked to burn together.

"They've taken Richard," Jack, trembling, managed.

"Lad, they need to hold someone responsible for what has happened. Those explosions, there could only be one thing round here that could cause that," Andrew said.

Jack turned on him. "The explosions have come from the church. We've nothing near the church. Everything is stored near the camp, you know that," Jack said.

"All I know is that we've got gunpowder, and that explosion was likely caused by it. How it happened I don't know, but the blame of it is going to lie at the Master's door unless we can prove otherwise," Andrew replied.

"You're right." Jack realised suddenly exactly the predicament his brother was in. "Come on, let's check the powder store."

The store which was to have been guarded at all costs during day and night, stood unattended. Jack cursed. After the explosion, every one of Richard's men had been in the village including whichever of them had been scheduled as a guard of the powder store that evening. Jack pulled the door open. The light from the moon lit the interior enough for Jack to be able to see that where there should have been four small casks of powder there were now only two.

"Christ, Andrew, there's two missing." Jack's face was white when he emerged.

Andrew pushed past him into the inside of the powder store. "Damn it! I knew it was nothing other than black powder that could have brought the nave down. Jack, we need to find out who was on guard tonight and how this could have happened," Andrew said, his face strained. "The Master was so careful. He recognised the danger and Master Scranton is meticulous when it comes to handling the powder. It must have been stolen or there is some other mischief." Andrew's voice shook. "When I find out who did this, it will be a day of regrets for someone."

Jack nodded in agreement. "Froggy will know who was rostered tonight. I was in there this morning with Scranton and it was all there then so it's been taken today. It shouldn't be hard to find out who has been in the store after me."

But as it turned out it was. Froggy knew exactly who had been on duty since the morning. It had been himself and then after the clock struck five it had been Pierre. Pierre swore that not a soul had stepped inside the powder store since he had taken over from Froggy, who was also likewise adamant that the powder room had remained undisturbed all day.

"It does not look good, Jack. They've taken the Master. They know we have been using shot and powder, and it doesn't take a clever man to work out that there is a connection between what happened tonight and us," Andrew looked just as frustrated as Jack. "Indeed it would take a clever man to persuade them otherwise."

"Do you think I should go? Explain that this has been an accident, that we suspect theft but as yet cannot find a culprit?" Jack asked quickly.

Andrew looked thoughtful. "It can't make matters any worse, can it? Perhaps offer to make amends. The Master is not without resources. I know that four good people have died, but perhaps you could tell Freiherr Gelfrat that we could offer some restitution to these people."

"I think you overestimate my brother's wealth!" Jack scoffed. "There are not just four dead people but a dozen homes have gone up in smoke, not to mention half the church has been reduced to rubble. I think setting that to rights might even stretch Richard's purse."

Andrew gave him a hard look. "Go quickly, lad. See what you can do. They do not know how much he has or hasn't got, do they?"

"True," Jack conceded. "I can try. There is little else we can do, and I can't just leave him in there, can I?"

So Jack rode, alone except for of a deep sense of foreboding, and readied himself to make as good an account of himself and his brother as he was able.

†

It was an hour later when news came back that Jack also had been arrested, and the general feeling was that it might not be long before the rest of them shared the same fate.

Andrew, taking control of the situation, made what they all felt was the most sensible decision.

"We can't just leave them!" Dan protested. "Why the hell did you let him go in the first place? He'd been caught poaching on Freiherr Gelfrat's land. They were hardly going to listen to his case, were they? You might as well have put him in the gaol yourself!"

"Dan, I know. I didn't think, I'm sorry," Andrew replied, his arms flung wide. "But we must leave. The Master would expect no less of us." Andrew clasped the big man's arms. "We take everything we have, follow the Master's course and press the knights to secure their release as part of the bargain."

"It will take too long," Dan growled. "They hold a court session on the first Saturday, and that's in two days' time."

"What other choice do we have, man?" Andrew reiterated his argument. "We cannot stay. If we do, we risk internment with the Master. We are too few so there is little we can do by force. All we can hope is that by persuasion if we move quickly, then we can free them."

"They've not got the time for you to do that," Dan protested angrily.

"I know it is a slim chance, and I will ride these men to their deaths to get them there as quickly as I can. What else can I do? Dammit, man, I feel your pain. I've known the Master since he was a lad, and if I thought I could take a blade in my hand and free him, I bloody would." Andrew's words were passionately spoken and heads around him nodded in agreement. "The best we can do now is take ourselves back on the road, quickly, and press his case." Andrew's face was grimly set. "The longer we stand here arguing about this, the less chance they have. I swear on my very soul I will do

everything in my power to bring them help."
Andrew paused for a moment. His eyes raked around the room, meeting those of the men intently watching him, and when he spoke next, his eyes were locked with Dan's. "Who is with me?"

There was an affirmative shout from Thomas and he was joined quickly by the others.

Andrew nodded, a satisfied look on his face. "Right, let us ride now and offer hope to the Master."

Andrew ducked through the low door and one by one the men quickly followed him out. Dan, still standing in the room, watched them go. He didn't even realise Lizbet was in the room until she spoke.

"What are you going to do then?" Her words bore an edge and revived his attention.

"God knows!" Dan dropped heavily onto one of the empty trestles, his head in his hands. He felt the table tilt as another sat opposite him, and raising his head, he was about to tell Lizbet he did not wish for her company when he found himself looking into the worn creased face of Froggy Tate. "Are you not going with the others?"

"I had a mind to, that's for sure." Froggy spat on the floor. "But it is a fool's errand. They'll never get there and back in time."

Dan nodded, accepting the truth of his words.

"There must be something you can do." Lizbet moved to stand at the end of the table.

Dan eyed her coldly, but it was Froggy who replied. "If there was, we'd do it. Andrew is right. We can't fight our way in, there are too few of us, and now there are only two of us left, we have no chance. We would need two dozen men to be able to force our way inside Bertradaburg, and then once you are in such a place you have to find them. That's often not as easy as you think."

Lizbet paled. She knew what it would be like inside – cold, isolated and worse, it would be dark. Jesus, poor Jack. "Why did Jack go, and on his own?"

"Andrew's idea. He thought Jack might be able to get Richard out, make a case of clemency," Dan provided.

"That bastard! Can you not see it? He's just got rid of the pair of them and ridden off with everything they had. Are you stupid?" Lizbet blazed at them.

"Lass, I'm not so sure it was quite like that," Froggy said. "Andrew means to help, and he's right. Taking the men away is the only safe thing to do or all of them will end up in gaol. We've been lucky they did not come and arrest us already. I'm not surprised most of the men went with Andrew. They are worried if they linger round here, they'll be soon sharing a room with the Master."

Lizbet's fist banged on the table. "He's not what he seems. He has driven a wedge between Jack and the Master and taken everything. Can you not see that?"

Dan caught her wrist, stilling her. "That might be so, but right now, at this moment, we need to think about how to get the Master and Jack out of gaol." Dan, turning his attention to Froggy, asked, "How come you didn't go with them?"

Froggy shrugged. "Don't know. You stayed, and so I thought someone should back you up, and I've got to agree with the lassie, there are a few things here that don't add up right."

Dan acknowledged Froggy's loyalty with a grim smile. "I'm glad of the company, but I truly don't know what we can do. Freiherr Gelfrat has the Master and Jack as well now, and there's little we can do. A gaol is unfortunately designed to keep the unfortunate in and the rest of us out."

Froggy let out a long loud breath and rubbed his right eye with the heel of his hand. "And we are most certainly not going to get anywhere near. If we make ourselves known then we will be tarred with the Master's crime and thrown in gaol with him, or worse."

"Or worse," Dan agreed.

"But you are going to do something," Lizbet said, looking between the pair.

"Lass, what can we do?" Froggy said

Lizbet glared at him. "I don't know. You're the one always telling me to keep my mouth shut and leave the deciding to the world of men."

"They've been arrested. Four people have died, woman, and I don't care what Andrew says, they'll want restitution and they'll be swinging from a rope soon enough, or worse!"

"It wasn't the Master's fault though," Lizbet complained.

Dan glared at her. "Fault isn't going to matter much, I don't suppose." He looked back at Froggy. "There's no way to reach them, not that I can see."

"You'd need to be Anne Archant to get to them now," Lizbet remarked.

"What do you mean? Anne Archant?" Dan turned his dark eyes on her.

"Anne Archant. She runs the Angel," she said, then when the two men looked at her uncomprehending, explained, "The bawdy house in Southwark? The Angel? You must have heard of it?"

"Why would that help us now?" Dan said slowly, his eyes watching her carefully.

Lizbet looked between Froggy and Dan. "For God's sake, I just meant dead men's luck."

"Dead men's luck?" Froggy repeated confusion on his face.

Lizbet took in their blank expressions. "For God's sake, where have you two been all your lives? Anne Archant'd take anyone who paid to the Southwalk prison for a tryst with a condemned man. She was famous for it. It is supposed to bring good luck. Don't suppose gaols here are any different. Pay enough and the curious can always get past a locked door."

Both men were now looking at her closely.

"What?" Lizbet exclaimed feeling their gaze upon her. Then her eyes lit up and a smile spread across her face. "So you think we need Anne Archant?"

Dan fished inside his doublet, brought out a purse and let the contents spill onto the table. "Froggy, what have you got?"

Froggy screwed up his tanned face and thumped down on the boards in front of him a few meagre coins. "I'm not left with much after that last game of cards with the lads."

Lizbet raised her eyes from the poor collection of coins. "Is that it? I don't think you are going to persuade a man to chance his life and liberty for that lot, are you?"

Dan scowled at her. "That's all we have. If you want to add anything, you can."

Lizbet did not back from his stare. She fished in the pocket of her dress and drew out a small hand sewn soft leather bag. Carefully pulling the draw cord, she opened it and let the contents spill to the table before her. The men's eyes widened as they watched the pearls, rubies and gems scatter on the wood.

"Where did you steal them from?" Dan gasped, his hand reaching across the table made to pick up one of the bigger pearls.

Quicker than the big man, Lizbet snatched it before his thick fingers could close around it. "They are mine and before you go accusing me of otherwise, the Master knows very well that I have them."

Froggy grinned at her. "Lass, that's a dowry I didn't know you had!"

Lizbet, ignoring his comment, was carefully putting the gems, that had once adorned a pair of shoes, back into the leather pouch. Smiling she said, "If you want me to be Anne Archant, I'll need a dress, lads, but I think there is enough in here to bribe my way into any castle."

The expression on Dan's face had changed. "You could bribe your way into Heaven with that little lot."

✝

It was a long time before he moved, and when he did, he found more of his body had gone numb than he had guessed. He was sitting on the floor with his back to the wall, knees drawn up. His heart was racing too fast in his chest, and his throat, dry and tight, was limiting his breathing. Richard took a slow steady breath, but it didn't help; his clothes were burnt and the smell reached his nose, an acrid reminder.

The vision of the boy's face, ashen, eyes closed, his body laid where Froggy had dropped him in the road in a tangled heap of limbs would not leave him. Dead. Choked by smoke and if he had lived, he'd have died from the burn that ran across his stomach where the flaming roof truss had fallen on him.

The smell of the boy's burnt skin replaced that of the odour of burnt clothing and Richard gagged.

There would be a reckoning. It was not a matter of guilt. That, he accepted as his. He alone had brought about the destruction in the village, the deaths. And for what? To further some pointless cause, to carve a worthless and transient niche for himself? To have again what his father had taken from him? It was this that had led to a crumbled church, a burning village and the deaths of children who had never even met him.

Even Scranton had lectured him on the sanctity of children. It was a twisted fate that had brought him to also be a part of the massacre of the innocents. The boy would have been no more than four or five years old. What sin could such a child have committed that God could wish to steal away his life in such a way? How could God punish a man with the death of a child?

Then there was Mat. Dead, his head panned in from an impact with the cart, and Lizbet, whose arm would bear the marks for the rest of her life where the skin had been torn open by the exploding flintlock. He didn't understand how it had happened, but the ultimate responsibility for it rested with him. Jack had made that painfully clear.

Jack... the rift between the two after the beating he had taken would never heal. He'd humiliated him, belittled him in front of the men, shown them all he had little respect for his brother.

He alone was responsible for his careless words that had driven Andrew to believe he was doing his Master's bidding. It was probably his own words threatening to cut the Alaunt's throat that had driven one of them to think they acted at their Master's direction. All careless words.

Richard tried to swallow again, and found he couldn't, choked by guilt. There would be an end soon. There would be a reckoning and he welcomed it. The sooner that blessed moment of payment arrived, the better.

Chapter 20
A Reckoning Welcomed

†

There were a dozen stone steps down to the door of the cell.

It's below ground! Jack could already feel his skin crawling with fear. His two gaolers had him held fast between them as another in front swore and fumbled for the right key on the ring.

"Come on, Erin," the man to his left complained. "It's freezing down here."

And it was. Even in the dim light, Jack saw his breath billow in a cloud before him.

Dark and cold. *Christ, not again.*

Erin, impaired by trying to hold a torch and twist a key, swore under his breath. The rattling of the lock and keys continued, and then there came the unmistakable click as the right key twisted tumblers in the lock. Erin swung open the door and the restraining hands propelled Jack towards the black oblong where the door had been. Missing the last step, Jack fell, sprawling on the floor, with his hands out before him to save himself. Behind him he heard laughter, which was abruptly cut off as the oak of the door was slammed back into the frame and the key turned once more, forcing the lock back securely into the frame.

Air caught in a choking gasp in his throat. A claw forced its icy talons into his chest, squeezing his heart, stopping the blood.

"There's light there."

The voice startled him, but the strong hand under his arm helping him back to his feet shocked him even more. Richard!

"There's a grill there. Can you see it?" His brother pulled him across the room and sure enough, high up in the wall was a grey square of night pinpricked with stars and moonlight glistening from the wet iron bars. The helping hand let go of its hold and by degrees, Jack's eyes became accustomed to the dark. He could pick out the silhouette of his brother where he had hitched himself up onto the top of a barrel.

"Good God, what are you doing here?"

"I tried to get you out. They would hear nothing of my words." Jack's heart was hammering in his chest so hard that his words were stilted and broken.

"Jesus! Jack, you should have left me. You have reason enough!"

"You got me out of Marshalsea. I had to try," Jack replied, his voice a little steadier.

"You owe me a debt?" Richard put the question.

"Yes, I do," Jack replied.

Richard tipped his head back and rested it against the wall. A debt, was that all that was left? After what had happened, his brother had still come for him, indeed he'd pledged his life.

"Andrew has taken the men with him. He hopes to plead your case with the Knights and secure your release. It is a noble mission but I knew he had not the time to make is succeed," Jack managed slowly. "He did not want to leave, but he had little choice."

"Jack, you should have left me," Richard replied wearily.

"Don't make me wish I had," Jack replied. The panic was beginning to subside and his heart rate was steadying.

Richard was silent, and after a moment Jack said angrily, "Do you have nothing to say to me?"

"Shush Jack, I'm trying to think,"

"I bloody well will not. I risked my life to try to get you out and I'll not have my words stilled like a child's!" Jack's temper flared.

"Well, that's the point, isn't it? Let me think how I am going to get you out of here then," Richard said through gritted teeth.

Jack's hands were still trembling as he pulled himself up to sit next to Richard.

The silence lengthened between them, but eventually Jack did speak. "They are going to hang you."

"That fact has been made painfully clear already, and now it seems it will be a fate we will share unless I can think of something," Richard said.

"I thought fate was not something you believed in?" Jack said. His head was still reeling.

"I didn't think I did. There are, however, a set of circumstances that keep on recurring and I am starting to believe that no matter how many times I elude her, she keeps on setting the same trap. Perhaps the end was always inevitable, and anyway this time I think I deserve it."

Jack shook his head. "What are you talking about?"

"Store rooms, always a bloody store room. Always," Richard replied as if somehow Jack was supposed to understand.

The next noise was a dull thud as Richard's boot heel banged against the cask he was sat on. "They are, it seems, not empty. I had been debating on pulling the bung out, but to drink on your own would sadden even Baccus, but now you are here that does change the situation somewhat."

"Are you sure you have not already pulled that bung free?" Jack kicked the cask he was sitting on and listened to the hollow noise. "Yes, this one sounds a good third empty."

"It's an attractive proposition. Do you think they would hang you if you were blind drunk?" Richard asked.

"There is only one way to find out, but knowing my luck it won't be malmsey in these casks, it will be pickling vinegar!"

"Ever the optimist!" Richard jumped down from this perch and began to feel around on the floor for a tool he could use. Exclaiming in triumph, he stood a moment later, an object in his hand that Jack could not make out. "Shall we find out?"

Richard had found a hammerhead that had lost it shaft. Hitting first one side and then the other, he used it to loosen the bung on the side of the cask. Before it was free, a trickle of liquid sluiced down the side of the cask and the odour of wine rose to their noses.

"It's not pickling vinegar," Richard announced. Cupping his hand against the stream, he caught enough to fill his mouth. "It is wine, and it's not bad either."

Jack's hand was next to his in a moment. He took a mouthful and followed it with another. His shaking was lessening and the cramped pain that always set upon his muscles was lessening.

Jack lifted his cupped hands to his mouth when Richard's sudden grasp on his wrist made him spill the liquor from his hand.

"Do you think they will let us stop in here if they knew we had loosed their Master's entire supply of wine over the cellar floor?" Richard said quietly in his ear.

"No, no, I don't suppose they would. However, how would that help us?" Jack said.

"Possibilities, Jack. Who knows?" Richard said.

"If we end up in the empty room next door, you do realise I will hate you?" Jack wiped his hands dry down the front of his hose.

"It is a risk I am willing to take. Anyway, we both know how much you like to extoll on my errors so at least you will be able to go to the rope primed with the injustice of the wronged. And should you meet Saint Peter you can then tell him with some certainty that you are there not at all through your own fault but through mine." Richard was laughing bitterly.

Very soon the gaolers sat at the top of the steps became uncomfortably aware that they had made a very bad mistake. The smell of the Master's stored wine was beginning to filter its way around the door frame to their noses. The noise of drunken revelry from within, interspaced with the noise of hammering followed by loud cheers, made them painfully aware that their captives were releasing their Master's wine all over the cellar floor.

It wasn't long before the door was flung open and a torch thrust in for them to see the carnage their captives had wreaked on the wine supplies. The cellar floor was standing in liquid, the fumes were eye watering and several of the barrels were now on their sides, glugging forth their contents.

Jack put up a good fight as they dragged him up the stairs, breaking one man's nose and earning himself a split lip and a grazed face from the stone wall in return. Richard took their shoves and pushes and kept his temper in check. Their new room was devoid of alcoholic indulgence, but it was above ground, warmer and drier, with two grilled windows letting nightlight flood into the room. The floor was dusty and Richard guessed it was used as a flour store for the bread ovens.

"So much for possibilities," Jack proclaimed to the room as the door closed behind him.

There was then a silence between them. Jack was, for once, lost for words, and Richard kept his own counsel. Indeed he sat propped against the wall, his eyes closed, and Jack was sure that he slept.

Both men, like dogs on guard, their senses heightened by their plight, heard the noise at the same time.

Laughter. Laughter and footsteps. A woman's laughter, higher pitched above the men's more guttural exclamations.

Richard and Jack exchanged a look.

The noise paused outside the door, and then a woman's voice spoke loudly. "You'll keep me safe, sir, won't you?"

"It's Lizbet!" Jack was on his feet in an instant, but Richard, next to him, placed a firm hold on his arm. "Keep quiet, Jack. Don't say anything." Richard shook him until he received an affirmation before letting him loose.

"Aye," they heard one of the men reassure her, "we'll make sure you are safe. We'll go in first. You just wait here."

She spoke again, loudly and unnecessarily. Both men realised what it was, a warning.

"Thank you, sir. You are both such a reassurance to a lady."

The door opened and the gaolers, one holding a vicious nailed club, pushed both men against the wall and tied their hands hard behind their backs. Jack felt the hessian rope bite hard into his wrists, and knew the bond would stop the blood to his hands. Their gaolers thought they were wary of Mal and his nailed club which would take a man's face off at one stroke, and leered at them both in satisfaction.

"They are safe now. You can come in."

An instant later a hesitant Lizbet emerged around the door frame. "Are you sure, sir? Show me I am safe. He's already laid his filthy hands on me once and I'd not have it happen again."

"He's trussed like a fowl," one said, and delivered a blow to Richard's stomach that sent him staggering back against the wall. "He can't touch you, and he knows if he does, Mal here will tear the flesh from his bones."

Lizbet stood straight, and an air of confidence settled about her. Taking three steps into the room, she announced, "Well then Master Fitzwarren, how does it feel to be at a disadvantage?" She took two more brisk steps towards him and before anyone realised what she meant to do, she slapped Richard hard across the face.

His gaolers laughed and she delivered another stinging blow.

"Careful Mistress, Master wants something left to hang!"

"Oh, I'll not kill him. I'll leave that to the drop at the end of the rope." Reaching up, Lizbet laid her hand on the side of his neck. "When the rope cuts into you, think of me, think of what you did to me, you bastard." Her face was close to his now and his impassive grey eyes held hers calmly. "It is for luck, so they say, to kiss a dead man." Lizbet pulled his head to her own, closed the gap between them, and planted her mouth on his to a series of cat calls behind her. Her other arm slipped around him, pulling him closer for a final kiss.

Lizbet had not expected his mouth to open beneath hers, not expected him to return the kiss. He couldn't pull her against him, but his mouth drew her hard towards his body, and a moment later she pulled away, breathless.

"Hit me again," Richard said under his breath. He had to repeat his words before Lizbet suddenly had the sense of them and slapped him hard again. His head twisted away from her and Lizbet prayed he caught the words she quickly whispered into his ear.

Lizbet put on a performance that had the men howling with laughter as she set about hitting and slapping Jack with every ounce of her strength. She finished off with a knee in his groin that dropped Jack to his knees and had the gaolers crying with mirth. Spinning on her heel, chin high, she stalked from the room leaving the gaolers, still laughing, to scramble from the room after her.

Jack, his shoulder against the wall for support, pushed himself back to his feet, and turned a clinical blue stare on his brother. "Possibilities perhaps?" It was a question.

"Perhaps." Richard didn't add anything else.

Jack continued to stare at Richard. "If there could ever be another word for loyal, it would be Lizbet, and God knows why."

"It's the story of Eve," Richard grunted, twisting the small knife Lizbet had pressed into his hand, and feeling the bite of steel as he set to cut the rope. "And an apple." A moment later, his wrists bleeding, his hands were free and Jack turned so he could apply the knife to the rope holding his wrists fast behind him.

"God love the woman," Jack said quietly over his shoulder as the bonds were neatly slit. "What else did she say?"

"Worryingly that they have a quantity of black powder and shortly they are going to ignite it."

Jack was grinning broadly. "How do we get out? The door's locked. Will they blow it off its hinges?"

Richard held up a small metal ring with three keys attached that Lizbet had dropped down the inside of his shirt. "I think she thought we might use these," he replied, returning his brother's smile.

It was the second key they tried that fitted the lock and slowly Richard turned it and the door, although still held by the tight fitting frame, was now open.

Impatient as always, Jack said, "How long do we wait?"

"Bide your time Jack. They'll wait until Lizbet is out and has let them know she has spoken to me before they do anything. It will take a little while. If they have it right, they will set a charge to cause as much confusion as possible and then we leave."

Richard, his weight against the door should anyone try the handle on the outside, was alert. His eyes were closed and all his concentration was on the noises beyond it. Jack's heart hammered in his chest. Like a beast in a cage that was too small, he paced and turned, again and again.

"Come on, Richard, something must have gone wrong. Let's go and not lose the opportunity."

"Patience is bitter, Jack, but its fruit will be sweet," Richard said quietly, still listening.

Jack swore under his breath. "Easy words to say."

"Not mine. They're Aristotle's, if you must know," Richard said, still blocking Jack's path to the door.

"I'll bet Aristotle didn't say that when he was waiting to find out if he was about to be blown into the hereafter."

"Probably not. I believe Aristotle lived a fairly risk free life in comparison to yours," Richard replied quietly.

"Was that meant as an apology?" Jack asked.

"Yes, I think it was. It was my careless words that made Andrew take a whip to you. Please don't blame him."

"Oh don't worry, I wasn't blaming him," Jack said bitterly as he tried to get closer to the door.

Neither of them though had long to wait. Jack was always sure later that he felt the blast before he heard it. The slabs beneath his feet seemed to tremble like the uncertain stepping stones in a stream. Then the unmistakable noise of a gunpowder explosion, like a dull thump, met his ears. Jack needed no invitation and he was as close as his brother's shadow as they opened the door and set off down the corridor. Half way along, there was a second blast that sounded like cannon fire and the windows on either side of them imploded into the castle, scattering shards of glass and lead, but the pair did not stop running.

The corridor ended with a set of steps and in a moment the men spilled into the courtyard. Richard had been right about the chaos. One of the charges must have been in a cart and the splintered burning remains were scattered across the yard, while the second must have been near the curtain wall as a huge plume of dark acrid smoke billowed from it.

Jack's instinct told him to run from the site of the explosion, but Richard ran straight towards it, and as they ran coughing into the anonymity of the smoke, he realised why. The third and final explosion was to their left and peppered both of them with stones and earth as the charge ripped away part of the chapel wall and sent a large quantity of roof slates into the air.

It was Froggy's uneven face they both saw coming towards them in the smoke. All around them were the shouts of men, the screams of woman and the panicked noise of livestock and horses.

Richard, a hand on Jack's back, pushed him toward Froggy. "Go, run."

Jack dug his heels in and stopped. Richard was already turning back the way they had come. Jack's eyes were wide. "Where are you going?"

"Run, I'll stop them. Just run, Jack. Now!" Richard said, taking a step away from him.

"No, we go this way, together." Jack had at first just a hold of Richard's sleeve but in a moment his hand clenched around flesh and bone, dragging Richard with him, further into the smoke. Froggy was shouting directions and Jack, with Richard in tow, blindly followed them.

Chapter 21
The Payment

Ech day me comëth tydinges thre,
For wel swithë sore ben he:
The on is that Ich shal hennë,
That other that Ich not whennë,
The thriddë is my mestë carë,
That Ich not whider Ich shal farë.

☦

On the ride from Bertradaburg they'd not even considered letting Lizbet ride her own horse; her skills were not sufficient for the flight they would need to make. She was forced to sit behind Jack, arms tightly wrapped around him, eyes closed in terror, sure that at any moment she'd fall from the galloping horse. They had ridden for hours, resting the horses, and then setting off again, putting as much distance between them and the castle as possible.

The pace finally slowed and they spent the next two days riding and resting briefly, resuming the journey south until Jack was sure they were now far enough away to have evaded any pursuit. They had not seen anyone on their journey as they had kept from the roads and he was sure there would be nobody to point Gelfrat's men in their direction.

Any elation he had felt over their escape did not seem to be one shared by his brother. He had seemed uncharacteristically quiet and happy to take direction rather gave it. Dan and Jack had exchanged glances and Jack had just shrugged. He'd no idea why Richard had suddenly become so withdrawn.

Jack brought his horse close to Richard's. "We are going to need to stop soon, to rest the animals and ourselves properly. We should be far enough away now. There's a village down there – should we see if we can stop there for the night?"

Richard met his eyes, but didn't seem to have a sense of what he'd been asked, and Jack had to repeat his words.

"Yes, it has been a long two days," Richard replied distractedly.

"Three," corrected Jack. Richard made no move and it became obvious Jack would need to go. "Here, take Lizbet. I'll ride down with Dan and see if it is safe."

Richard switched the reins to his left hand and accepted the limp form of Lizbet from Jack. Richard pulled her close, wrapping his cloak around her. The reins he kept in his left hand, and his right arm encircled the woman, holding her against his body.

Corracha was tired and his head drooped, so Richard held him to a slow walk as he waited for Jack and Dan to return and Froggy, equally as tired, rode next to him.

There was a warmth from her that he had not expected and a weight from her he had not been prepared for. Hooking the reins briefly over the saddle pommel, he used both hands to lift her to a more secure position in his keeping.

Lizbet moved in his arms and her arms snaked around him, one going to his waist while the other pressed under his jacket and his shirt. His own hold on her tightened, drawing her closer.

Then Lizbet spoke, her voice beyond tired. "Jack, I am sorry for being a trouble."

Did it matter? He considered it for a while, as her head rested on his shoulder and they rode on slowly. Not really, he supposed.

Corracha, raising his head, alerted his Master to the stream they had arrived at. Richard shortened the reins, guiding the stallion to the narrowest point. The horse picked his way across, and his jolting gait woke Lizbet; her head rose from his chest for a moment.

"Where are we?" Lizbet murmured.

Richard was about to answer, but before he could, Lizbet's eyes had fastened on the silver gilt buttons on his doublet. Realising it wasn't Jack she was riding with, Lizbet recoiled from him as if stung. She tore her hand from his shoulder where it had rested so gently on his skin, seeking his warmth.

"Sit still woman, or you'll have us both off!" Richard said angrily as she strained against his hold.

"Sorry... sorry," was all she could manage.

The body around which he still had an arm was now rigid.

It doesn't matter, he told himself. That a woman from the stews of London had a better liking for his brother than for him should be of little importance. So why then, did it rankle him so much?

Jack chose that moment to arrive back and saw the relief on Lizbet's face as she swapped horses to sit back in front of him. Jack had found an inn, secured rooms, and soon they were inside, out of the reach of the pelting rain, and shaking water from their clothes.

Dan and Froggy had insisted they ride on ahead to try and close the gap between the Master and Andrew with the men. Carrying Lizbet with them was slowing their progress, and after securing fresh horses, Dan was sure they could catch up with Andrew and halt their journey south.

†

Jack watched his brother closely. Richard was still quiet and when Jack had tried to engage him in conversation, Richard had provided curt replies and made it quite clear he was in no mood to talk. When he had left the room, a wench from the tavern in tow, Jack had watched his departure with dark eyes.

There had been no time during that flight for considered conversation. Lizbet had badly wanted to talk to Jack and riding behind him she had little opportunity to be heard.

"What's up with you?" Lizbet's words cut through his thoughts.

"Nothing, nothing at all," he said absently, his eyes still on the door that Richard had departed through, closed now.

Lizbet followed his gaze. "He's not in good humour tonight, is he?"

"God! Would you be after all that has happened?" Jack replied.

Lizbet leaned across the table and placed her small hand firmly on his wrist. "Listen to me Jack. Andrew… I tried to tell you he was not all he seemed to be, didn't I? He's taken the men, everything. Everything the Master has, he's got it all now."

"He had no choice. He's gone to plead Richard's case, woman. What else could he do? If he had waited, if the men had waited they would surely have been arrested," Jack replied. "Andrew is Richard's man, Lizbet. We just need to catch up with them."

Lizbet dropped back in her seat a dark look on her face. What had it been that Andrew had said to her? 'They'll never believe you anyway'. Lizbet knew she was going to have to pick her moment better to raise the subject of Andrew again.

"No, and I have no doubt there's much weighing on him, but there's something else tonight as well," Jack said, tapping his fingers on the table thoughtfully.

"He's not going up there to get drunk at least. He's taken a lass with him," Lizbet said. She was well acquainted with Richard's infrequent but debilitating bouts of drunkenness. Sometimes he drank like a man who wished to never rise again.

Jack was still watching the door thoughtfully. "He'll not drink. He knows we need to be gone tomorrow early so we can catch up with Andrew."

☦

The woman he'd taken to his bed liked him well enough. Her soft warm body didn't pull away from his. Wrapping a hand around her, he drew her face to his chest, and closing his eyes, he lay his cheek on top of her head of auburn curls for a moment. The head in his mind though had long chestnut hair that hung down her back and high cheekbones giving her face a permanently enquiring look. Richard smiled, but running his hand though the woman's hair, it stopped short of where it should have. He placed his palm against her cheek. It was plump and rosy and not finely boned like the one his mind dwelt on. He turned her on her back and covered her body with his. She was shorter, he noted as well, shorter than she should have been.

Jack saw the whore's reappearance in the inn room shortly after he'd finished his meal. She'd not been gone long. Lizbet was still eating, and Jack bid her wait for him. Crossing the room, he exited through the door Richard had taken and headed up the stairs.

Knocking, he received no answer. Jack knocked again, his eyes casting along the passage. Had he got the wrong room? Then from inside he heard the unmistakable sound of movement and banged on the door with his fist.

"Richard, open the door," Jack demanded.
Silence.
A sudden feeling of dread hit him in a wave and his hand grasped the handle but the latch was down and secured from the inside.

Jack banged again. "Richard, open the bloody door."

No reply.

Jack was aware of the fear now creeping through his veins and he waited no longer. Bracing himself, he shouldered the door and the insubstantial latch on the other side splintered and the door swung open.

The smell that met Jack's nose he recognised, but for that first moment, not the source.

Jack's first thought was that the woman had taken a knife to his brother before leaving him, but two more steps into the room and he knew that it hadn't been the whore who had ripped the knife across his brother's wrists.

"No!" Jack gasped.

Richard was pale and barely unconscious, blood pouring from his left wrist. The grey sheets on the bed and the rough wool blankets were sticky with it. He'd done an efficient job.

Richard's shirt was on the floor and Jack had it torn into two in a moment, and then bound his wrist punishingly tight to stop the last of his blood from leaving his veins. There was no response from Richard at all; he let Jack do what he wished.

Leaving him for only a moment, Jack took the steps back to the tavern room three at a time, appearing at the door and waving an arm to summon Lizbet.

Lizbet pointed down at her unfinished meal, a pained look on her face, but the expression disappeared in an instant when Jack held up his hand for a moment and she could clearly see his palm covered in blood and the look on his face.

Without a moment's hesitation she was across the room and following in Jack's wake.

"Close the door," Jack instructed. He was pulling the bloodied sheets from under Richard whose whole body seemed to be covered in smudges and stains of his own blood. Then he supplied by way of instant explanation, "There's no one to blame, he's done it himself."

Lizbet, dropping to her knees next to Richard, placed a hand on his chest. "He's still alive. God love us! Why's he done that?"

Jack shook his head. "Get some clean sheets from my room, he can't lie on these."

"Will he be alright?" Lizbet said, rising on shaking legs.

"I don't know. Why didn't we see it? Why didn't I see this coming? Christ, how much did I think he could take?"

Lizbet returned with the sheets from Jack's room.

There were tears on her face. "There's blood everywhere. Are you sure it's just his wrists?" Lizbet had the remains of his shirt in her hand. "It's all over your face, you foolish man." She tried to rub it away but it had already begun to dry and her efforts just smeared it across his cheek.

Lizbet swallowed hard. "What do we do, Jack? What does he need?"

Jack said. "What salve you can give a man who does not wish to live? I do not know."

"Should we get him a priest?" Lizbet suggested quickly.

"Are you mad, woman? He's just committed the final sin. A priest is not likely to like that very much, is he?"

"I suppose you are right," Lizbet replied. "Let me get some water. Please don't wrap him up like that."

Jack was folding blankets around his bloodstained body.

"Go on! Hurry up." Jack's voice was raw with emotion. With Lizbet gone, he knelt next to his brother. "You bloody fool. Always you try to face everything alone. Am I not equal enough yet to stand by your side?" His voice was angry. Jack saw that his brother's eyelids had flickered. "Can you hear me?"

The grey eyes opened and stared for a moment into the distance, not registering Jack before they closed on the world again. The words, when they came, sliced into Jack's heart. "I hear you." The words were spoken quietly, slowly, and Jack heard the pain behind them. "Let me go, Jack. Please. I need to pay for what I've done."

Richard's right hand moved to the bindings on his left wrist and when his bloodless fingers pulled ineffectually at the tightly wrapped linen, a sob escaped his throat.

"No," was all Jack could say. He picked up the lighter form of his brother and pulled his body hard against his own chest. "You'll not leave me again."

Richard marshalled what strength he had left, and spoke for the last time. "Please." It was just one word.

Jack held him then at arms' length in a brutal grip. His blue eyes bored into his brother's half-closed grey ones and Richard dropped his gaze from Jack's.

"Look at me," Jack growled and shook the lighter man. "Damn you! Look at me."

Lizbet returning to the room, standing transfixed near the door.

Richard raised his head by degrees and looked at Jack with an unsteady gaze.

"You'll not leave me. It wasn't your fault and I've forgiven you." Jack's voice was harsh.

Richard didn't reply and as Jack watched, his eyes started to close.

Jack shook him again. Richard's eyes opened a little further, a pained gasp escaping his lips.

"Swear you'll not leave me," Jack said, his fingers digging deep into his brother's arms as he held him.

Richard closed his eyes and his head dropped.

Jack shook him again. "Swear it, damn you!"

"Jack, stop it!" It was Lizbet's voice, but Jack ignored her.

Richard spoke quietly, his words little louder than a breath. It was only Jack who heard them. "You can't win every time, Jack."

Jack's eyes darkened, his face set hard. He ripped the knife from the guard on the inside of his wrist, folded the hilt in his brother's limp grasp and wrapped his own two hands around Richard's. The blade hung between them, the point scraping the skin on Jack's chest.

"Together then," was all Jack said.

"Sweet Mary! Jack, no!" Lizbet wailed.

There was alarm on Richard's face. He had been held up by Jack, but now that support was gone, his whole weight was against the knife's hilt. If Jack lessened his hold on the hilt and Richard's hands, the point would drive straight into Jack's chest.

"Swear it!" Jack said again.

There was a plea in Richard's eyes.

Jack began to release his hold on Richard's hands. The knife point stabbed through his skin and a red plume spread, staining his shirt around the point.

Jack tried one last time. "Swear it!"

Richard's lips moved, and he mouthed the words Jack wanted. Unshed tears dampened his lashes.

Jack pushed Richard back. Opening his hands, he let the blade fall to the floor. Richard's face was ashen and his eyes closed as unconsciousness claimed him. Jack collected him this time in a gentle embrace and carried him back to the bed.

Lizbet was white; she'd forgotten to breath.

Jack lay his brother down and when he released him, Lizbet saw his hands were trembling.

Chapter 22
The Search For A Knave

✝

Catherine didn't see Morley at Durham Place when they arrested Kate Ashley. It had been a day when she had kept herself very much out of the way, so she saw nothing of the search and the resulting arrest. When she had heard of the arrest, Catherine had paled, but everyone was shocked; the taint of heresy was a worrying one for servant, or Master, to be tied to.

Catherine had expected Morley to appear sooner than he did, but he left it for nearly two weeks before she saw his smiling face peering at her through the closed window to the kitchen garden. As usual, any other servants had mysteriously absented themselves. Catherine glowered at him which seemed only to make his smile broaden. Morley's face disappeared from view only to reappear a moment later as he stepped round the open door and out into the kitchen garden to join her.

"Good day to you, Mistress," Morley's cheerful voice announced, "and how are you this fine day?"

Catherine didn't return his smile or his greeting.

"Oh Catherine, don't look at me so. I have good news," he said, hitching himself up onto the edge of a wall.

"Good news? I can hardly believe that." Her voice was icy.

Morley fished into his pockets and produced from it a shining coin that he held up for her to see.

"I am not a child you can buy with trinkets," she said in the same cold tone.

"I never thought you were," Morley said. He flipped the coin high up into the air and both their eyes followed its spinning journey until he snatched it back into the palm of his hand and ended its flight. "But lass, this is yours, a thank you from my Master."

He flipped it with his thumb towards her. Catherine resisted the instinctive urge to catch the coin, and instead it bounced off her apron and landed with a metallic tinkle on the paving.

Morley smiled and then shrugged. "It's your choice."

"If I take it, you'll want me to do more and more," Catherine blurted.

Morley's face twisted in a not unkind lopsided smile. "Lass, you'll do it anyway. I think we've already dispensed with your lack of choices so you might as well take it."

Catherine watched him leave before she stooped and retrieved the fallen coin. It was a silver crown, worth five shillings and certainly worth having. Whether she liked it or not, she was working for Morley and she needed as many of these as she could get.

†

Panic had receded and now Elizabeth had herself back under perfect control. Her face, schooled by necessity, gave nothing away as she sat, apparently at ease, facing Edward Gage and Robert Rochester both members of the Privy Council, and neither of them sharing in her apparent calm state of mind.

"Lady Elizabeth," Rochester repeated, "Mistress Ashley has been found in possession of Knox's papers. We have to ask, were you yourself aware of this?"

"So where were these found, on her person? Was she seen reading them?" Elizabeth returned.

"They were found in a search of her room, secretly hidden," Gage replied.

"Or secretly placed there without Mistress Ashley's knowledge more like," Elizabeth replied, and Gage although he was inclined to agree with the lady kept his counsel. "So who saw her with these and led to you mounting a search of her rooms?"

"I cannot disclose our sources. I have to ask again, Lady Elizabeth, did you see Kate Ashley in possession of these papers?" Rochester pressed.

The gaze that Elizabeth forced on him made him drop his eyes to the desk between them.

Elizabeth hid a smile. "Of course I haven't." Elizabeth leaned forward slightly. "Because you and I know perfectly well that they were placed here with one purpose in mind. To take Mistress Ashley from my service. I have scarce enough comfort in my life and it is a sorrowful shame that your Masters should feel the need to rob me of what little companionship I do have."

"Aye, well, I am sorry that you have suffered by this, and I'm told Lady Travers is to appoint another to take her position," Rochester said.

"Mistress Ashley…" Elizabeth kept her voice level with difficulty. "Where is she now?"

"In the Fleet Prison," Gage replied a little too quickly

Elizabeth tried not to let out a huge gasp of relief. At least Kate was not in the Tower.

The woman stood in the doorway, her arms folded tightly, observing the servant as she knelt to set the fire in her bedroom. The girl was small and mousey, dark brown hair restrained neatly within her cap. She knelt with her apron rucked up to keep it clean as she swept last evening's ashes from the grate. Elizabeth had spoken to her once before, months ago, shortly after she had joined the household but not since. Since then she had seen her, but only as part of the mobile furniture of Durham Place.

The kneeling girl finished her task. The fire set, she stood, hefted the ash bucket in two hands and turned to take it from the room.

Catherine put her brush in the top of the ash bucket and lifted it. Turning to leave the room she found the exit blocked by Lady Elizabeth standing in the doorway, her eyes fixed upon her, and a look on her face that made Catherine start.

The handle of the bucket in her hand slipped through her fingers and the copper pale fell to the floor, ash plumed in a grey fog around her.

Elizabeth looked towards the ceiling.

"My lady, I am sorry," Catherine stammered, a hand ineffectually battering away the fine grey mist. The acrid ash caught in her throat. Catherine coughed and her eyes stung. Finding the handle, she picked up the bucket.

"Leave it, woman," Elizabeth commanded, looking at the servant surrounded by a billowing silent cloud of grey ash. "Put that down and come here." Elizabeth unfolded her arms and pointed at the carpet in front of her.

Catherine obeyed, putting the bucket down. Eyes downcast, she walked to across the room to stand before the Lady, wishing very much she could be elsewhere, and wondering if Elizabeth indeed knew who had concealed the papers in her beloved Kate's room.

Elizabeth's first words let Catherine know this had nothing to do with sedition and Knox's writings.

"Some long time ago we spoke about how you came to enter my household, do you remember?" Elizabeth stated carefully.

"I do, my lady." Catherine replied quietly, wondering where this was going.

"You came here at the behest of Richard Fitzwarren. Are you still in contact with him?"

Catherine didn't mean to but she raised her eyes from the woven carpet to meet the lady's.

"Well? When was the last time you saw him?"

"When Durham Place was on fire, my lady. I saw him outside for a few moments," Catherine supplied truthfully.

Elizabeth nodded. "Do you know where he is now?"

Catherine shook her head in reply.

"When was the last time you spoke to him?"

"The night of the fire, your lady, but it was but a few words." Catherine cast her mind back to that evening, and then added, "He was looking for you, my lady."

The corner of Elizabeth's mouth twisted for a moment into a wry smile before returning again to a hard line across her face. "And you've not seen him since? Do you know how to contact him or where he is?"

Catherine shook her head. "I wish that I did. After his brother died, I rather think he forgot about me."

"Died?" echoed Elizabeth.

Catherine looked up and met her cold gaze and realised she had said too much.

"Who died exactly?" Elizabeth pressed.

"His brother, Jack," Catherine replied quietly.

"How do you know that? How did you get such news," quizzed Elizabeth.

"Just before I came here, he was extremely ill," Catherine said quietly.

"What makes you think he's dead? Did you get news of this?" Elizabeth pressed.

"No, my lady. I knew Jack well, and I don't believe he would have left me here, alone. So I truly do not think he recovered," Catherine stated, with effort, keeping her voice level, keeping from her mind the image of Jack stricken, stinking and shivering on the bed in Richard's rooms last time she had seen him.

Elizabeth nodded thoughtfully. There was a cushioned window seat to her right. Arranging her skirts she seated herself, all the while keeping her eyes on Catherine. "So, tell me, how did he become so unwell?"

How much to say? What should she keep to herself? So many traps. It would have to be the truth, she had at least learnt that much from Morley.

"He had been in Marshalsea, my lady," Catherine provided.

Elizabeth's eyebrows raised a degree. "Why does that not somehow surprise me?"

Catherine was about to speak but stopped herself. Did Elizabeth know Jack? Had he been here, to Durham Place with Richard? What had happened?

"You look puzzled, child. I have met your Jack, and I can well believe he is a debtor's rogue," Elizabeth said reading Catherine's face. "He's not dead, although he probably deserves to be."

Catherine's mouth opened, and remained so.

Satisfied. Elizabeth continued. "So, you last saw him just before you came here, which was last year. I last saw them in February, but not since."

"February!" Catherine gasped. He was alive, in London and had not come for her! The blow was physical.

"I have not seen them since. If you hear word from Richard Fitzwarren, or his brother, you will tell me directly. I would speak with him," Elizabeth said.

Catherine's brain was stalled. February! Nearly six months and he'd never come near her. Where was he now?

"Did you hear me?"

Catherine managed a mumbled reply. "Yes, my lady."

Elizabeth waved a hand in dismissal and Catherine went to retrieve the ash bucket.

It was nearly a year since she had helped Richard drag him from Marshalsea. She'd mourned him. At night, in the dark, she'd pressed her hands into her eyes to stop the tears. Jack wouldn't have left her, she'd been so sure. But he had. He might even still be in London with Richard.

Then she groaned – Morley. She'd told Morley where they were. Maybe he had found them both. She'd told Morley she thought Jack was dead, and he'd never mentioned him again. She needed to find out if Morley had caught up with the brothers.

Catherine did not have long to wait. She heard Morley before she saw him, quipping with a servant in the corridor as he came, no doubt, looking for her.

"Mistress De Bernay." It was the first time he had addressed her by her proper name.

Catherine's eyes narrowed. What was he up to?

"Good day to you, sir," she replied, not sounding at all like she meant it.

Morley smiled, his face happy, his eyes twinkling. "Do I detect a few teeth today? Should I be a little wary?" Then he laughed. "It seems, Mistress De Bernay, that you are indeed the lady you say you are. I've no reason to disbelieve you."

"So will you help me? Can you get me from here?" Catherine stammered.

Morley shrugged. "I might be able to help. As you have already told me yourself, the situation is very complicated. Your father's brother believes you dead. He has annexed Assingham and has his own steward there managing the estate. His main lands are some distance away in Surrey, it seems."

"I know. Richard wrote to him, and then Robert's lawyer as well. So he must know I exist. Can you not help me, sir?" Catherine was desperate. Here was hope and she could not let it slide through her fingers. "I've helped your Master, sir, can you not help me? Or can your Master not offer me some help?"

Morley smiled. "Let us take a walk in the garden while I think about this."

Catherine was forced to follow him as he set his feet towards the empty kitchen garden. At the end of the small garden was a gate in the high wall that opened into Durham Place's private garden. It wasn't locked, but no servant would dare to lift the latch and step into a world that lay beyond their own. Morley pressed the gate open and held it so Catherine could step through and onto the neat gravelled path on the other side. Before her lay the precise green jewelled tapestry of Durham Place's garden.

Morley broke the silence as they strolled along the path. "It's quite beautiful, isn't it? So peaceful it is hard to believe we are still in London."

"I can never forget that I am in London, sir, and always trapped," Catherine replied, then she returned to her earlier entreaty. "Can your Master not see his way to help me?"

Morley threw her what seemed to be a sympathetic smile. "Not all men of power, my dear, are men of honour, and even men of honour like to champion causes that will advance their own. I fear it might be difficult to persuade them to take an interest in your situation."

"But I've helped your Master. I could do more, surely you can see that?" Catherine sounded as desperate as she was.

"Yes, me dear, and a coin or two he might throw you, and a promise not to reveal your identity and thereby preserve the roof over your head. But if you think he is going to transport you from here, and turn the wheels of the Court of Chancery to reinstate your inheritance, I very much doubt it."

"Well then, sir, there is little more to speak of, and I have work to do." Catherine lifted her skirts and made to turn back towards the gate.

"Don't be so hasty, my dear." Morley lay a gentle but restraining hand on her arm to stop her. "Maybe if you could be useful to my Master then there may be a day in the future when he could look favourably upon your situation."

"I thought you just said he would not be interested. Sir, you need to make up your mind," Catherine said.

"At the moment he is not, but in time, if you show him loyal service, he might be more inclined to help," Morley said, knowing that this was the key to retaining the girl's obedience.

"Aye, but no promises." Catherine's voice was bitter. "I've heard that before."

"Not a lot I can do, I'm afraid." Morley sounded sympathetic, although Catherine very much doubted he meant it.

"My choices are, it seems, limited," Catherine replied, then she asked the question she very much wanted the answer to. "So, did you find him?"

"Who?" asked Morley, even though he knew exactly who she was talking about.

Catherine raised her eyebrows. "Richard Fitzwarren. I told you where the inn was."

"No. No, I didn't," Morley conceded, then he asked, "Do you still believe he could be a champion for your lost cause?"

"Is that what I am? A lost cause?" Catherine spat back. "If that is true, then there is little to make me want to help your Master is there?"

"Well, a roof over your head might persuade you. If you are known to not be Mistress Ashley's niece, I doubt you will remain at Durham Place long, and then where will you go? Onto the streets? You haven't any money, you've told me that yourself, and the crown I gave you won't last long, will it? So staying here and hoping to sweeten my Master's regard for you is the only route I can see. Richard Fitzwarren has gone, and what a trail of wreckage that man has left in his path."

"Really?" Catherine tried to sound surprised.

"Wanted for murder now in London as well. Do not rely on such a man as that, lass."

Then Catherine asked. "And his brother, Jack, did you find news of him?"

Morley smiled. "So you have place in your heart for that rogue too then?"

Catherine blushed. "I have a care for him, sir, as a friend. I cannot believe if he had recovered he would have left me here."

"Well, he did, my dear." Morley saw the confusion on her face and continued. "He both recovered and he left you here."

Elizabeth had not lied, he was alive.

"My Master would know where they are as well. If you hear from him, I would like you to let me know of it," Morley pronounced.

"He left me here. It's been nearly a year, sir, and I've heard nothing, seen nothing. It is not likely that he will come here now, is it?" Catherine replied.

"True, I admit. However like the rabbit warren, if you stop up all the holes even the old ones that look disused, you will eventually get the rabbit you seek pop out of the one you have your eye on," Morley said smiling.

They had drawn to a mutual halt at the far side of the formal garden. Had Catherine known it, the wall she now rested against was the one in February that Jack had scarred his knuckles against trying to ward off a terror attack in the garden while he had waited for his brother.

"I will walk back with you, my dear. I have other business at Durham Place, and while your company is always entertaining, my Master has expectations that I need to fulfil." Morley took her hand, placed it on his arm and steered her back towards the gate, chatting all the while about a grand scheme his own wife had for a garden such as this at his own country house.

Catherine did not hear a word he said.

"He appears to have disappeared, along with his bastard sibling," Morley said in response to Cecil's question.

"Your contacts at Durham Place? Are they aware you are looking for him?" Cecil replied, only half his mind on the conversation, the other given to the correspondence laid before him, all of it begging his own penned replies. Some issues could not be trusted to clerks.

"They are, and if he is in London, which I very much doubt, then I will hear of it," Morley remarked as he pulled his gloves from his hands and lay them smoothly across one stockinged leg.

"Where does your nose tell you he has gone then?" Cecil enquired. He peered at Morley over the top of his glasses. Only his very near sight had suffered, which he blamed on years of reading in dim light.

"I doubt very much he is hiding in the city or indeed in the counties around it. Over the last two years he has left a trail across England from Assingham. Then falsely securing Her Majesty's approval, he obtained a manor and land from her at Burton. He further tried to expand his wealth by keeping the De Bernay girl close. His treasonous intent was revealed, as was the plan he executed to steal those papers from under Gardiner's nose. The he finds himself back with his bastard sibling in the heart of London, and, after murdering two of the inn's clientele, disappears," Morley said. "I suspect he has tried to blackmail his father, but I cannot be sure."

"What I do know, " Cecil said thoughtfully, "is that such a man was in London for a reason. Perhaps the murdered men came between him and that reason I do not know. But what I do know is that such a man does not simply cease to be a threat. It means the threat has just moved and we need to find out where to."

"So far all enquiries about the murdered men have revealed them to be of little interest. They may have been working for him. They were local trouble makers of ill repute, but so far there is little to tie them to him, other than the man who was pressed into helping them remove the bodies from the inn," Morley supplied.

"Have you spoken to his brother Robert yet? Cecil asked.

"Not yet. He has been absent from London. As soon as he returns I will speak with him," Morley said.

"I know you spoke of an enmity between them, but they could still be working together," Cecil warned.

Morley nodded.

Morley found Robert Fitzwarren to be both stupid and arrogant, a fairly lethal combination he generally found. Robert wasted no time in providing Morley with a catalogue of his brother's ill deeds. Morley was left in no doubt of the genuine hatred he felt for his brother. When Morley had mentioned Jack, then Robert's temper had properly flared. It seemed he was one of his father's by-blows that

Richard Fitzwarren had, for some reason, recruited to his cause.

So it seemed that both men had tried to profit from the girl, Catherine. Her family had indeed been supporters of Mary and there was a part of him that felt genuinely sorry that she had ended up misplaced and abused in Elizabeth's household.

Robert had no idea where Richard might be.

It did however prompt Robert to pay a visit to his lawyer. It had been a while and there had been no news forthcoming. His useless steward might have lost the girl, who was probably now whoring herself around the dockside in London, after the stupid creature had run from his door. But he had her signature already on the documents Clement had prepared, so there was no reason why Robert could not still press his case. The loss of the De Bernay wench was a problem he would face later. He was sure he could find a woman to take her place if the need arose.

It had been weeks, and the dreaded name Fitzwarren was one that Clement had managed to stop dwelling on. The acidly charming Richard and his dog, Jack, had not reappeared and there had, so far, been no reply to the letter he had sent to the address he had been provided with. He'd fulfilled his part of the bargain and he was very much hoping they would stay away. Robert also he had not seen for weeks, and his heart hammered now in his chest as he heard Robert's voice swearing at Marcus outside his office door.

Moments later the door swung open and the frame was filled with Robert Fitzwarren.

"Good day to you, sir," Clement managed, trying to avoid Robert's eyes.

"It had better be, for your sake," Robert threatened. "Have you good news for me, lawyer?"

Clement knew he was going to have to play for time. He'd filed the paper with Chancery, but the wheels turned so slowly, he would not expect to hear back for at least another month. The Courts and their systems were never going to be fast enough for Robert Fitzwarren, Clement feared.

"I was going to write to you, sir. The Court have replied and there are a few papers the lady needs to sign before we proceed." It was a lie, but at least Clement hoped it sounded like progress was being made. "I can draft up the necessary papers and if you bring the lady we can get these signed and progress on to the next stage."

Robert looked at the lawyer, his face furious, and his voice when he spoke shook with rage. "She's been here, you've recorded her bloody signature. What else can you need from her?"

Clement blustered, "It is just Court procedures. There are processes we need to follow."

"Give me the papers, I will get them signed," Robert demanded.

It was plain that something was very wrong. Clement might not be the shrewdest lawyer in London, but he was certainly no fool. "Yes, of course, I will have them drafted and delivered to you tomorrow if that would be acceptable?"

"Does it matter whether it is or it is not? You fool, you should have got these papers signed as well when she was last here."

Robert left, and slowly Clement's heart rate returned to its normal quiet level. *So he's lost the girl then?*

Clement sat back in his chair and thought about how best to use this information. He could play along with Robert for a while, if he'd no longer got access to the girl, any case would fail as soon as it came to Court. This might also be a useful piece of information he could feed to the other brother to keep him peaceable and at bay. There was nothing to be gained from volunteering it now so he would keep it to himself until there was a time of need.

He could press the issue with Robert, ask him for the girl's signature on some fictitious papers he could say he needed. He was, after all, in control of the case. He could even force events quickly to the point where Robert would have to produce her in Court. Robert's discomfort was a fleeting pleasure that Clement could savour for only a few minutes. The facts were such that he was in no position to toy with Robert, no matter how delightful that would be. He needed to tread a quiet and careful path through the turds strewn before him by the Fitzwarren family. Bastards to a man.

Chapter 23
The Fallen Knight

☦

Dan had halted Andrew's advance south. Riding through the night, they had finally caught up with them. Andrew had been on his feet in a moment, delighted that the Master and Jack were free. Dan and Froggy, with their mission complete and too tired to argue, gave Andrew the directions to find Richard. He insisted on riding alone to bring Richard and Jack back to where the men were billeted and waiting. Within the hour, he was on a horse and headed back north following the directions Dan and Froggy had given him.

Andrew's journey north was longer than he had thought it would be. He had expected to meet them as they travelled south, and as he closed in on the inn where Dan had left his Master, he began to worry that he missed them. Surely they would still not be here?

"He did what?" Andrew's face was ashen.

"He felt he was to blame. When we escaped, he brought their judgement to bear on himself. You've known him since he was a lad, can you not help?" Jack practically pleaded.

"Those blessed souls' deaths would weigh on anyone. First Mat and then those poor people in the village. I don't know what I could say that would ease his conscience," Andrew said, his arms flung wide and expression of helplessness on his face.

"Well, you could try telling him it wasn't his fault," Jack said pointedly. "He'll listen to you. He won't even hear my words."

"He feels a great guilt for what he did to you as well. That I feel is something else his conscience is wrestling with."

"I've forgiven him," Jack said quickly. "I've told him, but he seems not to listen."

"He feels that these events are his fault and that is what is weighing upon him. I am not sure my mere words could…"

Jack cut him off. "And you think it is his fault as well. Mat's death, the explosion?"

"I didn't say that," Andrew replied hastily, then added, "You are right, I can try. Please let me try."

Jack nodded and stepped back so Andrew could mount the steps to the room above where Richard, ashen and still, lay alone on his bed.

Lizbet watched the conversation with alarm between Jack and Andrew. She was sure Andrew had not seen her, and as he disappeared up towards Richard's room she ran on unsteady legs, grabbing Jack's arm.

"Where's he gone?" Lizbet jerked Jack's arm painfully.

"Jesus, woman, will you let go? He's gone to talk to Richard…"

"Are you mad?" Lizbet didn't wait for a reply. Pushing past Jack, she took the stairs two at a time.

†

Andrew pressed the door open slowly and stared at the room within. He made no effort to bring himself down to the level of the prone man, but remained standing above him. Richard's eyes were closed, his head turned to one side, the sharp cheekbones standing out even more in the harsh dark shadows cast by the light from the candle.

"Can you hear me?" Andrew was rewarded by a stirring from the man on the bed. "Good. Jack has bid me counsel you. I would rather not, but he is beside himself and feels he cannot help you anymore. I am not sure that I can either." Andrew let the silence lengthen before he spoke again. "What you have done is an affront to God. There are no amends you can make on earth that can heal the wrongs you have committed. To take the lives of first Mat and then the villagers is a sin you will have to bear and I cannot give you hope you could ever be absolved of it. Jack told me you tried to take your life. That would have been right, a sin, but one given the gravity of your crime that would have been just."

A moment later a knife appeared in Andrew's hand, fierce and serrated. He twisted it before his eyes, and then changed his gaze to meet that of the man laid on the bed.

"I shall leave you this. If you let your conscience guide the blade then perhaps you will do a better job a second time." Richard's hands lay limp on the cover, and reaching down, Andrew pressed the knife into his hold. "I give you the means to find some salvation for your soul."

Through cracked and dried lips, Richard said one word. "Kells."

Andrew's brows furrowed and then when Richard repeated the name of Lizbet's Alaunt, he laughed out loud. "Oh so maybe you have a little too much understanding." Andrew snatched the knife back from Richard's hand, the blade tearing a ragged cut in his palm as he extracted it. "Maybe you need a little help. You are such a fool!" Andrew started smiling as he saw realisation settle on the other man's face. "You've finally fitted the pieces of the puzzle together, have you?"

"The explosion in the church?" Richard said. "All of it was you?"

"Your whore of a sister caught me in your room and I forced Scranton's horse into hers. Unfortunately that useless bastard, Jack, fished her out." Andrew sounded quite annoyed. "I switched the guns, getting round the lock wasn't hard, and levering the cart down the hill to Mat was fairly easy. Stripping the flesh from Jack's back wasn't necessary, and neither was killing the dog, but God I wanted to make you suffer and it did make you suffer."

"And the pheasants?" Richard asked.

"Yes, that didn't quite work properly. I didn't think you'd manage to get him out of there alive. I thought it more likely they'd hang him or cut his hands off," Andrew said matter of factly.

"You didn't need to get rid of Jack though, did you?"

"I might have driven a wedge between you, but that bitch of your sister never quite believed me and she'd fed Jack just enough for him to doubt me. So I sent him to beg for your release knowing full well they'd not let him back out again, and especially not after I sent them a message that it was he who had brought the powder to the village in the first place."

Richard was quiet.

"I have just one question for you? Who is Christian Carter?" Andrew asked, his eyes fastened on Richard's face; the reaction from the man on the bed was answer enough – Andrew knew immediately Carter was the key he needed.

Richard pushed himself up on one elbow but Andrew's palm in his chest shoved him back hard onto the bed.

"Are you not going to ask me why?"

Richard's grey eyes met Andrew's dark brown ones. "Go on then. Why?"

"Because of you Seymour fell. If you had left them well alone that day, he would have taken her, made the bitch his whore and saddled a brat on her. Elizabeth would have been his next wife. But no, you have to get involved. Elizabeth was placed out of reach and Seymour pegged his hopes instead on Edward, and we both know how wrong that went. If you had left Seymour well alone, he would not have tried to abduct the King and I would have had a place, a future, and bloody good life!" Andrew's temper flared. "Within just over a year it was finished. Seymour threw everything he had away, and I was left with no choice but to flee. All because you wanted to save that bitch's honour."

If Richard felt shock, it didn't register on his face.

A moment later Andrew's hand clamped across Richard's face, blocking the air from his nose and mouth.

The woman listening at the door was alarmed enough by the sounds of the pewter wine flagon being thrust to the floor by Richard's out flung arm to press the door open.

Andrew spun his head around as soon as he heard the door. "He's delirious. I cannot make him stay in bed. He made to take my knife from me and turn it on himself again. I'll restrain him. Get Jack! Go, woman, go!"

The door closed with a bang and Andrew turned his attention back to the man on the bed. "Let's do this quickly, shall we?" In a moment he had the pillow ripped from under Richard's head and rammed it over his face.

He didn't however get the chance to apply any pressure to it.

Lizbet had slammed the door but remained inside the room and the chair that she swung at his head impacted just beneath his temple and sent him into a heap at the side of the bed.

"Mary Mother and all the Saints!" wailed Lizbet, still holding the chair.

Lizbet ran screaming to the corridor, Jack's name on her lips. In the same moment that Jack mounted the stairs, Lizbet felt a hand planted violently on her back. She lost her footing and was propelled forward, falling headlong, screaming, down half a flight before her fall was halted by Jack coming up them. Past them both, almost unnoticed, went Andrew.

Jack extricated himself from under Lizbet but not before the pair of them had slithered painfully down another half a dozen of the steep wooden steps. Lizbet was shouting in his ear, but her words made little sense. He had heard her shouting for him before they had collided on the stairs. He had a sense of Andrew passing them, but could not even guess at what had happened. He had only one goal in mind, to make it to his brother's room.

The door stood open and when he rounded the frame, the room he saw was in disarray. The table next to the bed lay on its side, the earthenware jug had broken and the wine, acrid, was spreading across the boards. His brother lay on the floor in a tangle of sheets, breathing heavily.

"Jesus! Richard, what's happened?"

"He tried to kill him!" It was Lizbet at the open door, her voice shrill.

"Andrew?" Jack's blue eyes bored into his brother's. "You tried to kill him?"

Richard still breathing heavily was shaking his head.

"No, you fool! Andrew tried to kill him." Lizbet pushed Jack out of the way and, kneeling, offered her shoulder as support for Richard to help him sit back on the edge of the bed.

Jack, shaking his head, took two steps back from the pair. "What's going on?" Jack had his hands pressed hard to his temples.

"It seems I have been Cicero's fool," a quiet voice said from the bed.

Jack, hearing Richard speak, turned upon him. "Christ! What have you done?"

"Nothing it seems," came the reply, and then. "For God's sake, help me get up!"

Richard was trying to stand and it was Lizbet who offered a supporting arm.

"Andrew, he'll head straight back to the men?" Lizbet said.

"No one is going anywhere. Lizbet, pass my clothes."

Lizbet just looked at him in disbelief.

Realising he was going to get no help, Richard took two unsteady steps towards the table where his shirt and doublet lay neatly folded. On the third step he felt his knees buckle, the fourth his senses swam and the fifth he never made, plummeting instead to a heap on the floor in the centre of the room, surrounded by Lizbet and Jack.

Epilogue
A QUEEN'S KNIGHT

✝

"We've waited too long already." Jack's temper flared. "That cur has everything, the money, the bloody flintlocks, the men… everything! We have literally what we are standing up in!"

"Not quite," Lizbet said. "I've still got some of this." She pulled the leather bag from her pocket that held what was left of the jewels from Elizabeth's shoes.

"God love you, lass. You should have kept your money and left the pair of us to rot," Jack said, his anger fading.

"I tried to tell you," Lizbet said.

"I know, and the blind fool that I am, I didn't listen to you," Jack said.

Lizbet looked shocked.

"What's that look on your face for?" Jack said.

"I think that's the first time I've ever heard you admit you were wrong!" Lizbet's eyes were still wide. "Mind you, they do say there's a first time for everything!"

"He had us all fooled," Jack said sadly, and then looked closely at Lizbet. "Why not you?"

Lizbet shrugged, "He never liked me. Mind you, I think I know why now." Then quickly before Jack could say anything she added, "Do you think Dan and Froggy will come back?"

"I don't know. It depends on what Andrew tells them," Jack replied. "Andrew will want to keep them with him if he can."

"Especially Froggy. He's the one with the skills to make the flintlock balls and if Andrew intends to take the Master's place and still put this deal before the Knights, then he needs Froggy."

Jack nodded. "Andrew has everything. The only thing he does not know is where the rest of the guns are hidden. Richard wouldn't even tell me that."

"I caught Andrew in the Master's room weeks ago going through his papers. Could he have found out then?" Lizbet asked.

"Oh God! When did that happen? Not that it would matter much anyway, he's got the coffer that Richard kept all the papers in so…" he trailed off. "Oh for God's sake…" Jack realised suddenly that Andrew had the papers signed by his father proclaiming him as heir. He groaned loudly, pushing his hands through his hair.

"What? Tell me," Lizbet said.

"He's got everything, literally everything."

"What do you mean?"

"Oh God." The enormity of the situation began to dawn on Jack and he sat down heavily, a tight knot in his stomach. The face that looked up at Lizbet was white. "He knows who I am. He's got all the papers Richard took from his father, he's got the communications from the lawyer in England. Richard's letters from the Order are there as well and the chances are that there would be something in there that will lead him to where the guns are hidden in London."

"What do you mean? He knows who you are?" Lizbet was utterly confused. When he didn't answer, she placed one of her small hands on his shoulder and shook him. "What are you on about?"

"I'm John Fitzwarren, Richard's older brother and William Fitzwarren's heir. That, however, is not that important at the moment. What is important is that Andrew has enough at hand to be able to pass himself off as Richard, or if not, to still have enough at hand to press for a deal. I have to assume that he thinks he knows where the guns are, otherwise he'd not have tried to kill Richard. So there must have been something in the coffer that told him where they were."

Lizbet was just looking at him blankly.

"What are you staring at woman?"

"You...? John...?" Lizbet sounded confused.

"It's a long, long story I would be glad to tell you, lass, but not now. Right now we need to find a way to stop him. So let's think about this. He's going to want to keep Froggy, and he'll not want Dan coming back here either to help us, so what's he going to do?"

Lizbet thought about it for a moment. "Dan's loyal to the Master. He'd not leave him, and he'd not watch Andrew press on without him."

A grim expression settled on Jack's face. "That's what I thought as well. He'll need to rid himself of Dan and persuade Froggy to stay with him."

Jack stood suddenly.

"What are you going to do?"

"I need to ride south, catch them up. Warn Dan at the very least, and if I can, stop Andrew."

"What with, for God's sake? Jack, you've got nothing! Not a sword or a knife. You've not even got a jacket."

Jack was smiling now, and reaching out a hand, he ran it down her cheek. "Life has been a lot worse. I've got my brother with me and I've got a lucky lass with a purse filled with pearls."

"There's not much left after we used them to bribe our way into the castle, but you are welcome to them." Lizbet fished into her pocket and handed Jack the leather pouch.

Jack shook out what there was left into his palm. She was right, there wasn't much left.

"We were in a hurry. I didn't get anything for them near what they were worth," Lizbet said sorrowfully.

"I will fill that purse for you again, trust me." Jack put an arm round her shoulders, pulled her close and planted a kiss on her forehead. "I'll be back soon. Don't leave him alone while I'm gone, and make sure he stays put."

Richard was dressed and standing in the room arguing with Lizbet when Jack returned.

Lizbet looked to Jack for help. "I told him to stay where he was but he wouldn't listen to me."

"Be fair to the lass, she's only trying to do what I told her to," Jack said, but then seeing the look on his brother's face, he added, "You are not coming with me."

Richard's eyes were unusually dark, while the skin on his face was pale and tightly drawn. "I am coming with you."

Jack threw his arms wide. "We have between us two horses and one sword that's blunter than Thor's hammer." He tapped the sword he had just acquired that was buckled to his waist. "And we have with us, do not forget, our gracious sister." He gestured at Lizbet. "Who has neither horse nor money. I cannot take care of both of you!"

"I said I am coming with you," was all Richard said.

Lizbet looked Jack squarely in the face. "Looks like we are both coming with you."

Richard and Lizbet walked past Jack, leaving him staring at the wall. "Nobody ever listens to me. It must be a skill!" Jack grumbled to the empty room before turning to follow them.

✝

Printed in Great Britain
by Amazon